The Thompson Body

Dick Wingate

This novel is entirely a work of fiction. The names, characters and incidents are the work of the author. Any resemblance to actual persons, living or dead, and to events is entirely coincidental.

Copyright © May 2023 Dick Wingate.

All rights reserved.

Cover design uses a print of a watercolour by Dick Wingate

Book design by Dick Wingate

All rights reserved. No part of this publication may be reproduced, distributed, or transmitted in any form or by any means, including photocopying, recording, or other electronic or mechanical methods, without the prior written permission of the publisher.

For permission requests, write to the publisher, addressed below.

Published by dw.books

Contact dickw.books@gmail.com

Although every precaution has been taken in the preparation of this book, the publisher and author assume no responsibility for errors or omissions. Neither is any liability assumed for damages resulting from the use of information contained herein.

ISBN 9798386450311

This novel is by Dick Wingate who spent nearly fifty years in the town planning profession including ten years as a private consultant.

He was born and spent his first thirty years in Suffolk, and now lives in Norfolk with his wife, Maggie. They have four daughters, ten grandchildren and, so far four great-grandchildren.

Dick is hugely grateful to his daughters and to Maggie for their continued support and encouragement.

Especial thanks are expressed for the agreement of the Norfolk Wildlife Trust to focus this novel on one of their finest and unusual reserves.

May 2023

As with Dick's previous novels *"The Malthouse" and "The Mystery of the Leaves of the Woods"* this book is dedicated to old friends and colleagues in the planning profession and to those who continue to battle away at the coalface in an age when social media allows more access to proposed developments, but also gives access to those who wish to criticise without knowing all the facts.

FRIENDS

Not everyone can be your friend. It must be someone as close to you as your skin, someone who imparts colour, drama, meaning to your life.

A life without friends is no life, however snug and secure it may be.

    Henry Miller

Chapter 1

The village of Easthoe was a settlement of some 900 souls that was situated to the south of the A11, roughly midway between Norwich and Thetford and just far enough away to be sheltered from most of the noise from the main artery into Norfolk.

The church of St. Ethel was a half a mile away from the nearest dwelling which historians decided was a sign of a deserted settlement and the rebuilt village after the Great Plague.

Churchwarden Myra Plater, a woman in her late sixties wore her age well and her clothes even better. She prided herself – even if pride was allowed for a churchwarden – in spending her late husband Arthur's pension fund in the pursuit of 'Country Smart'. Her speciality was in her large collection of silk scarves, many made especially for her by a local farmer who specialised in growing woad, making dyes, and creating his own patterns.

Five foot four, slightly stooped, her greying blonde hair 'a little too long for her age' one of the villagers had said, but her bright sparkling blue eyes shone through the wrinkles and crows' feet of a once smooth porcelain face.

She had retired from a position in a local solicitor's office which had given her many opportunities to carry our research regarding clients' wills.

The cottage that she and Arthur had bought thirty years previously was of warm red brick with black pantiles. The garden allowed for a vegetable patch as well as a few apple trees amongst the overgrown lawn. There was just enough room beside the cottage for Myra to park her six year old Jeep Cherokee.

With her busy life she had no time – or inkling – for any pets. She and Arthur, at least Arthur had entertained the company of a chocolate Labrador called 'Woolfy'" who had developed arthritis and became so lame that he was put to sleep.

Not long after, Arthur, who had been an actuary in one of the big national insurance companies, found he was unable to provide the necessary accuracy for his own demise at the age of fifty-nine and at the hands of a brain haemorrhage.

Myra didn't want the tie of any pets and despised the neighbours' cats that came and 'did their business' in her garden borders. She had resolved herself to her widowhood with a clear stoicism, and busied herself in her various researches.

Her father had been a postmaster in the village and had passed away following his second heart attack at the age of seventy-three. Her mother, Elsie a staunch supporter of the Church, was in her nineties and lived in a church sponsored Care Home in Bury St. Edmunds, some twenty miles away. It had been a difficult decision, but this was the nicest Home that they had found for her. Fortunately for Myra it was not on her doorstep.

Myra visited her as a rule on Friday afternoons, unless, of course, there were more important things to do. Mum was in a very confused state and wouldn't have noticed anyway.

What little time Myra gave to herself was spent pottering in her cottage garden or watching crime dramas on the television and reading similar themed books, when she prided herself on the number of correct guesses she made as to the final chapters of the actions of the perpetrators.

Myra knew the village well. Brought up in the neighbouring Wrotham, she met her husband at the local youth club in her teens, married at nineteen and produced three daughters and two sons. Her late entry to the Open University was rewarded with degrees in Human Geography and Psychology. The sheer intensity of her research increased her interest in investigations of all sorts. Nothing got past Myra, and the villagers knew it. Those who were "below her station" called her Myra the Meddler.

Myra knew what Myra knew, and she knew what she found out. Being in the right places at the right times, hearing the right things.

She was a stickler for catching up on the local Parish Council's minutes, and often went along to the meetings to gather whatever snippets she could, and she also kept close tabs on the District Council's planning discussions. Certainly, she knew what was going on, what might be going on, and even those things that wouldn't be going on at all.

Towns, villages, and the City of Norwich as well. Nowhere was free from Myra's knowledge.

Myra knew.

Myra knew that her two elder daughters were safe and secure with supporting and loving husbands. At least, that was what they told her.

Patricia lived on the north Devon coast with a successful entrepreneur in electronics and a son who was training with the Olympic sailing squad. Olivia had a well paid job in marketing and was married to Damian who was a journalist and author in Northumberland. They were unable to have children, which at one point saddened Myra but she saw how their freedom gave them joy in their work and their travelling.

However, she had two major areas of sorrow.

Firstly, the perishing of their youngest daughter through engaging in the wrong company whilst at university and becoming riddled with STOs and the effects of snorting "those awful powders".

Secondly, the pathetic little wives that her sons had dragged into her family.

She saw little of her boys as they were doing very well for themselves, earning big bucks in finance and civil engineering in the Middle East. She had managed to put them to the back of her mind for most of the time.

She used the front of her mind to examine the lives of the locals and the stories that confused the residents of the wider area but, particularly the villagers. Things they didn't know

However, Myra knew.

———

The Norfolk market town of West Kenning in the centre of Norfolk had a history of heavy engineering and malting, with little left to show of the former, but with one of the old malting buildings still in use and another converted to dwellings.

The town centre has a marketplace, mainly used for car parking except for market days, a few Georgian buildings, shops, restaurants, opticians, banks and a few pubs and hotels, and is the main bus terminus with its links to Norwich, Peterborough as well as the surrounding villages.

West Kenning sits within the Local District of Paston which is made up of towns, villages such as Easthoe and open countryside with varied landscapes and uses, dependant on the underlying soils. There are areas of rich agricultural land, some of the country's oldest woodlands and a large area of heathland.

It is not the most affluent in the county but tries its best.

Like many towns West Kenning is pressurised into accepting more and more housing development without the normally accepted level of both physical and social infrastructure. Traffic increases to the annoyance of many. Doctors, pharmacies and dentists are understaffed, Charity shops are multiplying, and life still manages to go on despite the frustrations.

And Myra Plater knew it and made sure she kept up to date with all the goings on.

———

Dave Wakefield was having to adjust.

At sixty-eight, six foot tall, balding, eyesight deteriorating, beer belly far from deteriorating, he was coming to accept the fact. Adjustment it had to be.

Six years previously he had retired as Chief Planning Officer at Paston District Council with a decent pension and in the last few weeks he had tied up the ends of all the paperwork to close down his sole practitioner practice as a Planning Consultant.

He had become disillusioned with a job he had loved by the many and regular changes to policies, protocols and petty politics which had pissed him off to the extent that the money he brought in wasn't worth the hassle.

His wife Michelle at five-foot four, a Norfolk native with a variety of shades in her once brunette hair was delighted that she was going to get him back as he used to be but found that his indecisiveness and the signs of boredom were unsettling.

They rattled around their large 1970s four-bedroomed house on an estate in West Kelling where Michelle had made up beds for any of their four daughters or grandchildren to stay, and who never did.

That fact didn't worry Dave, who was happier without others living with them, but he still missed time with the girls. Not that they live that far away. Rose and Suzanne in Norwich, Annie living locally in Swinton village and married to Sam Chambers. Meanwhile their eldest daughter, Jade lived in Yorkshire and she was as close as FaceTime allowed.

Dave's ageing body and creaking knees were signs that his younger days of athletics, football, rugby and hill walking were at long last calling in their debts.

"I just can't do this anymore," he said one day last summer when they were walking in the hills on a short break to the Lake District. "I used to be able to pull myself up those big buggers every day, even with a forty-pound pack on my back."

"But, dear, you have to take account of your age, your time away from doing that sort of exercise, and the fact that you have put on more than a few ounces of weight," Michelle had said to him.

"Can't do this, can't do that, can't play my sport, pissed off with working. What the hell am I going to do with my time?"

"Relax, Dave," Michelle said to him with a gentle smile. "Enjoy being alive, enjoy time for yourself. You don't *have* to do anything. You can read, write, enjoy working in the garden with as much time as you want. We can go out for days, either to the coast, or to the woods, there are plenty of National Trust properties and gardens we've never been to. We can go and see the kids, think about downsizing and look for a smaller place, you can join a crib team and have an evening with a few beers, join a choir, join a conservation group."

"That's all bollocks. It's not being productive."

"Look, you've worked your arse off for over forty years and it's right and proper that you – in fact we – should enjoy time together, and separately as we want to."

He grunted.

"You know want you need, Dave, you need a Plan!"

"Hah, very funny!"

"But you really do, Dave, it's part of your nature! But, you love your garden. That is productive."

Dave was quiet for a few minutes thinking about his vegetable plot, his greenhouse and the borders that had taken years to develop as he wanted, and then said, "I guess you're right and I can put more focus to the garden. But we need to do this together."

"Great, that's a good start. Fancy a good walk?"

Early Spring in the heathlands of Norfolk brought the usual flush of so many shades of green, this year "oak before ash", the clean light of the new larch growth, harebells and heathers, rabbits abound, the deer moving stealthily through the trees, the meres full from the winter rains and the crooked shapes of the scots pines, once grown as hedgerows and which now formed such an iconic feature of the area.

It was a place and a walk that Dave needed to clear his mind.

Chapter 2

Jane Seabrook was in her early forties. A vivacious woman with dark hazel eyes and chestnut hair that was kept that colour with the help of various sachets of hair products. Divorced from John and after a difficult time getting him to pay appropriately for their two teenaged girls' support, she was a slim five-foot eight professional person working at Paston District Council as the head of the section in the Planning Department that dealt with planning applications. Living on the edge of West Kelling she could walk to the office on days when she was not travelling to meetings.

She had considered applying for the Chief's job when Dave Wakefield retired but decided that she preferred the day to day interest in the caseload and had realised when chatting to her girls that she didn't want additional pressures to the ones she was used to.

For a number of years, she kept a close relationship with Jim Prentice who was approaching his fiftieth birthday and was a senior geography teacher at Westgate High School. He was also a prominent Labour councillor at the District Council. Jim had lost his wife to cancer a few years back and had been happy and enriched in Jane's company.

Jim's two children, Zac, who had been through a difficult time, dabbling in the local drugs scene and troubled by his mum's illness and eventual death, had matured into a decent young man and Phillipa and known as Philly, who had overcome the terrors that some teenagers felt and was studying History and Philosophy at the City College.

Jane and Jim had become so close that they had tried to share a home, with the Prentices moving into Jane's large house which she had negotiated as part of the divorce settlement. However, with the four teenaged children, all with different interests and attitudes, everyone got under each other's feet and on their nerves. The situation was fraught with tension and so they eventually agreed to abandon the experiment. Jim and his children moved back to their home in the village of Swinton, a few miles north of West Kelling.

Nevertheless, Jane and Jim arranged the occasional meal out together and had enjoyed a couple of weekends away at their favourite hotels on the Suffolk coast.

Jane's work in managing her team, dealing with the District Councillors who were often pulling for their constituents rather than upholding the planning policies that they themselves had adopted, and contributing to the departmental management team all led to the knowledge that she had developed a strong sense of trust in her team, and they in her. She felt entirely comfortable delegating responsibility and knew that any of the team would seek her views if uncertainty raised its head.

She was happy to accept the role of keeping a close eye on particular proposals where the politics would be involved, those that were likely to cause more of a stir in local communities and dealing with any aggravation that was caused.

She had previously stood firm against the former leading councillor's bullying ways and her reputation across the County had ballooned as a result.

One of the friendships she had developed was with Avril Danes at the Broad Norfolk Post, and she was always ready to answer questions from the media regarding issues that arose and from those individuals who seemed to want to have their voices heard.

She was well aware of the likes of Myra Plater.

Early mornings, looking out of the bedroom window, Dave Wakefield let his mind wander as he watched a man jogging down the road, with heavy feet, and guessed he was a rugby forward. Then young wives taking their dogs for the early morning obligatory walks with thin blue plastic bags dangling from their waistbands. He was reminded of a friend who had mused about why we never saw any white dog shit like he did in days past.

The cackle of a magpie and the fluttering of bloody

pigeons brought him back to the present and to his feeling of missing out. No cases to work on, no arguments to have, no lunches out with his clients. He *was* missing work.

The recuring thought at this time of day was 'what am I going to do today?'

Michelle had warned him before his retirement from the Council that she had been used to the house being her domain while he was at work. They would have to be careful not to trip over each other. Dave's consultancy work had given him the opportunity to get out and meet with clients, and to use his office downstairs with a measure of privacy. It had worked well for both of them, and the fees received from clients helped towards their holidays and fresh cars.

They agreed on scrambled eggs and mushrooms for breakfast and then sat in the conservatory drinking their mugs of tea and thinking about their programme for the day.

It was a bright but cool morning and Dave said that would spend time in the garden, getting the greenhouse into shape and sorting out the shed, which was a real mess, full of old flowerpots, seed trays and his essential bits of machinery. He knew now that he had plenty of time on his hands for the jobs he had put off for years.

Michelle said she would ring the daughters and see how the families were all getting on.

Dave knew that that meant the whole morning.

―――

It was over a couple of months since young Geoff Pulling had left his post as a reporter at the Broad Norfolk Post, and Avril Danes, the Chief Reporter at the local office in West Kelling had become brassed off with the number of different temporary staff she was being sent from the paper's headquarters in Norwich.

There was no consistency, and whilst the nature of news was that it should be fresh and newsworthy, she was certain that very little progress was being made in enhancing the reputation of her team's contribution to the premier County newspaper. Indeed, her last chat with the editor had confirmed that, and she had pleaded for a permanent appointment to be made and that she should be involved in the interviewing process.

She had been approached by other publishers and had also been offered a measure of promotion at HQ, but she enjoyed the 'big fish in a small pond' feeling of being in charge of her own crew, however small, ferreting away at local stories, highlighting the good – and the bad – of her patch, as well as contributing to countywide and national features.

Whilst the job often called upon her time when she would rather have spent it with her family and with the village community in Holme, a half a dozen miles south of West Kelling, she liked that style of living.

It was worth something.

In fact, it was worth a lot.

Her husband, Jake was in IT and worked from home with occasional trips to his main office in Cambridge. Avril's normally early starts meant that Jake was in charge of the school run, when he took their two boys to Southgate High school.

This morning Avril was in a fine mood, for she had brought a new reporter to the office as a permanent addition.

And she had a feeling that it would not be long before a big story would hit her desk.

Darren Prescott was a postgraduate in political studies and had worked for his first four years for the West Yorkshire Globe, before landing the job as Avril's right-hand man. A big lad, rugby player who also enjoyed a good old sweat session in the local gym. Six foot four he was to become a critical feature in the West Kelling Rugby team. With a full black beard over his swarthy skin he gave a somewhat piratical appearance and was not one to be trifled with. Avril was delighted to have helped appoint him and the first two months proved that he was a thoroughly enthusiastic member of the team.

He had a surprisingly good nose for sniffing out stories that others might have missed, and very quickly established great contacts through the Rugby Club and the pubs.

"I'm going to work hard at this, boss" he said to Avril after his first three days of learning the way the office operated, the way the people of the town and its nearby villages went about their daily lives.

"That's what I want, Darren, but I am Avril to everyone here and around the District, so that's what you'll call me." she said. "There is only you, me and Jenny giving us the admin and comms support we need. We are a small team where working closely together is critical. No secrets, no ego, and no bullshit. OK?"

"Thanks indeed, Avril. That's great with me!"

He spent the rest of the week ploughing through the old editions of the paper and trawling the internet to get a better understanding of the past, and the likely issues that could arise.

He found tales of earlier drugs problems in the town, unfortunate deaths when an undetected World War II bomb had exploded killing a drug dealer and four others. The local cricket team that had once been a potent force in East Anglia was struggling to retain a place in the lower leagues, whilst the football team was climbing up their table. The local military base had changed services over the years and was currently under real threat of closure giving no small measure of concern about what that would mean for employees, the houses on site and the remainder of the land.

There were new roads planned by the County Council and the environmentalists' opposition to them and the continual underfunding of support and social services.

He had noticed that the same old names always appeared in the 'Letters' page of the paper's weekly editions and guessed that they were the people that might prove useful contacts in the future. Perhaps they liked seeing their names in the paper; perhaps they felt they could influence political opinion; or even like the idea of stirring the pot.

In particular, he noted the names of Mike Stevens, Myra Plater, Colin Brunby and Vice-Admiral Sir Douglas Ewart-Robinson.

Chapter 3

The town's Police Station was a hive of inactivity.

Apart from a few speeding offences, and the inevitable trunk road accident, the feeling, contrary to the rest of both the country and the rest of the County was that crime was on the decline. Certainly, the number of arrests had fallen, and successful convictions were at an all time low.

Whilst some of the coppers felt that this was a new norm, many of the local critics were of the opinion that there was not enough effort being applied. The Covid-19 pandemic had delayed so many cases in court, that offenders who were waiting for cases to be heard had slipped off the registers and were living their lives without the yoke of court appearances in the near – or even far future.

PC George 'Dolly' Parting, a twenty-four year old and relatively puny in his stature was constantly moaning about the situation. "What's the bloody sense in us catching the buggers if no one does anything after that, Waste of our time and the public's money."

Sergeant Sally Parmenter was much longer in the tooth and told him to get his head down, and to "stop whinging about things, 'Dolly'. You'll still get paid!"

Sally was a well built woman with shoulder-length wavy auburn hair with a tinge of red in it, with brown, almost black eyes and an ample bosom which she partly displayed when not in the public eye.

In her late thirties she was married to Ed, a mortgage advisor, and had been unable to have children. Ed was more upset about that than she was, and once that diagnosis was absolutely clear she had put all her energies into her weekly work.

She had worked her way from desk duties, through traffic and a short stint with the anti-drugs team at headquarters and had found herself in charge of the satellite office at West Kelling under the supervision of Detective Inspector Tony Lovelace who was based at headquarters a dozen miles south in the town of South Bardon.

Whilst she acknowledged that apart from the normal concerns about the amount of drug taking, things had been quiet recently and she had a feeling in her water that something was bound to bring some tasty action before the month was out.

She was right.

Thompson Common lies some fifteen miles south of West Kelling and is an unusual area of high conservation status. It is primarily damp meadow land and contains over four hundred strange depressions within which water levels rise and fall and where a huge variety of wildlife especially dragonflies, damselflies and pool frogs enjoy their environment.

These pools are called pingos, and were formed after the ice age, when their containing and expanded ice formed mounds which had been covered with windblown sand and soil. When the ice eventually melted it left these shallow pools.

Local conservation volunteers were assisting the County Wildlife Trust in the maintenance of the area, and in a new project to excavate those mounds that had excessive soil coverings and had not reverted to the pools. These were called 'ghost' pingos.

Three days into the project and after the earth shifting machinery had removed the top half metre of soil, Jed Ford who was working on one of the 'ghost' pingos was shocked when he hit a large bone with his shovel and called the supervisor to announce the find.

"Benny, I'm not sure what this is, 'cos it's either a big animal, a vast bird, or God forbid, a human."

Benny took off his safety helmet and peered at the end of Jed's shovel.

"I think you're right, but we need an expert. I suggest we rope off this part and leave it until we get one of the archaeologists here."

"It's funny, as I wondered why the soil on this one seemed less compact than the one we did last week", said Jed, as he trudged back to his car.

Within two days it was confirmed that the bone was indeed human, and great care was taken by special archaeological staff to excavate the whole body and take it to the forensics laboratory for further examination.

―――

Easthoe was one of a few villages that had grown over the years and had most of the facilities that the community required. Evidence of a once simple agricultural settlement was clear in the older cottages with their warm red brick, some with flint and with red or glazed black clay pantiles on steep roofs which indicated that they had previously been covered in thatch. Their once wide long cottage gardens had been infilled by dwellings of varied ages, some fitting in better than others.

Within the village the post office was situated in the general store, and the butchery situated around the small Market Square all provided most necessities, although the shopkeepers knew they were under threat from the increasing use of online delivered supermarket produce.

There was a doctors' surgery with its small pharmacy, and a school for the little ones, a bus service for the older ones to get to High School and an hourly bus service to West Kelling and to Norwich.

It was a thriving village and a target for house builders. Indeed, the planners had identified it as being suitable for some new development because of its facilities and easy access to main roads. One of these sites was on the eastern edge of the village next to a former grain store and was on the radar of developers.

Preliminary drawings had been submitted to the planning department of Paston District Council for discussion and informal comment.

Through his chats with some of Jane Seabrook's staff in that department Darren Prescott from the Broad Norfolk Post had got wind of the proposal and thought it might well generate some interest amongst the villagers and discussed it with Avril.

"Mmm, that's an interesting one. I'll have a quiet word with Jane. See what the story is. Might well be worth following up," she said with an encouraging smile.

Chapter 4

The body in the pingo had been thoroughly examined and found to have been in the ground at least five or six years and had been subject to a series of knife attacks prior to burial. It was male and aged in its thirties.

The investigation would be led from Police HQ by Detective Inspector Tony Lovelace and a Cold Case team, supported from the local Station which meant Sally Parmenter and 'Dolly' Parting working alongside Tony's team. It was hoped that DNA could be extracted and some indication of the origin of the man would be revealed.

Tony was in his late forties with dark hair showing flecks of white at the temples. He was a big man standing six foot one with broad shoulders and with a slightly sneering smile. He had been married to Rita for nearly twenty five years and with two strapping sons who were both at university.

Sally and 'Dolly' had met with Tony's team in his conference room, and the discussions resulted in an agreement that the first thing for the team was to identify the body. The primary port of call was the missing persons records from a few years around the suspected time of the death. This task was given to 'Dolly'.

"All I bloody need, to be stuck in front of computer screens for hours," he moaned.

"Good training for when you want to become a detective, 'Dolly'."

"I suppose so."

"And once you have found out who he is, we will need to know who his main associates were."

"I might need some help there."

"Then we will ask the Inspector for specialist help. Go on, let's get back to the office and you can start on it."

Sally was not particularly confident in the likely outcome but thought the press would want to know what's going on.

She rang Avril.

———

When Darren got back to the Broad Norfolk Post's office from his drive around the District to familiarise himself with the area, Avril was working on the new story about the body in the pingo and was quick to update him on the news.

"What?" he exclaimed. "Didn't expect to get involved in one of these so soon, and in this part of the world."

"Don't think that all life is rosy round here, Darren. Life is pretty grim for a lot of folk, as you will find out."

"No, I'm sure that you're right, especially from the comments I've picked up so far, but this is going over the top! What progress is being made, then?"

"They're still working on trying to establish who the body is. I can't say that I remember any concerns about anyone being missing, even that long ago. I was here but I can't recall anything about it," said Sally.

"So, are you going to ask if anyone remembers it?"

"No, not yet. That's the job for the police. We'll wait and see what they say when they hold the press conference. We'll just do a short leading piece just to whet appetites."

So, to keep the pot boiling, she wrote: -

> **Body found in special conservation site.**
> *Whilst excavating a series of mounds at Thompson Common, a special area of conservation value, a volunteer hit upon a large bone that was suspected to be human. Indeed, after uncovering the whole, it was confirmed that the skeleton was indeed that of a man, probably aged in his thirties.*
> *Police Sergeant Sally Parmenter told us that it had looked as though the person had been stabbed and then buried. Further detailed investigations are being carried out, and a full press statement would be given once there was clarity into the death.*
> *We will keep the public informed of all information that we gather.*

Dave Wakefield read the short piece in the Broad Norfolk Post and his mind wandered to a time just after he left the Council's employment and started up his own planning consultancy. He had been asked to assist an old friend, Frank Pack in his architectural design practice, and following a surge in interest in solar farms, Frank had added the development of these to his portfolio. His extensive list of contacts in London had put him in touch with a Chinese company who were willing to fund such developments so long as Chinese manufactured solar panels were used.

It was fascinating work for Dave, assessing sites that Frank's landowner contacts wanted to put forward for one of these relatively new solar farms. The main issues were: - What was the likely visual impact of the scheme? How could it be improved? What were the problems during the construction process? Who was likely to oppose it? What was the traffic impact? Were there ecological or archaeological issues to overcome?

It certainly made a change from neighbour disputes over extensions to houses!

Whilst recalling those days Dave remembered that there had been something odd that occurred. One of the Chinese company's sub-contracted surveyors had gone awol. He had apparently been employed from a bank of specialist surveyors to assess the potential for successful and profitable solar farms across Europe, and then just disappeared.

Was this a coincidence?

Hey, Mich," Dave called out to his wife, "look at this bit in the Post. Do you remember me saying about this bloke who went missing?"

Michelle read the piece, thought a while, and said, "Yes, I do. There were some people who got pretty upset about it at the time. Sounds a bit dodgy, doesn't it?"

"It does indeed. Not sure what to do, and I seem to remember that there was another scheme in Cambridgeshire where one of the guys disappeared too."

"Is there someone who can help?"

"Yeah, I think there might be. You remember old 'Red' Herring, don't you?"

"Indeed I do. I think he was a bit sweet on me back in the day!"

"He was sweet on every woman!"

"Oh, Dave," Michelle said, changing the subject, "I know there was something I meant to tell you, only I forgot."

"Mmmm?"

"Remember I rang the girls the other day? Well, when I spoke with Annie she was in a right old stew. It seems that Sam has got himself in a state over some family issues. I think that the two of them are OK together, but there's something going on in Sam's side of the family. Give her a ring sometime, would you?"

"Sure, I hope their kids are all right and I do need to ask Sam something anyway."

In the afternoon Dave contacted a long-standing friend from his days in Round Table, ex-Chief Superintendent Rob "Red" Herring, and they agreed to go for a pint at the Rat and Rabbit, so that Dave could see if there was any sense in progressing his thoughts.

Chapter 5

The heathlands around Easthoe and for many miles west and north were a botanist's dream. Sandy soils that sucked storms so quickly that you could hardly see that it had rained at all, and which had the effect of bringing out blooms and refreshing grasses that provided food for the deer and rabbit population to strengthen them and help them to breed like, well, rabbits.

The drainage of these lands enabled the ground water aquifers to replenish and keep the hosepipe bans at bay, whilst the lightness of the soils meant that many gardens required large quantities of compost to add goodness and to provide some water retentive qualities.

Just outside the village on the south side of the A11

sits the red brick Victorian pile that is Snetterbrook Hall, the home of Vice-Admiral Sir Douglas Ewart-Robinson and his very own Lady Hilda.

Well into their seventies, they both liked to parade their status around their circle of friends and acquaintances.

Lady Hilda maintaining her appearance in her plaid skirts and silk headscarves was a great believer in recycling and was a member of the Easthoe Recycling Group which organised the gathering of 'no longer needed items' and taking them to charity shops in any of the nearby towns. Unbeknown to the Vice-Admiral she would take a few of his items that she thought she knew he never used, holding her breath for the day he looked for them. She also ensured that the neighbours heard the sounds of the recycling bin being emptied every fortnight as it disgorged the numerous bottles of Sir Douglas' favourite beverages into the refuse collection vehicles.

She had become a fervent advocate of composting and had three large bins created for her by Dibber Eke. Dibber was her gardener and handyman who had taken the place of old Albert who had suffered from gout and eventually passed away after a heavy drinking session. Hilda was certain she had heard that it wasn't necessarily alcohol that brought on gout, and had heard that orange juice was a normal culprit, but she refused to tell Douglas. Nevertheless, her old friend Albert was no more.

Dibber helped her with the heavy work. The Vice-Admiral left the gardens to her and her 'man', and saw little benefit in gardens anyway, unless it was a place to stroll round after dinner and break wind whilst Hilda and her friends were attached to their sherry and bridge table.

Dibber was a man of the countryside, born and bred in Easthoe, and knew the way the days and the seasons varied with the weather. Short, stout and still very strong after his fifty-five years, with ginger hair that was thinning, but sporting the strongest possible beard underneath a bulbous nose. Always with a long-sleeved grey shirt and sleeveless pullover, grey baggy trousers with a wide brown leather belt. And black wellington boots. Whatever the weather it was always black wellington boots.

Turning the compost bins every few weeks kept Dibber's heart churning nicely, and the sweating gave pleasure as well as giving way to Hilda's home-made lemonade.

"Phew, tha's a decent owd job, Lady" he croaked as he thanked her for the drink.

"Good man, Dibber, you've earned it, that's the truth. Want a drop of gin in it?"

"Better not, Lady. I'd hate to get caught by the rozzers drunk in charge of me boike!"

"Well, get you off to your family, and have a nice evening."

"Thanks, Lady. Dew, I will dew thet."

―――

Tariq Antoine Browne – known in the trade as TAB – was a drug baron from London but operating mainly in East Anglian cities. He also had many feelers into the various market towns and villages. County Lines police teams across the counties knew of him but had not managed to catch up with him.

Yet.

One of his main men was a guy called Fat Robbie who

did the dirty work, recruiting the kids who were looking for a few quid to carry stuff around the streets and distributing it to the local dealers and consumers.

Despite his size Fat Robbie was difficult to find. No flash car, no personalised number plates, no sharp suits. Fat Robbie was basically a slob, but he made enough money soldiering for TAB, and would probably say that he sent all his profits to his mum.

He was known to visit West Kelling on an irregular basis, but always let his contacts know when and where he would be by encrypted text messages. There were no rumours about TAB visiting the town, so it was assumed that he gave Fat Robbie the goods either in London or somewhere in Essex.

Sgt. Sally Parmenter and 'Dolly' and their colleagues both in the town and at Police Headquarters had spent months trying to infiltrate the groups of users to find out how to get some sort of handle on the movements of all concerned. So far, they were just spinning their wheels.

No success.

―――

A few years back, Jim Prentice had resigned as a District Councillor during his wife's long illness and had taken over a year grieving after her death, despite the comfort of family and friends, and not least of Jane Seabrook.

Once he was back to his mental level best, he was eventually persuaded to stand at the next available by-election by his Labour Party colleagues. Such was his popularity and with the sympathy of the public that he romped home, coincidentally in the same Ward as previously. By happy coincidence (for Jim, but not for Alec) the sitting councillor, Lib. Dem. Alec Fosdyke had been involved in a tragic car accident on the M25 whilst on his way to visit his daughter in Kent, and apart from his own physical injuries he was traumatised by the death of the driver in the other car. As a result, he felt that he was unable to carry on and resigned his seat on Paston District Council.

Jim had been intimately involved in his previous stint as vice-chairman of the Planning Committee when, unusually for a predominantly rural area, the Labour Party had been in control. Well-liked by all parties, Jim was welcomed back to his former seat and was co-opted onto the Planning Committee. Jim knew his stuff, he asked the right questions and thought deeply about an issue before he made up his mind.

Which was more than could be said for some of his colleagues.

However, his relationship with Jane was an open secret and there were some comments about the appropriateness of him taking decisions knowing where the advice had come from. Was he gaining inside information from a senior officer?

These comments were seen as being politically motivated, and the Council's solicitor had made it clear that any Councillor was entitled to seek advice from any of the appropriate staff, and to ask any question they had.

And so it was that Jim was having his say on new developments, on historic buildings and on issues relating to the towns, villages and countryside within the District.

Including proposals at Easthoe.

Chapter 6

'Dolly' Parting was fading fast. The hours spent in front of his computer screen scouring databases, examining press records, phoning retired detectives and forensic scientists were getting to him. He had found barely any time for a coffee and a walk in the fresh air and his mind was a haze.

Sally Parmenter breezed into the office from a liaison meeting with the DI and the Cold Case team with a burst of enthusiasm that brought 'Dolly' well and truly out of his fug.

"Got anything 'Dolly'?"

"Not really, Boss. It seems that no-one said anything, or everybody said nothing. It's as if it never happened. I'm wondering if the guy was killed somewhere well away from here, whoever he is. Do you think we should be alerting all other forces or looking for mispers elsewhere?" 'Dolly' was catching onto the jargon, albeit slowly.

"Maybe we'll have to", she replied, her earlier enthusiastic manner jolted into quiet consideration. "There was little to gain from the Cold Case team either. I suppose I ought to see if the DI wants to expand the search."

In her normal manner of organising her work, Sally opened her diary which had a page for each day so she could write lists of actions she needed to perform. Sally liked lists.

She rang Tony who was less than delighted with the prospect of spending more unbudgeted funds on a case that had aroused no-one at the time of the victim's demise. He told her to put another couple of days into the search for information and to discuss the next steps then.

During her time on the anti-drugs training seminars, she had met with officers from other Counties' forces and kept in touch with a few. Ravinder Kapur was in the force in neighbouring Cambridgeshire, and she hoped that Rav may be able to do some digging for her to see if anything similar had been recorded in that County.

―

Needless to say, the story of the body in the pingo was one that set Myra Plater's juices flowing, and she was thinking of ways she could help. Her specialist knowledge of 'solving crimes before TV detectives can' would be bound to help, and she was wondering if she should offer her services to the local police. But no. She would do her own investigations and make sure she had something worthwhile to share.

She spent some time in her garden deadheading the daffodils and weeding her planters of emerging alliums before making a pot of Earl Grey from loose leaves bought from the travelling tea vendor that visited her every month. A couple of slices of lemon gave it that little bit of piquancy that she needed to focus.

"Why bury the body there?" she mused, "The offender must have been aware of the place. Might be a local. Might be a local who has moved away. Might be a naturalist who had discovered the special interest at Thompson Common. But which is it?"

A visit to the site might clarify things, so Myra popped on a light fleece jacket and climbed into the Jeep and was soon on her way. It was a bright late spring afternoon, and she enjoyed the trip through the lush countryside.

She supposed it was inevitable, but on her arrival the local traffic police were moving on all vehicles away from the site and its access.

"Excuse me officer, but is the whole of the Common out of bounds? I am trying to complete some survey material and I have to be away in a couple of days," she said with her usual measure of authority.

"I am sorry madam, but there will be no access to the Common for a number of days, I'm afraid."

"Well. That is so unfortunate. I suspect my clients will not be happy with this."

"Not half as unhappy as the poor bugger that lost his life here," the officer thought to himself, but took a moment and bit his lip.

Myra had no option but to turn round and make her way back to Easthoe.

But at least she had seen where the main entrance to the site was. And that was extra knowledge.

———

The Rat and Rabbit is a typical market town pub. No frills, wooden board floor, simple bar, three hand pumps for locally produced ales, one lager and a Guinness, jars of pickled eggs, optics on the back wall, frumpy woman serving regulars, owner chatting to drinkers.

Dave had ordered a couple of pints of Poppy's Best, a beer from a nearby microbrewery and was sitting at a table facing the door ready for when 'Red' Herring would come in.

When that time arrived a few minutes later, Dave got to his feet and greeted his old pal with a handshake and a warm hug.

"Long time, no see. I've missed you, mate."

"I don't know how time goes so quickly, and we miss the important things like friendships."

They sat and supped, talking for ages about their work and their families and social lives over the period of at least ten years since they had last met up.

"So, what's the story that you want my thoughts on, Dave?" asked 'Red' at last, with a satisfying smile.

"I'm sure you must have seen the story of the body found at Thompson Common. It's just that I remember a guy who was surveying for a solar farm company that I was carrying out some work for. As I remember it, he just seemed to have disappeared about five or six years ago, about the time they think that body was killed. I also think there was a similar case in Cambridgeshire within a year or three of that. Is it just a coincidence? Should I mention it to the police? I remembered that you were involved in a case when a couple of students went missing in France and how you went on the investigation. I thought you would know what I should do. Sounds a bit pathetic, right?!"

"Not at all. It's interesting, Dave. My guess is that this will be with the Cold Case team at Police HQ, I remember a guy called Tony Lovelace. I'll have a word with him and let you know."

"Great, 'Red', that's a bit of a weight off my mind. Another pint?"

"Better not, mate, I've got a long drive tonight."

"OK. Where are you off to?"

"Going down to Dorset to see an old police colleague who moved down there when he retired to be near his daughter."

"Well, safe journey, my friend. We must catch up again soon.

"Absolutely. Give my love to the gorgeous Michelle."

And with that he left the pub, while Dave ordered himself another pint and gave himself some time to think.

He thought about his friend and wondered how it was that 'Red' ended up with such a large house and was clearly well heeled. Perhaps it was an inheritance, but he didn't think his parents had done particularly well. Perhaps it was all those clothes he used to sell. Perhaps they had fallen off a lorry.

"Oh, don't be such a bitch, Wakefield," he muttered to himself.

Chapter 7

At the Police press conference, Detective Inspector Tony Lovelace indicated that the search through the missing persons databases for a two-year period either side of the suspected death had found no evidence that provided a match to the size of the victim or of his dental records. DNA had been extracted from some of his remaining hair and the depleted bone marrow, and it matched no other records. However, the investigation into the DNA suggested that there was some evidence that he may have been of eastern European extraction. He indicated that experts were constructing a facial reconstruction of the victim and asked the public to bear down on their memories and to let the police know of any thoughts that they had.

Within days there were a number of potential leads and also the usual calls from cranks who either were deluded or mischief-making.

Avril and Darren had been at the press conference, and they inserted a piece into the next edition of the Broad Norfolk Post: -

Murdered body of possible foreign origin

Police Detective Inspector Tony Lovelace today indicated that the body in the ghost pingo at Thompson Common had not yet been identified but analysis of its DNA and of the body's remains suggested that the man probably had light coloured hair and blue eyes, It was possible that he was eastern European. The Inspector said that he welcomed any information that members of the public may be able to dredge up from their recollections of about six years ago. Any information should be sent to the Police or to Crimestoppers.

He indicated that a facial reconstructed image would be made available shortly.

Local people are understandably anxious. Should they have noticed anything at the time?

Darren was getting the hang of the place and people who, by and large were friendly and, despite the financial pressures were relatively calm and kind to each other.

Except, that is, when it came down to the drugs problem.

One local wag had wondered how it was so easy for users to get their drugs, but the remainder of the population struggled to get theirs from understaffed pharmacies.

It wasn't just the sight of spaced out youngsters but the same old story of poor old folk who sat in shop doorways and looked thirty years older than they were. Darren wanted to drill down into the matter and find out why people got into that unenviable state, and how they could be helped. He had enjoyed the odd high himself in his late teens but had managed to ensure that it didn't become a habit.

One day after work, he went for a pint at The Dark Horse, and bumped into 'Dolly' Parting who had just come off shift and fancied a quiet Diet Coke. Darren got himself a pint of Guinness and introduced himself to 'Dolly' who introduced himself as George. 'Dolly' was a name that was restricted to the Force.

"So, what's the lowdown on the Thompson Common murder, George?"

"Still fairly under wraps at the moment, but there may be more news next week. Anyway, what news stories are you looking into now?"

"I'm trying to get tabs on the drug scene, not for me, you understand, but the wider issues. What are you guys able to do about it? I saw a couple of really sad looking old blokes yesterday."

"It's a real problem, Darren, partly because there's not

enough coppers, social workers, probation staff, and then if we do catch and arrest anyone, the court system is so understaffed that you can't get anyone in front of the Magistrates, let alone a Judge and Jury. It's a real nightmare."

"I can imagine. Is it a lack of funds as to why there are so many vacancies?"

"Not just that, you know that the government is hell bent on reducing posts in public services. I expect we will be privatised soon!"

"I'll talk to Avril and see if we can do a feature on it. Anyway, back to the drug issue, are there any of the main players you can get your hands on?"

"Plenty of rumours. County Lines certainly operate round here, and the drugs squad at HQ are spending crazy amounts of time trying to improve the problem, even if they are unable to solve it. There's one chap around here who seems to pop into town fairly regularly, but we haven't got a lot of bodies in our local team here to keep a constant watch."

"That's crazy. Do you know who he is?"

"No, but we've heard names. Fat Robbie is one name on our files, but we've not seen him."

"Can you speak with any of his customers? You know, someone who needs a friendly face?"

"Don't think any of the punters want us poking our noses into their lives. Shame, but there it is. We're mostly not welcome in that community."

"Well, good to bump into you, George. We must keep in touch." And with that Darren drained his glass and walked back to the office.

"That was useful. Now for some research."

Chapter 8

It was early on a warm sunny morning and Dave Wakefield phoned his daughter Annie to see what was going on with Sam and she said it was something to do with Hannah, Sam's sister and he couldn't let go of the matter.

"Anything we can do to help, Annie? You know we're always here for you."

"I know, Dad, but I think it's one for Sam to sort out himself."

"OK, but let him know if he wants a chat, I'm happy to lend an ear."

"Bless you, Dad, thanks. Must go, there a delivery at the door."

"Love you."

"Love you too."

Dave went into the garden where he headed for the greenhouse to tend to his new tomato and cucumber plants and see how the seedlings of some of his favourite flowers like zinnia, sunflowers and bidens were coming along. He started preparing his own version of a compost for the next stage, which he enjoyed telling his friends was 'having a little prick out'.

"Dave, DAVE," called Michelle from the conservatory door, but Dave was so immersed in his horticultural thoughts that he didn't cotton on to the command from his wife until he spotted her from the corner of his eye as she approached clutching a telephone.

"Dave, didn't you hear me? There's a call for you."

"Oh, OK. Who is it?"

"It's 'Red' Herring."

"Chatting you up again, is he? Dave said with a grin.

"Just talk to him, will you," she replied giving a poke in the ribs.

―――

In the Planning Department of Paston District Council Jane Seabrook was sifting through new applications and checking the progress of the current caseload with her team leaders.

One proposal that was causing some local aggravation was one for a major storage building to house batteries that would store electricity from offshore wind farms for its gradual transfer to the National Grid. The site was in open countryside a few hundred yards from a small hamlet. Here was a case of national interest versus local concerns. It was a big and ugly feature that would certainly spoil the appearance of an attractive part of the district.

The expected questions were being asked. Why did it have to be there? Why not on the coast? What happened to the idea of a coastal ring main?

The team discussed other questions that needed to be asked of the applicants, and they agreed that Jane should talk with the District Councillor about it.

This was likely to be one of the more controversial proposals for the Planning Committee when the time came for that discussion.

———

In West Kelling and its surrounding areas, people had performed wonders sending lorryloads of clothes, medicals. Toys for the kids and other essentials to the poor souls in Ukraine who were under the most intense pressure to live reasonable lives under the Russian attack on their country.

Those same Norfolk people had then found themselves in difficult times with the cost of fuel for their cars and businesses and for heating their homes, as the global financial situation caused tremendous rises in the ordinary costs of living.

Supermarkets made big profits, the fuel companies even more and were seemingly more concerned that their shareholders got their dividends rather than helping the ordinary folk who struggled to keep wolves from their doors.

People were getting angry and depressed.

Some were moved to very desperate measures, and more than a few had every right to feel anxious for their futures. Where and how could this end?

In more ways than one.

Temptations abounded.

Some youngsters fearing for their futures had taken a sorry way out and had succumbed through the misery of it all. A very few found their way to a relatively comfortable life.

And there was some whose anger was more powerful than most and, in those families, it showed.

Georgia Stephens was one of those fraught folk. She was a forty-six-year-old woman who lived in a rented terraced house in West Kelling with her three children. She had an elder brother, Charlie who was fifty and worked in construction in Thailand, had married a Thai girl and appeared very content. He had no children and hadn't wanted them anyway. Her younger sister Zoe was forty four, single through her own preference and a teaching assistant in Norwich.

Georgia was short at five foot one, dark hair and with stunning pale green eyes. She had married Kyle Martin, an up and coming professional in the financial world fifteen years earlier as they tried to settle down as a nuclear family, having lived together in a few rented houses in Norwich.

Their two children, Tyler and Rebecca were lively and a bit of a handful, and Kyle's stressful business, together with too much drinking after work often left him in a bad temper with them. Resentment grew.

Tyler, at seventeen was again tall but slim with skin that tanned so easily and with a body that showed that he trained well at the gym. He was one for finding small jobs to earn enough for his designer clothes. Tyler was one of those youngsters who worried little, and was resourceful enough to enjoy his life, and help support his mum through her more difficult days.

Becca, for that was Rebecca's preferred handle was fourteen and the opposite of Tyler, being pale, blonde, growing slowly and struggling all her expected hormonal changes. Despite that, she was bright, well liked and heading for a successful time at school and college.

After some months, Georgia became more than suspicious that Kyle was dipping in and out of affairs whilst he was away for work, and there were tales from some of his friends that got back to her confirming those concerns. He was also gambling away too much of their income, and the finances within the household were at stretching point.

Georgia main concern was for the welfare of her children she had had enough and told Kyle to get out and stay away, and that she wanted a divorce.

The drinking and the late night gambling was at the root of Kyle's downfall in that one night after a long and unsuccessful poker session in a friend's house on the outskirts of the City, and together with too much whisky he stupidly got into his car. Going too fast and fuelled by alcohol and adrenaline he failed to negotiate a bend in the road and slammed himself through the windscreen as the car barrelled into a huge oak tree. Neither stood a chance.

Kyle was gone.

Georgia was devastated. This was the father of her three children, and yet there was a measure of relief that the terrors she had faced most days in recent months were no more. Divided in her emotions she tried to concentrate on the welfare of the children. Kyle's death had hit them hard, and many tears were shed.

In particular, Becca was in a bad way, and the trauma had a negative effect on her digestive system. Tyler however was the resilient one and was able to give Georgia much of the comfort she needed.

Having been the life and soul of any gathering, Georgia was now downbeat and almost beaten. Life was a drudge with no level of enjoyment. Kyle had not invested in any life insurance and there was little money from his small pension. All was worry.

Worry about money, worry about her children, and worry as to where it was all leading.

What she was not, though, was one to give up and she had been determined to put her energies into the development and welfare of the kids.

After a while of getting used to her predicament, Georgia and the children had moved to West Kelling to get away from Kyle's connections and the influence of his friends.

Chapter 9

On one of the new estates in the village of Swinton, a few miles north of West Kelling, Sam Chambers woke early, and immediately felt grumpy. "Nothing much to look forward to today," he thought. "Why am I feeling like this? No real problems. What's not to like? It's springtime. Clear sky. Light south-westerly breeze. Perfect. Why do I feel so irritable?"

Sam was forty-five. Mid-life crisis? What's missing? Twenty four years in the same job. Decent income. Good people to work with. Few pints after work on Fridays. Just a few snotty emails chasing up payments at the weekend.

Sam ran a successful plumbing business in the town. Always someone with a leaking washing machine or needing replacement taps; replacement boilers; ways to keep energy costs down. Always plenty of work. No real money worries. Kids had moved on and caused only a little aggravation. Didn't they? So, what is it?

He was about to get out of bed and take a cool shower, when his wife of twenty four years, Annie stirred and rolled towards him, throwing a long slim arm over his chest.

"Hello, you," she said.

"What?"

"Pardon? What do you mean *what*?"

"Oh, nothing really. Just woke in a funny mood. Grumpy."

"Is that so unusual? What's up Sam. I know there is something wrong, but I don't know what," said Annie, leaning up onto one elbow, "Mum and Dad have noticed a change in you and are both concerned."

"What have you told them?"

"Only that you are not yourself and that there is something that is bothering you, but you haven't told me what it is."

"I'll get over it. Don't you worry."

Sam wasn't sure if he should be telling Annie what was on his mind, but said, "I promise I will tell you later."

He crawled out of bed and felt better after that shower and a shave.

―――

Jim Prentice had arranged to meet Jane for dinner at the Kashmir Kitchen and over a cold beer and poppadums they were working their diaries to find a date for their next weekend away.

During the Lamb Madras Jim asked if their respective positions as Councillor and Senior Professional was causing any concerns amongst the staff. The last thing he wanted was to jeopardise her future.

"Jim, I am contacted by almost every Councillor about planning issues in their wards. I am very happy to chat, answer, question and talk about the issues on any proposal. It is no different with you – except of course that I love you."

"That's what I thought. Just wanted to be sure. And you know I am devoted to you," he replied.

"It may be interesting when we get to a point where our opinions differ, especially at a committee meeting!" she said with a smile.

"In that case we must both be prepared to state our case. No strings"

"Absolutely."

Jim's palate was stinging from the curry and ordered another cold beer.

As expected, 'Red' Herring's discussions with Tony Lovelace concluded that there was indeed plenty of merit in Dave Wakefield talking with his team, and it was suggested that the local station was the best place for the first informal chat.

So it was that Dave was invited to a meeting with Sergeant Sally Parmenter who had asked 'Dolly' to be present to take notes.

"Many thanks for coming in, Mr. Wakefield," said Sally, leading the way to a grim and stuffy meeting room. "I gather you may have some useful information to discuss with us. Have I understood that correctly?"

"Perfectly," said Dave, and sat on a very hard and uncomfortable chair beside an equally uninviting table.

"Would you care for a coffee? George can get it."

"No thanks, but a glass of water would be good, unless you have a decent pint of bitter handy!"

That broke the ice, and they proceeded to chat about the town and the news of the Thompson Common body when Dave told them the story that he had outlined a couple of days earlier to 'Red' Herring.

"So, Mr. Wakefield it looks like you feel that we should be trying to find out who this surveyor was. Is that right?"

"Well, if it's not a wild goose chase for you. Oh, and please call me Dave."

"Chasing geese is what we do, Dave, whether they're wild or not. Do you know if the Chinese company went ahead with any of the schemes? Where was the bank of surveyors based? Are both still in business?"

"To be honest, I don't know. I've thought through all these sorts of questions, but each time I come up with nothing. I only know that the Chinese guy I met with my architectural contact left the country soon after our meeting in London. I must say that he was a very strange man. I didn't warm to him at all."

"Do you remember his name?"

"No, but I can see if I can find out a bit more."

"That would be most helpful. Thank you."

"My pleasure. I hope that will lead to something of use to you."

Sally opened the door and showed Dave the way out.

He was glad to be out in the fresh air.

The potential housing development at Easthoe had always been a possibility and Avril's discussion with Jane had indicated that there was no secret about the proposal. Jane thought that some publicity would alert those who were not aware of it, and that it would help to see if there was much in the way of local support for the idea. In order to push things forward, and as she had a mountain of paperwork to get through, Avril asked Darren to find out as much as he could and to draft a piece for the weekend edition of the Broad Norfolk Post. After he had spent a morning in the village chatting to residents, they discussed his draft, and agreed the following for publication:-

New development proposals at Easthoe worth discussion

Draft proposals for a new housing development to the east of the village of Easthoe are raising both some concerns and some benefits amongst the population. Our brief survey of residents and commercial enterprises indicates that the following issues head up the local thoughts:-

- *It was a good idea so long as there were affordable houses for local youngsters.*
- *It was a good idea if funds are provided to increase the capacity at the doctor's surgery and pharmacy and if sufficient space was created at the school, as well as the teachers to support the children of new residents.*

- It was a good idea if it helps to ensure the presence of the shops and other facilities.
- It was a bad idea because it would change the way the village feels, the way the communities might struggle to integrate the new residents.
- It would devour agricultural land which was needed to feed the country.
- It would change the landscape.
- It was the wrong thing to do.

The Broad Norfolk Post would welcome your thoughts on these arguments.

One person who had taken a particular interest was, of course Myra Plater.

———

Ravinder Kapur had been as good as her word and had spent many off-duty hours trawling through old records of the Cambridgeshire Police and the local newspapers' archives.

She rang the West Kelling Station with her notes of her research and asked to speak with Sergeant Sally Parmenter. Sure enough Sally was at her desk, engrossed in research on the origin and history of the pingos and picked up after a few seconds.

"Hi Sally, how are you getting on with your strange case?"

"I'm doing OK thanks Rav, but it certainly is a mystery, and I can't see a way through it. Have you got anything for me?"

"Not much. In truth very little. However, I did find a record of a surveyor going missing about seven years ago. Could this be the same man, or are we looking at a case of a number of missing surveyors? Our missing man seems to be at least a year earlier than yours."

"Mmm, sounds like that's likely. You know, that's interesting, because I've just finished talking with a guy who was acting as a planning consultant on these solar farm projects, and he thought he remembered something about a similar case in your County. Any idea what work your person was employed on? Was a name given?"

"No, it was a very short piece in the Peterborough weekly paper, and I couldn't trace any follow up. The reporter named was Paul Cooper. Do you want me to see if he's still there?"

"That might be very useful, Rav. Thanks a lot. Take care."

"You too. I'll let you know as soon as."

Sally thought for a while and wondered if this missing surveyor might be the same person who was transported cross-county to the Common. She would pass this on to Tony once she had heard again from Ravinder.

Chapter 10

Dave rang his friend Frank Pack to see if he knew anymore regarding his solar farm portfolio and the Chinese company that they had worked with all those years ago. Frank was in his mid-sixties and had built up his practice from a one man band in a converted cart shed at his house in the countryside to a practice with half a dozen technicians and designers in Norwich.

Nearly six foot tall with a greying beard Frank's ability to chat with clients and with authorities alike made him a popular figure, and while he was no national treasure of an architect, his down to earth approach and accuracy of detail was appealing to many.

"Dave, I'm really sorry, but I'm up to my eyeballs with

bloody complaints from builders who are getting grief from owners of some of our new houses about their drainage not working properly. I've barely had time to scratch my arse. Sorry to sound so unhelpful. Bloody civil engineers got it all wrong, but the builders and the householders blaming me!"

"Frank, that sounds awful, but this is about one of the surveyors who was doing the technical surveys of the sites. He disappeared. Do you remember?"

"Vaguely. Why?"

"Have you heard about the body found at Thompson Common? They reckon it was put there, one way or another, about the same time as that feller went missing. I've had a chat with the police, and they are interested in chasing this up. If I can give them the detail of the Chinese company, it might well help."

"I'll have to call you later. I'll have a think about it. I've made a note. It might be a while, and you know what my filing system is like!"

"Tell you what. How about you letting me come over to your office and go through the relevant files. I don't want to pry, but this thing is intriguing me and these days my brain has little else to stimulate it. What do you say?"

"Well, OK, come over on...." he checks his diary, "next Tuesday morning. I should be here."

"Thanks, buddy, will do. See you then."

———

At the liaison meeting at Police HQ, Tony Lovelace and the Cold Case team, together with Sally, and a new face that she didn't recognise were settling down with their notepads and coffees. Tony introduced the new member of the group as Reuban Blanche, which Sally thought was somewhat ironic as Reuban was clearly of African descent. However, he was an expert in profiling, and with his Midlands accent he told the gathering that he was pleased to be part of the team and hoped he could help in solving the crime.

The Cold Case team had spent hours delving through records of visa applications for surveyors back to six years ago, all to no avail.

Sally then explained that there had been a similar disappearance in Cambridgeshire and that she was awaiting further information from one of her contacts there. It seemed that this may be a different and earlier case, but that it could be possible that they may be linked. She asked how much longer it would be before they had the facial reconstruction.

Tony didn't know but would check when this meeting was over.

He suggested that the team should see if there were any local surveyors who may have moved to Cambridgeshire, perhaps to get away from the scene in that time period and admitted that this was a long shot. But he added he knew there were no short shots.

Reuban Blanche told the group that whilst he was here on a temporary secondment, his early examination of the files suggested that they were dealing with a revenge killing. He would be spending time at the site on Thompson Common and researching any other similar cases before he came to clear conclusions.

Sally asked how much longer her team should be involved as they had other regular duties to carry out but she didn't get a meaningful response. She would chase Tony later that day.

———

Dave and Michelle Wakefield were having a morning out in the countryside and had decided on a stroll through Wayland Wood, where legend said the story of the Babes in the Wood was based. So peaceful, so green, the sound of woodpeckers, the rustle and dash of roe deer, so many songbirds, butterflies, and wild orchids it was a delight, and their spirits were as high as they had been for ages, and their conversation light.

Until Dave asked, "What do you think is wrong with Sam?"

Michelle looked at him quizzically and after a moment said, "Annie was loath to say when I spoke with her yesterday, but I think he has got himself wound up over something to do with his sister. I think it would be a good idea to have them over for lunch at the weekend. What do you think?"

"Either that or we pop over there. Might be better on their turf, and we can come away when we want to. In the meantime, though, I'll give him a ring this evening and see if he's picked up any gossip particularly about the missing surveyor from his lads, or his mates at the golf club."

"I'll see what Annie says. Look, there's a tree creeper on that silver birch. Pretty little thing."

"Lovely bird. Tell you what, though and changing the subject, I'll be pleased when I get to hear more about that poor bugger who was killed and buried at Thompson. It's just down the road, shall we see what's going on?"

"OK, if you want to. Though I'm more than happy

staying here."

"Ok, I'll do that some other time."

They kept walking round the wood, and it was a spectacular diversion to his obsessive thoughts.

Back home and after their evening meal, Dave rang to speak with Sam. "Evening, Sam, I just wanted to pick your brains. How are you doing, by the way?"

"I'm OK thanks, Dave. What can I do for you."

"You know that business of the dead body found at Thompson, I have a sneaky feeling about it as they are saying it was put there about the time that I was working on advising on solar farms. Do you remember?"

"Well, I remember you saying that was the sort of work you were up to."

"Apparently there were surveyors who worked for our clients who just disappeared off the face of the earth, and I have been wondering if it might have been one of them that they found. Your guys at work haven't picked up any useful gossip about the underworld around here, have they? Or maybe any of your golfing buddies?"

"I don't know, Dave but I'll have a word and let you know."

The police had finally released the picture of the reconstructed face of the pingo victim and as suspected it showed a blond man with blue eyes, strong chin and rounded jaw line, lobeless ears, rounded nose and a short philtrum.

Avril was part way through a corned beef and pickle sandwich when Darren arrived from his walk around the town unsuccessfully looking for information or people who would talk to him about the drug problem.

"Hi, Avril. Any news?"

"Yep, I've just got the picture of the possible victim at Thompson from the police."

She passed it to him and waited for a response.

"Pretty boy, eh? Fancy him, would you?"

"Don't push it, sonny. The poor bastard is not my type."

"Especially as he's dead!"

The phone rang, and Jenny who had just returned from her lunch break answered, "No, I'm sorry she is in a meeting at the moment. Can I take a message? Oh, OK I will do that. Many thanks."

She texted this to Avril, 'Sgt. Parmenter rang. She'd like to talk with you re new picture. Please ring her.'

Avril had just finished her sandwich and was contemplating a couple of chocolate digestives whilst draining the last of her tea.

"Tell you what, Darren, you have a crack at drafting the article to go with the picture. I've just had a request to ring Sally," she said, with one of her quirky smiles.

Darren looked pleased, and said, "Will do. It'll take my mind away from the frustration of finding nothing about the drug scene."

Avril asked Jenny to get hold of Sally for her and a few minutes later, they were chatting away, and eventually agreed the gist of the statement that should appear in the Broad Norfolk Post.

Half an hour later, and with a few additions to Darren's draft they agreed on the following: -

This is the murdered man.
Do you know who he was?

The picture below shows the face of a man who the police are sure was murdered before being placed in a grave in a ghost pingo at Thompson Common. DNA indicates that he is probably Eastern European, or at least from such parentage. He was believed to be in his thirties.

Anyone who thinks they may know who this person was is asked to contact the County Police Cold Case team at the South Bardon Police Headquarters, or to contact Crimestoppers.

Your help is certainly requested.

(Picture of facial reconstruction added)

Chapter 11

Within a week, Sam Chambers was grumpy again as soon as he woke, and admitted so to Annie and told her that he'd had a rough night and that he would talk with her in the evening.

Sam was one of the sorts of bloke who heard stuff and remembered it. At work they called him Sponge because he heard gossip and information that he stored away and didn't forget. It helped him gain new work projects, and his memory of his customers and their installations either at home or at their businesses was legendry.

It was the same at the Golf Club, where at weekends he enjoyed the exercise, the banter, and the gossip. Not that he always enjoyed his lack of accuracy, as he sprayed one ball to the left, then one to the right into the long grass, never to be seen again.

"Bugger the golf, at least I picked up some juicy titbits and a couple of new jobs," he thought as he drove home.

However, this ability to remember also gave him an overload of thoughts and some stuck at the forefront of his mind when he didn't want them to.

One of those consistent thoughts was personal to him. Sam had a sister, his only sibling who was named Harriet and was two years younger than him. She was a tall shapely black haired woman with brown eyes and had married Murray Flanagan, a lad from Essex with Irish roots who had impregnated her after they had only been living together for a matter of months. With help for the deposit from Sam and Harriet's parents they had bought their first house in an estate of small homes in West Kelling.

Their elder child, Daisy was born with a rare neurological illness, and for years preparations for her to receive specialised treatments had been supported by 'just giving' pages on social media, by local businesses and pub landlords who had gained reputations for supporting folk in need. There were times however when those preparations weren't needed as Daisy's condition varied as she went in and out of pain, but still the financing for the treatments continued to flow in.

A couple of years after Daisy had come along, their son Oliver was born, thankfully in excellent health.

Murray was in the construction industry and had worked as a sub-contractor for a series of firms before setting up his own business in the roofing trade. His knowledge of general building work and of innovative construction methods soon gave him an entry into larger firms and he was often away for a couple of nights negotiating contracts in other cities. He became a name that companies would go to for a quote for their work.

However, he also focussed almost entirely on his work, and family time became less and less. Work, and money. Those were the things he existed for, in particular lots of money - and largely for himself.

Despite that, Harriet was still forced by him to seek help for funds to support Daisy.

Quietly, and after so many years Sam seethed knowing that Harriet and Murray had plenty of money, and that evening he had shared his anger with Annie when he bemoaned a system that allowed people to beg in such a public way when they had plenty.

She told him she understood how he felt but thought that it was not their business to worry about it. Sam had said he would try and put it to the back of his mind and poured himself a second beer.

Later in the week it was different.

"I'll bloody well spill the beans one day," he screamed at Annie one evening after a stressful day working on the plumbing system and replacing the water tank in the heat of someone's loft space at a temperature of forty-six degrees. "Why the hell didn't they ask us for help?"

Annie looked at him under her curtain of shiny black hair and shook her head. She knew he was right and that he was conflicted by the ties to his family.

Murray Flanagan was a big man, standing six foot three and weighing over sixteen stone he sported a shaved head and a goofy smile. He had an interesting history coupled with a fiery temper, having been involved in fights at a city football match, and had been hauled in by the police for a series of serious chats over his connections with some of his friends who had been convicted of assault, drug charges and of fraud.

He could charm the pants off anyone he fancied, but the underlying rage could, especially if fuelled with alcohol, rush out and present a completely different person.

One of the many problems was that Murray was charming the pants of too many other women and however surreptitiously he tried, people noticed. Some of Harriet's friends either saw or heard. And eventually enough of these stories got back to her.

She could hold back no longer and one rainy evening and after a couple of glasses of Malbec, she confronted him with what she had heard.

The tempers spilled out. She screamed. He had lashed out and caught her in the mouth with the back of his hardened right hand.

Swearing. Both of them. Tears, blood, snot, the lot.

And the kids had heard it all, and the effect on them was profound.

Sam was still getting so very agitated and was frightened that he might do something he'd regret.

He was becoming a danger and Annie could see it. Perhaps he was being jealous, or just put out because he hadn't been involved. It all seemed a bit over the top, and she decided that there was a good case for a family meeting, or at least for Sam to have a talk with her dad Dave.

And so, at the following weekend Annie and Sam Chambers invited Dave and Michelle for a Sunday afternoon tea, and after a glass or two of cool Chardonnay in the garden, Michelle and Annie went indoors to prepare food, leaving the men together with the second wine bottle.

Dave asked after Sam's business and was amazed at the hours he and his team were having to work to keep up with demand. Dave had thought that plumbers, like undertakers would always be in work. They talked cricket, drink, prospects for the city's football team, and Sam and Annie's three children and then Dave approached the difficult subject.

"Sam, Michelle and I are so sorry to hear that your sister's family are causing you a bit of distress. I can well understand that you might be upset, and whilst I don't know any of the details, I can empathise with any problem that crops up between family members. However, my man, you mustn't let that gnaw away at you as it would destroy your enjoyment of life. You work bloody hard for the benefit of your family, and we know that. You must give yourself time for you to find your own peace. One thing I have always been, and Mich is far better at it than me, is that we can listen and lend a shoulder to lean on if you want somewhere different to let off steam."

"That's very kind, Dave, and yes, it is eating away. Annie is taking it hard too. It just feels so wrong. Raising funds for treatments that might not ever be needed when they have plenty themselves and have never discussed it with us or asked if we can help."

"Sam, there is far more to life than money. You are doing OK, and Mich and I are comfortable enough, but the way things are in the country at the moment there are thousands of families who have four fifths of bugger all. That does nothing to take away any concerns you feel, but you have the responsibility to look after the future of your own family that we love so dearly. We think that you really need to let it go. If you feel you need help in reducing the anger inside you, there are specialists who can give you all the advice you need. We are happy to help. You know that."

"I know, but it's part of my family and I can't ignore it, can I?"

"It's not unknown for families to fall out, Sam. It's more common than you might think. You grew up together, there is blood that ties you together. Of course, you can't forget them but putting some space between you for a few months may just give you some peace. I think after some time of calm, and some thought, you'll find that what your emotions are doing to you is probably just a storm in a teacup."

"Thanks, Dave. I'm not sure I agree at the moment, but I promise you I will think on what you say."

Come on, there's more wine there and I expect there's some decent food waiting indoors."

There was no doubt however, that the anger that Sam and Annie felt of that issue was tempered by their love of his sister's daughter, Daisy and of Harriet herself, who was appearing more and more stressed and miserable.

And, not surprisingly there was more to come.

It was saddening but inevitable when, after a while Harriet had told them that she could not put up with Murray's infidelity that they had suspected for some years, and that she had told him to leave the home and that divorce proceedings would follow.

She told them that she had confronted Murray with these allegations to see if he would deny them. Far from being apologetic, he had snarled, said he hadn't loved her for years, told her that the children were a hindrance to all he wanted to do, and forcefully shouted to her that he would make her life hell.

He was right. He would.

And young Daisy and Oliver had heard it all.

Sam and Annie were devastated and knew that there was more help that they would have to give his sister.

Hence Sam's continued grumpiness.

That was all six years ago, and with the divorce settled, Harriet was having to look after her daughter's welfare on her own. Again, she had not called on her brother for help, but kept in close contact with her Dad, Jack Chambers.

However, Daisy was now an attractive eighteen year old with a penchant for colouring her pixie cut hair various shades of pink or mauve. Completely accepting her physical and medical shortcomings she really enjoyed, when her health allowed, to be out and about with her friends from college. Whilst there were still days when she was bedridden, she had found more confidence and had become much more outgoing.

And then there was their son, Oliver. He was at an age, nearing seventeen, where like so many teenage kids who were trying to find out who they really were, and trouble had been following him around. He had been vulnerable to all sorts of temptation, and often succumbed to it, often being at the wrong place at the wrong time.

He had not done well at school, and while he was not a

disruptive lad, his mind was rarely on the subject at hand. Concentration was not a strong point. However, he thrived on the sports field as well as in the workshops for the more practical subjects and had become a skilled student on the joinery benches.

Thus, Oliver Flanagan had managed to secure an apprenticeship with one of the national house builders operating in the County. Ollie was on the up.

Physically, he had shot up over the last twelve months and now stood just over six foot tall. He was obsessive about football and as well as playing six-a-side during the summer months, had signed up to the football team as a goalkeeper in the village of Swinton. Maybe he had turned the corner.

Maybe. Or maybe not.

Despite some measure of positivity, Harriet knew she needed help. Whilst she and her children had moved into a Housing Association semi-detached three bedroomed house in a different part of the town, and had settled well into the neighbourhood, there were still overbearing problems, not least of lack money, and Murray was not helping on that score.

She needed advice and knew that her dad, Jack would be there to give it if she asked. She had also chatted to her sister-in-law, Annie to get her thoughts, which were supportive of that idea, and Annie had said that her dad, Dave would always lend an ear, and was interested to help anyone in the family.

One evening, after their evening meal, Dave rang to speak with Sam. "Evening, Sam, I just wanted to pick your brains. How are you doing, by the way?"

"I'm OK thanks, Dave. What can I do for you."

"You know that business of the dead body found at Thompson, I have a sneaky feeling about it as they are saying it was put there about the time that I was working on advising on solar farms. Do you remember?"

"Well, I remember you saying that was the sort of work you were up to."

"Apparently there were surveyors who worked for our clients who just disappeared off the face of the earth, and I have been wondering if it might have been one of them that they found. Your guys at work haven't picked up any useful gossip about the underworld around here, have they; or any of your golfing buddies?"

"I don't know, Dave but I'll have a word and let you know."

Chapter 12

Jane Seabrook had left her office and walked to the local Portuguese restaurant in town where she had arranged to meet up with Dave Wakefield for their regular update and general chat. Jane had been part of Dave's senior team before he retired, and they enjoyed the time to catch up with the gossip. Dave now had no casework, and his newfound freedom gave Jane a few pangs of jealousy.

After the usual updates about families and Jane's team, Dave asked if there were any discussions about the Thompson Common body and explained his uncertainty about the missing surveyor.

"Obviously I know about it, but no details and it's not had any impact on our work…yet," she said.

"What about the countryside team? Have they been involved?"

"Oh, didn't you know? That work was abandoned when the Council twigged that your scheme - to use the excess of the fees after all the costs for Building Control work - had been ringfenced for the environmental projects that I know were a passion for you. That money now goes into the central coffers."

"Bugger. That was one of the best things we did. Change of control at the top then!"

"I guess so."

"So, what about this proposal for more housing at Easthoe? Has it created much fuss yet?" Dave asked.

"Not yet, but you can bet it will,"

"Good one for the Vice-Admiral to get his teeth into then!"

"Yep, and the others!"

"Well, good luck to you with that, and all the more reason for me to keep focusing on the pingo person."

―――

The story of Georgia Stephens was troubling, and she was both at the end of her tether, and close to telling the tale to the local paper. It was two years since the bitter divorce, and she had reverted to her maiden name, whereas Tyler and Becca had retained their birth certificated names and retained their Martin surname. The mention of that name burned holes in her heart every time she thought about it. She just couldn't shake off the memories of what Kyle had put her through, and she wasn't moving on with her life.

"What else can happen?" she often thought to herself.

And then this.

She had just got home from a morning working at one of the local estate agents, and immediately saw water on the floor of the kitchen in front of her. "Oh, no. What now?" she screeched. Then she assumed that she had left a tap running and that the plug had blocked so that the sink had overflowed. She was wrong. Something made her look up and saw water dripping from the ceiling through the light fitting. She dashed upstairs to the bathroom which was situated over the kitchen and found that floor soaked, the bath empty and no signs of taps dripping or the toilet overflowing.

Panicking, she rang Tyler's mobile to see if he could come home and take charge of the problem, but he wasn't answering.

Again, she looked up and saw water dripping from a bulge in the ceiling and realised that she needed help. She rang the landlord's agents and a horrified receptionist said she would get in touch with one of their sub-contracting plumbers to come to her as soon as possible and suggested that Georgia should try and find the mains stopcock and turn the water off.

"Where the hell is the stopcock?" Georgia asked, panic clearly showing in her voice.

"It might be under the sink in the kitchen or near the downstair toilet," came the response.

"Thanks, I'll see what I can do. Bye"

Indeed, the stopcock was under the kitchen sink at the front of the house, and she managed to shut off the water supply before she slumped down waiting for the plumber to arrive.

Within half an hour a young lad named Ryan appeared

at the door and said he was from Chambers Plumbing and asked how could he help. It was as much as she could do to stop herself giving the plumber a hug, but she let him in to the house and showed him the way to the hatch to the loft space, where he quickly spotted the problem. A bird had found itself into the roof-space and had drowned in the water tank which had not been covered properly and had blocked the overflow. In the hard water area, the ball valve had seized and caused the overflow into the floor of the roof-space.

Ryan came down to the lounge where Georgia was mopping up and explained that he had fixed the problem, had found a lid for the tank and that all should work well in the future. He turned the water on at the stopcock and told Georgia that he would send the bill to the landlord's agent and advised her how to get help to dry the house and to claim for damages on her house insurance.

It was then that she realised she had not renewed her insurance cover for her contents of the house. She thought for a bit and wondered if it was covered in her rent. would have to check with the landlords and their agents.

―――

In the offices of Frank Pack in Norwich, Dave had chatted to a few of the faces he remembered when he had worked with Frank on a number of tricky cases where his knowledge of the planning system had proved useful.

Now he was ploughing through a series of boxes of old files and was particularly looking for the cases relating to the many solar farm projects they had worked on. He was trying to recall those that had involved the Chinese investors, and it took over forty minutes before he found the right box.

Eventually, Dave came across a couple of familiar cases and recognised the sites involved. Draft plans for the site and his notes regarding the possible issues that could arise from the planning point of view. However, he was particularly looking for any surveys or appraisals of the technical problems that might occur, but he found nothing. He recalled that this was not necessarily unusual as Frank's team's job was to get planning permission for the scheme, and the technical and financing matters were for the developer to sort out.

He ploughed on through the box and found a detailed file involving a Chinese operator which did have a technical report showing the effect of some shading on the site which would lessen the effectiveness of the solar panels, the likely production of energy over the lifetime of these and the arrangements for attaching the site to the main Grid.

The report was signed with an indecipherable squiggle with no printed name to identify the surveyor.

"Bollocks," murmured Dave, mainly to himself. He wasn't too surprised at the lack of the required result of his search, but it would still have given him something to give to the police. Nevertheless, he wrote down the name of the Chinese company and would try to contact someone there.

Chapter 13

Harriet was totally fed up and feeling most odd. It was almost as though she was going to feint, but she seemed weirdly in control of that. Her thought processes were all over the place, and nothing seemed to be what or where it should be. Maybe this was what a panic attack was like.

Daisy was having a couple of days where she felt quite unwell but with some courage, had made her way to college, and Harriet had a a feeling of fear that she was losing control of Oliver.

She was wandering the streets, trying to clear her head of her worries, and not least about her finances. Murray had stopped paying her maintenance money for some long time, and she didn't know why. He wasn't returning her calls on his mobile and when she found his home number there was just a recorded message in a West Country woman's voice. She had to find out more. That bloody man was right after all; he was ruining her life.

And then this bombshell!

Her son, Oliver had called her to say that he had a problem.

"Mum, I need some help."

"What's up? Where are you, Ollie?"

"I'm in the City with Jimmy Patel."

"OK, so what's the problem?"

"A gang of boys came onto us and started chanting racist words at Jimmy."

"Yes, and what then?"

"He lashed out at them, and they caught him in the face. There's a lot of blood."

"And what about you?"

"I had to defend him. Mum, he's my mate."

"OK, and are you hurt?"

"Just a few scrapes."

"What do you want me to do for you? Did you call the police or ambulance?"

"They did as soon as people came to help us."

"So, is Jimmy OK now?"

"Shaken up and wants to go home."

"And what about the police?"

"Don't think they were very sympathetic because we fought back. Would have been OK if PC Parting had been here!"

"But he isn't. Ollie, what do you want me to do?"

"Can you come and get us? Please."

"Darling boy, I can't. I'm working. Tell you what, I'll see if Grandad Jack can come and get you."

And he did.

Harriet and Sam's father, Jack Chambers had retired from a senior post in the education department at the County Council some three years earlier. A tall man with light brown hair which was thinning rapidly.

Jack had lost his wife to bowel cancer a year before his retirement, and the memories and stress of caring for her had left their mark. It had also ruined their plans for their future together, for their love of travelling and the countryside.

He remained living in the family home, but painful memories occasionally left him disconsolate.

And the loneliness.

No-one to share the joys of a day, no-one to share the frustrations.

Jack, however, was always on the ready when the family called.

And Harriet called.

———

Early on a Tuesday morning the Vice-Admiral was poking about in the large former cart shed that had been converted into a garage for their three cars, Hilda's little runabout – a six-year-old Clio, the old but trustworthy Land Rover Defender that he had bought in exchange for his even older Discovery, and Douglas' pride and joy, the twenty five year old Bentley.

He was dressed in an old worn pair of navy blue corduroy trousers secured by a pair of plain black braces over a maroon work shirt, and he shuffled a few old paint tins around, trying to remember which rooms were painted with what. He found a pair of pliers and a small hacksaw on a bench where they shouldn't be and replaced them where they should be.

The dust made him sneeze which he managed to catch in a dark blue handkerchief, and he had to stabilise himself against the door of the Bentley. He brushed through his silver hair with the fingers of his left hand made sure he was steady enough and went out towards the Hall.

As he walked indoors, he called, "Hilda!"

"What is it, dear?"

"Just wondering if we should get the Bentley out and give it a spin. It's not been out of its covers for a month or more. It will do it good to have a run."

"Lovely. Where do you want to go? I heard someone talk about the Water Gardens the other side of Swaffham. How about that? You would like that, the water I mean. Memories of your boats."

"Ships, Hilda, it's always ships, and don't be so silly."

"Are you alright? You look as if you might have a summer cold coming."

"Just the dust in the garage made me sneeze, that's all."

"Oh, that's all right then. What about a garden centre then. Dibber says that our soil is perfect for rhubarb – or '*roobub*' as he calls it – and we could get some plants for him to put in for us."

"What on earth do we need rhubarb for? My insides work perfectly well enough, Hilda without rhubarb, thank you very much."

"Because it makes a nice change for pudding, or I could make some rhubarb and ginger jam."

"Why don't you just buy a jar of rhubarb and ginger

jam?"

"Oh, Douglas, don't be so awkward."

"Anyway, why is he called Dibber?"

"I think he helped his dad on his allotment and liked playing with his."

"Playing with his what?"

"His dibber, of course."

"Is that what you call it?"

"Stop it. Are we going for a ride out or not."

"I'll get changed."

One evening Myra Plater was thinking.

She had enjoyed a good day.

A brisk walk would do her good, she had mused to herself after a breakfast of bran flakes and muesli, and so she had donned her stout walking shoes, and walked the lanes around the village before making her way to the general store in the centre of Easthoe where she bought her provisions for the next couple of days.

And so, that evening, as she rested after her day's exertions her mind went back to the body at Thompson Common.

"They said 'skeleton', but no mention of clothes. Surely after five or six years the clothes wouldn't have disintegrated or decomposed. So, was the body dumped there naked? Is it a sex crime? Mmmm, this is getting complicated," she thought to herself as she poured her second glass of Pinot Grigio, staring out of her French windows onto the spring flowers as the light began to fade.

She took a large sip of her wine and thought that she had to focus more on this matter as she wanted to create a spotlight for her skills and the deficiencies of the police and other agencies. "Arthur would have wanted me to solve this," she said to the garden.

The shrubs agreed.

―――

Ravinder Kapur had eventually found time to try and track down the reporter in Peterborough and told him about the case in Norfolk and asked if he could recall the story that he wrote some seven years previously about the disappearance of a surveyor in Cambridgeshire.

Paul Cooper, fortunately, was still working for the same paper and was one of those people who kept his old notebooks in a meticulous chronological order. Having understood what Ravinder was looking for he said he would look through these and if he was able to track down the specific notes and if successful would ring her back in a few days.

It was in fact a week before Ravinder was able to call Sally and pass on Paul's information.

"Hi, Sally. Paul has been really helpful and found his notes of the time he wrote his report about the missing surveyor in Cambridgeshire. Apparently, the man was working for a solar farm company that was, indeed from China. It wasn't clear who had reported him missing and it sounds as though there was an anonymous tip off. He had never been traced, although very little pressure was placed on the police to carry out further investigations. He seemed to have just disappeared, and it seemed that there had been no effort to follow up the story."

"Oh dear," Sally replied, "Good of you to have done what you have, Rav, but that seems to be it."

"I know. Very frustrating, isn't it?"

"Well, it often is in this work, eh?"

"I know. Sally, it would be good to catch up sometime. Keep in touch."

"I certainly will, Rav. Good to talk with you, and thanks again."

―――

After his visit to Frank Pack's office, Dave was feeling somewhat underwhelmed, and decided that the only thing to do was to pass the details of the Chinese company to the police, and so he rang Sally Parmenter to check if he should pass it to her or to DI Lovelace.

Sally said she would take the information and would pass it on. As it was thought that the victim might have been of East European origin, she thought that Interpol might be able to put some time into probing the mystery of the pingo body. In recent years Sally would have used the European police cooperative body, not surprisingly called Europol, but since the UK had left the EU after the still debated decision to carry through the Brexit result, the international Interpol had to be the organisation to be involved.

Tony Lovelace was out of his office when Sally rang, and she spoke to his secretary Julie Paxton who said that he should be back before the end of play that day. She said she would get him to ring back.

However, it was six-thirty or thereabouts when Tony rang Sally's mobile, apologising for the delay. Sally had just finished her evening meal with husband James and their two children, both of whom moped about wanting to take their meal to their rooms where they were in the midst of some game with others remotely on their X-boxes.

"Hi, Tony, I just wanted to see how you wanted to play this. Dave Wakefield has tracked down the name of the Chinese company he was working with, but not the surveyor. He wanted to know who was best to see what they could about this company. My hunch is that it is one for your team, and we were wondering if there was a case to involve Interpol at this stage."

"Sounds like a possibility, Sally, but yes please email the name over to me and I will talk with my team. I'll be in touch. Bye for now."

"Oh, Tony, before you go, I must just tell you that the other disappearance of a surveyor in Cambridgeshire wasn't taken any further. There was no pressure from any one to ask the police to do anything. I just have a feeling that these two must be linked. I'll let you know if I hear more."

"Yes, please do that. Goodnight Sally, have a good evening."

Chapter 14

In his black seven year old Ford Kuga, window open so he could let his cigarette smoke out, Fat Robbie looked like any family man driving into town to see his mum. Worn jeans, black Nike trainers and maroon tee shirt he appeared as nondescript as he wanted to.

His dark hair hung over his collar and his fat face was pitted with old acne spots. Still, he whistled as he drove, listening to the police radios on his especially adapted media centre in the dashboard.

He had sent encrypted texts to Johnny McNeil, his main contact in West Kenning and had arranged for them to meet on the rough land behind the railway station where there was no CCTV coverage and where money would pass in one direction and a bag containing a series of plastic packages would pass in the other.

The delivery complete, Fat Robbie then left at a sedate speed and drove towards Norwich for another delivery in a nearby village, before he made his way home.

―――

Within forty minutes Jack Chambers had arrived at the car park beside the Theatre in Norwich and saw the two boys looking very sorry for themselves. Whilst Ollie just looked a bit tearful and clearly had a scrape on his arm, Jimmy had a fat lip and a swollen left eye.

"Come on here, you lads," said Jack opening the passenger door for Ollie to slip in and then, checking that Jimmy was merely feeling sore and had been cleaned up, he opened the rear door and helped Ollie's mate into the back seat.

Once on their way, Jack asked, "So what was the fighting all about?"

Ollie quickly said, "They were bloody racists. One of them walked right up to Jimmy and stared into his eyes and told him to go back to where he came from. Then Jimmy just said that he came from Norfolk, and the bloke started punching him."

Jack was incensed. "Any idea who these lads were?"

"No, as soon as people started to gather round us to help, the bastards ran away."

"Probably best that you don't go there for a while, boys."

"I know."

Jimmy was very quiet.

―――

Myra Plater had, like most people been concerned about the horrendous rise in energy bills and was doing her sums. The energy company that provided gas and electricity to her cottage wanted to increase his monthly payment from £65 to £200. She had kept clear records of her energy usage since the warning of increased prices and had worked out that she would not use more than £5 a day averaged over the year and offered to pay £150 a month.

The company argued. Myra argued back.

She adjusted her direct debit to the £150 a month previously offered and went through her figures again, fiddling with the newly installed smart meter to see if it would give her any assistance and prove that she was right. She wasn't.

She had misinterpreted the way gas was recorded and realised with some horror that the company wasn't far off. She corrected her figures and decided to get back to the company and see if they would agree that a figure of £190 a month would be nearer the mark.

It was.

She didn't like it, but at least she knew she could afford it, thanks to Arthur's pension.

Myra knew that there were families where both parents were working, albeit at just above the minimum wage and were having to use foodbanks to feed themselves and their growing kids. The Vicar had told her so on a number of occasions. In fact he had mentioned the shameful situation in one of his sermons – where someone had muttered something about loaves and fishes.

She also knew that some of those poor people had considered borrowing from firms offering loans at stupid rates of interest. The Vicar had told her that too.

She thought of her own children trying to manage their own families, especially the girls, and knew that she would probably have to help them out at some stage.

Myra knew she was one of the lucky ones and could afford to help. Just.

Myra knew.

She went into the village centre to do some careful shopping and arrived home, cursing how much the cost of everything had shot up. Her pack of favourite cheese, Cambozola had gone up by twenty-five pence, and she was sure that the package was smaller than before.

Usually, she was one of those shoppers who saw something she liked and threw it into the trolley, but now she was being a bit more careful. Even when it came to getting her wine, she was looking at the lower shelves rather than those nearer the top. She had decided that the own brand Soave was nowhere as nice as her preferred bottle of Pinot Grigio, but it still did the required job.

As she unpacked the groceries, she noticed an unexpected piece of paper that seemed to have been slipped under the kitchen door. This seemed odd as she thought that the door was constructed in such a way that nothing would get through any gaps. She had not noticed any draughts, but she would test that later.

The piece of paper was a plain sheet of A4 torn in half and folded twice. She opened it and found, scrawled in red, which looked like it was done by a Sharpie, the words *'Leave well alone'*.

Somewhat shocked she opened the bottle of Soave and poured a large glass, finished packing away the shopping and took a long gulp of the wine.

"Whoever did that? Why? Leave what alone?" she said to herself.

No-one replied.

———

Darren Prescott had been in touch with George 'Dolly' Parting, and they had agreed to have a catch-up drink at The Brown Bear after work one evening. As before Darren was nursing a pint of Guinness and George had got a Diet Coke.

"Are you not a big drinker, then George?"

"Not really. I'm OK when I'm on holiday, but you never know in this job when you might get a call out."

"No real time to relax, then. I'm not sure I could do that. Anyway, I'm getting nowhere trying to find out more about the drug scene. There must be someone who would be able to kick off my investigations."

"I'll ask the boys in the anti-drug team and see if they would contact you."

"Yeah, that would be useful. There must be more than one drug gang operating in the County. Do they cooperate with each other or are they competitive?"

The genial constable looked at him, smiled and said, "I'm sure that must be right."

"Anyway, is there any progress on the pingo body case?" Darren asked.

"Not much, in fact there's just about bugger all. At least that's as much as I know. I do know, though that the Sergeant has been in touch with the DI, so there must be something going on."

They found some easy talk about football and sport in general, and Darren asked if his new friend had contemplated playing rugby. Whilst George was slight in stature, he did look fit.

"I've tended to use the leisure centre in town for a swim and a bit of gym work," George said. "You never know when you might need to chase after some villain, just like the old cop shows!"

"You would make a great scrum half, I'd reckon, and as you can guess I'm a bit of a second row forward!"

"I can see that!"

"Are you from around here, George?"

"Not really, although I am a Norfolk boy. I was born in Great Yarmouth. What about you?"

"I was born and brought up in West Yorkshire in a village outside of Halifax. Strange name, Luddenden Foot."

"Bloody hell, that's a bit of a mouthful."

"Lovely spot actually, but I moved to Leeds for Uni, and got my first job at the West Yorkshire Globe. Fancied a change and we had taken holidays down here when I was a kid. So, when I saw the ad for this job, I got in touch, liked the people, and joined them. Must say that I love it here."

"So, are you on your own?"

"Oh yes. I've got plenty of time to think about settling down. Huge responsibility is that, and I'm not ready for all that! What about you?"

"I'm not sure what my plan is. I think you need some financial security before you think about getting tied down with someone else. I've got plenty of time to think about it too."

"Anyway, good to chat, but I want to get back. There's a good match on tele tonight." Darren finished his pint.

"I shall be watching too. Got to wash my hair first!"

"Good for you, ducky! See you, George."

Chapter 15

Myra Plater had taken a tough decision. She was going to see her mother and was on her way to the Care Home in Bury St. Edmunds.

Before Arthur had died the two of them had spent many hours traipsing around Norfolk and Suffolk checking out the Residential Homes, Care Homes, retirement villages and any other facility that would be able to give the old dear a comfortable and supportive future for her remaining years. They had chosen the Goldcrest Home in Bury.

As she entered the drive to the substantially enlarged Edwardian villa, she prepared herself for the aroma of boiled cabbage and stale urine as well as the expected confused conversation ahead.

She parked the Jeep and on entering the entrance hall, she was pleasantly surprised by the scent of citrus, partly from the potted lemon trees and partly from the lavishly used air spray, but above all by that unctuous smell of home-made steak and kidney pudding.

She knocked on the office door, introduced herself and chatted politely with a member of staff who was called Sharon and asked where she might find her mother.

"I'll take you to her room," said Sharon, rising steadily from her computer chair. Sharon had one of those kindly faces but with a very wide waist and backside.

Myra thought that with all the walking round the Home, Sharon would have walked off a few of those inches. Perhaps it was the steak and kidney puddings.

Sharon led the way along a corridor with a bright maroon carpet patterned with lemon-coloured flowers, and up the stairs, similarly carpeted and onto the landing of the first floor overlooking the well-tended gardens.

The room was named 'Nuthatch' and there was a label stating that the room was occupied by Mrs Elsie Roe.

Sharon knocked on the door and opened it gently and said in a cheery sing-song voice "Morning again Elsie. You have a visitor. Would you like to go into the visitors' room or stay here, dear?"

"Yes."

"Which would you like to do?"

"Eh?"

"Where would you like to sit?"

"In my chair."

"OK, dear. You stay here, then. There are Myra. There's a button on the cabinet beside Elsie's bed you can press in case you need anything. Can I get you a coffee?"

Myra gritted her teeth at the thought of a weak instant and said that she would be happy with a glass of water.

"Hello Mum. How are you doing?"

"Yeah."

"Are you comfortable here, now? They seem very nice, and the lunch being cooked smelt lovely."

"Half past ten."

"Pardon?"

"What?"

"I asked you if you were happy here."

"I know that. Who are you? What'ya doin' here?"

"It's me, Myra. Your daughter, Mum."

"What?"

"It's Myra, your daughter."

"Forty-seven. Half past ten."

Myra sat, dumbfounded. The monthly email from the Home hadn't suggested that she was this bad. After a few minutes she knew she ought to speak with Sharon again.

"I'm just going to the loo, Mum," she lied as she opened the bedroom door and went back to the office to see if Sharon was still there. She was.

"Hello again, Myra. Everything all right?"

"No, it's not, Sharon. I wasn't expecting to see her like this. How long has she been as confused as this?"

"I know. It has got worse quite quickly. The doctor is coming in soon, and I expect you would you like to have a word with her when she gets here?"

"That might be very useful, thanks Sharon."

Myra went back to her mother's room where she found that Elsie was sitting on the edge of her bed, totally naked, her clothes strewn over the floor.

"Oh, mum, what's this about? Let's get your clothes on again, shall we?" she said picking up the underwear, stockings, skirt and blouse and her favourite orange cardigan. And then she realised how wet they were.

"Oh, Christ on a bike," she thought, and then regretted her language. "This is bad."

Within ten minutes the doctor arrived at Goldcrest Home and registered her arrival at the reception office, where Sharon told her about Myra's visit and her concerns.

Doctor Polly Grainger was surprised and asked if Myra was still there, and asked if she could she have a private space to talk with her. Sharon took her to a small meeting room and went to fetch Myra, where she found her with her head in her hands weeping. Elsie was still sitting on the edge of her bed and still naked.

"Myra, the doctor is here and she would like to have a chat with you. Come along with me, dear."

Sharon called to one of her staff to go and try and get Elsie cleaned up and back into bed and took Myra to the meeting room.

"Myra, this is Doctor Polly Grainger," she said, and left the room.

"Hello, Myra. I understand from Sharon that you have increased concerns over your mother's health."

"I certainly do, Doctor…. Or may I call you Polly?"

"Whichever is fine with me."

"OK. Well, I've not seen Mum for a few weeks, and she is much more confused than when I saw her last." Myra then told Polly about the latest episode of the wet clothes.

"Mmm. It certainly sounds as though she is worse than when I saw her last week. I will give her a thorough check. I suspect she has a urinary infection, but we better check everything."

"Many thanks, Polly. Will you let me know?"

"I will report back to Sharon and ask her to let you know."

"That's very kind. Thank you so much."

"You're welcome. Bye, Myra."

"Bye"

Myra went to thank Sharon, got into her car and drove home in a blur.

Once there, and the Jeep safely parked, she sat in her favourite armchair, drank two large glasses of wine, cried and fell asleep.

Chapter 16

The response to the invitation to write to the Broad Norfolk Post about the proposed housing development at Easthoe was inevitable.

There were voicemails left, some of which were of such an obscene nature that they were scrubbed from the recordings, others agreeing with either the pros or the cons as set out in the earlier article in the paper, and the usual responses by email as well as a handwritten letter from Vice-Admiral Sir Douglas Ewart-Robinson.

Avril was also not surprised to see an epistle from Myra Plater.

By email came a letter from Colin Brunby, who was one who wrote in nearly every week.

Sir

It was with great interest that I noted your request for comments about the proposed housing in Easthoe.

You only have to look at the housing market to know that there is not enough supply to meet the demand. This situation does nothing to help our children, let alone grandchildren and it is imperative that more housing is encouraged. What do your readers think of the prospects for their offspring?

It's not just granting permission for the development but making sure the dwellings are built. Leaving the land undeveloped with permissions like so many landowners or developers have done in order to increase its value is nothing short of scandalous.

Let's get this done!

Yours

Colin Brunby

West Kelling

From The Vice-Admiral on his thick, headed notepaper and written in a green ink from a well used fountain pen came this: -

Sir

I understand that a terrible catastrophe is about to befall my nearest village. How in the name of Jehovah is the village of Easthoe meant to absorb another vast number of inhabitants? I despair.

No doubt the woolly-headed councillors will

ensure that half of these new people will be migrants coming here to sponge on our already feeble benefits system.
I say that it is imperative that we look after our own.
Yours
Sir Douglas Ewart-Robinson (Vice-Admiral Rtd.)
Snetterbrook Hall

Myra's email was direct, if not quite so offensive: -
Dear Editor
Thank you for the opportunity to speak about the proposal for new homes in Easthoe. Many of my fellow residents are appalled at the prospect of more traffic within the village. There are not enough jobs here to provide for the new folk who would be bound to have to travel to their work.
The village works well now; the community is one of togetherness.
Please do not make our village worse.
Enough is enough.
Yours faithfully
Mrs Myra Plater
Easthoe

Avril had asked Jenny to copy the most relevant of these and pass them on to Jane and her colleagues at the Planning Department, where they were received with both a measure of cynicism and inevitability.

"Right, where are we going, then?" asks Lady Hilda.

"What?"

"You said we were going out in the Bentley. So, where are we going?"

"Oh, don't be so awkward, Hilda."

"Awkward? Me? It's you who is the awkward one. I merely asked where we were going. It's not that difficult."

"I don't know. You said you wanted to go to a garden centre. Is that still what you want? If so, which one? And.... please don't choose the most expensive one, like you usually do."

"They're all about the same."

"I'm damn well sure that they are not."

"Anyway, what do you know about them. You leave all the gardening to me."

"And Dibber," he retorted.

"Well, yes. Good old Dibber. I do like that chap. He's a good sort with a very nice family. Although his granddaughter, Phoebe I think her name is, she can be a bit of a handful."

How do you know that?"

"Because I talk to him, Douglas. It's more than you do."

Douglas grunted and raised his dark bushy eyebrows.

"You don't need to grunt like that. You only do it when you know I am right," she continued. "So, now then, where are we going?"

"We will go up to Holt and see where we go from there. Pop into The Feathers for coffee and a small glass of malt."

"Drinking and driving, Douglas? Tut tut."

———

Depression was a constant companion to Harriet, but she was strong enough to concentrate on the important things in her life. Her kids.

In particular she was consumed with giving as much of her time and support to Daisy as was necessary. There were times however, when she thought that the eighteen year old should have come to terms with all her physical problems that she had been born with. She had tried to instil resilience into girl's life with the help of the consultants and physios at the hospital. However, Daisy still demanded so much of Harriet's time to provide the support and comfort she craved.

And then there was Ollie with his easy knack of finding himself at the wrong place at the wrong time, and not least with his latest engagement supporting his friend. Not really at fault but caught up in trouble.

Many were the times when Harriet had cursed the way Murray had left the family and was sure that Daisy's insecurity was a result of losing the father figure she needed so much. It was time she had another word with her Dad, Jack.

However, it was his laid-back attitude to life that gave him his real character. The involvement in the fracas was an expression of him standing up against what he saw was wrong. Prejudice in all its forms was something he was certainly learning about and his support for Jimmy Patel was testament to his growing maturity.

The difficulties in her life were getting Harriet down, even though she knew there were many others much worse off than she was.

———

DI Tony Lovelace had talked through the latest information that Sally had passed to him with his Cold Case team and they agreed that there were two main areas they needed to concentrate on.

One was the need to get clarity on the identity of the pingo victim and there was a general level of support to involve Interpol in the tracing him through the facial reconstruction photograph, and Pete Evans was tasked with making contact and sending the details.

The second strand was to talk with their Cambridgeshire equivalents and try and persuade them to open an investigation. Tony said he would speak to his oppo and try and persuade him or her to the importance of doing so. No doubt there would be an issue of funding, and Tony knew he would have to argue his case with his bosses before he contacted the neighbouring county.

The team had tried to find out more about the Chinese company that Dave had passed on to them, and whilst they managed to find a London address, it was clearly a company created purely for the developments in England and Wales. The Chairman was a man called Nan Gong Xin and the Chief Executive had the hardly oriental handle of James Smith. No current phone numbers were available, and there was little for the team to get to grips with the issue.

What was also nagging away in Tony's mind was the issue of the alleged 'bank of surveyors' from which the disappeared men had allegedly been plucked.

He had a horrible suspicion that this was a fantasy, and that the Chinese companies had recruited their own men, probably at cheaper rates who would write their reports with an extraordinary slant towards the answers that the companies wanted. It was certainly not unknown.

"I bet that's it. How many authorities had the special knowledge to be able to challenge these reports when they dealt with applications?" he wondered. "Dave Wakefield was in that business. Must talk to him in the next few days. Oh yes, and make sure I know who the best person is to talk with in the Cambridgeshire Force."

At a meeting of Paston District Council's Planning Committee, the councillors had made decisions on sixteen applications, many involving robust discussion. On two occasions it had proved necessary for Jane to make it clear to them that they had to make those decisions in accordance with the law and within their own established policies, rather their views of either the applicants or obscure issues raised by objectors. Wanting to help someone out of a muddle of their own making was not a good reason to depart from the Council's policy. The councillors nodded in agreement with her, knowing that they would do just what they wanted when circumstances demanded.

The most controversial proposal was for a battery storage facility to accumulate electricity from offshore wind farms before sending the power to the National Grid. This involved a series of large buildings which impacted on a rural landscape and a small group of dwellings.

Needless to say there was much opposition, and after a quarter of a hour of comment and argument, the committee did its favourite thing and deferred making a decision so they could go and have a look at the site, outside the village of Ballington in the south of the District.

At the end of the main agenda, Councillor Jim Prentice

asked when the application for the housing development at Easthoe would come before the committee. Jane advised the meeting that there was likely to be a public meeting in the village, and so it might be at least a couple of months of discussion and, hopefully revised proposals before it would be ready for discussion.

Chapter 17

Work on the restoration of the pingos at Thompson Common had been halted for a couple of months whilst detectives continued their search for clues as to the identity of the victim.

The team of volunteers had then been moved to a scrub clearance project on a nearby wildlife site comprising a mature woodland. Work was required in order to create more light to the woodland floor which would allow the overshadowed plant life to regenerate and provide its colour, scent and wonder in the following spring.

Long handled loppers, and pruning saws were at work cutting back goat willow, hazel and elder. Over mature trees which had shed dead branches were either felled or given another chance with careful removal of other dead and dying limbs thanks to the skills of specialists wielding chain saws.

A good fortnight's work by all concerned and whilst it looked brutal at the time, confidence for the future was high.

———

There was little else said on the drive home from Norwich. Oliver sat looking out of the passenger window, and Jimmy was nursing his wounds, saying nothing after the thanks to Jack for the wet wipes and tissues he handed him.

It had been arranged that Jimmy's mum would pick him up, and she had already arrived at Harriet's home and was enjoying a thankful cup of coffee when Harriet's phone rang. It was Jack saying that they were ten minutes from dropping the boys off.

He parked the car and they went round to the back of the house, and Jack opened the kitchen door.

"Hello, we're home."

Nothing.

"Go and see if you can find your mum, Ollie," Jack said, gently.

"Don't want to."

"Look, what's done is done. No sense in trying to pretend otherwise. I expect she will wonder what really happened, and she may not like what you have been up to, but she is still your mum, and she still loves you."

"I can't face it."

"You are learning big lessons today, my boy. Better

than anything you would learn at college. Just go and get it over with. Just remember that you and Jimmy did nothing wrong, other than defend yourselves."

Oliver crept into the lounge and found his mum sitting on the settee with Jimmy's mum.

He knelt down next to the sofa and put his arms round Harriet and whispered, "I'm sorry, mum".

In the meantime Jimmy's bruised face was swelling further, and his mum took him to the bathroom to get some cold water on the damaged areas.

Harriet had rehearsed the tongue lashing she wanted to give Ollie, but the softness of his words, the hug that he pressed around her softened that speech.

Leaning towards him, she said, "Ok, Oliver, tell me your side of the story. Please."

"Not now, mum. GD is still here." Oliver had called Jack that from an early age, and the title had stuck.

"But he went to support you, and you know how much he wants you to succeed in your life."

"I do know that."

"Then, go and give him a hug and thank him for helping."

"OK."

Oliver went back to the kitchen, where Jack was sitting at the kitchen table with a glass of cranberry juice in his left hand. "GD, I'm sorry for causing you this trouble. I love you."

"Ollie, Grandads are there to support their children and their grandchildren. The good thing is that they don't have to live with them!"

"Wish you did, GD."

"Do you really?"

"I think, it might stop mum being so ratty."

"Darling boy, she has so much to think about, bringing up children on her own, especially with Daisy being so ill and not knowing from day to day how she will be. It's not easy. In fact it is really hard, and I bet she worries about how she can afford to run the home. I'll try and have a word with her in a few days."

With that he opened the kitchen door preparing to go home, as Oliver came forward and gave him a massive hug. "Thanks GD," and Jack could see damp eyes in the lad.

"See you, Harriet, love," he called to his daughter. "See you later, Ollie. I hope Jimmy will be OK."

"Laters, GD. I love you."

―――

Six weeks later and Dave was getting used to his new lifestyle and the extra hours he was able to enjoy in each day.

The occasional pub lunch, bit of essential decorating that had been put off for months, a few phone calls to old colleagues for a catch up, cajoled into playing bowls which ended up with a few beers, and he had made contact with the County Wildlife Trust to see what he might be able to do in the way of volunteering to help.

On one of their evening strolls over the surrounding fields he turned to Michelle and said, "Do you know, I'm beginning to like this. Tell me, though, do I get under your feet?"

"Sometimes, but in fairness you are beginning to see your own way to your enjoyment on your own, as well as the things we like to do together."

"We'll get there, girl. It really is a massive change but

I'm sure we'll get there."

"You will Dave. I promise!"

"I know," Dave stood still with his ears cocked.

"Listen," he whispered.

They stopped and listened.

"What to?"

"Almost nothing!"

It had been some time since the Broad Norfolk Post had published the picture of the best attempt of reconstructing the face of the man buried in the Thompson pingo, and there had been little response other than the usual jokers who suggested Lord Lucan, Robert Maxwell, Denis Thatcher or the usual Mickey Mouse.

Jenny had giggled at these as she passed the messages on to Avril.

"Same old, same old," she said.

Surprisingly, at least to Avril and Darren was the fact that there had been no response from Myra Plater.

"Do you think she's ill?" asked Darren.

"It wouldn't stop her saying something though."

"Or Colin Brunby!"

"Or indeed the Vice-Admiral."

But the odd email did prompt some interesting thinking, and the three musketeers in the Post's office gathered around to try and make sense of any of it.

Firstly, an anonymous lady suggested that there had been a surveyor from one of the big Norwich firms who had surveyed her house before she bought it about seven years previously and who she thought looked very much like the man pictured in the paper. Secondly a handwritten note that had been posted through the office door one evening, again with no address or name suggesting that the man was one of a pair of brothers who had been scamming their way around the County.

Under normal circumstances Avril would have told Jenny to destroy these. If folk couldn't be open enough to put their name to suggestions and accusations, they were probably cranks and jokers. However, this time she thought that any whiff of an idea might just prove useful, and so she rang the Police station to talk with Sally, who was having a few days off, and so she had a quick word with her secretary and agreed that she would pass the information straight on to Tony.

Chapter 18

The Bentley gave as smooth a ride as ever, despite the state of some of the back roads, and the Ewart-Robinsons turned into the main street of Holt, which as ever in late Spring was heaving with vehicles and pedestrians, some of whom found it difficult to walk on the pavements.

"Look at those thoughtless buggers. Why can't they take their time and walk in the proper place?" cried out the Vice-Admiral, waving his gloved finger at a young man in shorts and sandals who was almost in the middle of the road.

"Never a problem like that at sea, eh Douglas?"

"Don't be facetious, Hilda. This place is blocked with cars, and I'm not going to bugger about in the little streets round here to try and find a parking spot."

"Thought you wanted to go to the Feathers."

"I did."

"Don't they have a car park?"

"I'm not going to try that with all these vehicles about. Might scratch the Bentley, you know."

"So, where do you want to go then? Home?"

He thought for a while and then decided that they should continue the ride. "It's early in the day. Why don't we go to old Coke's place. You know, what's it called?"

"Holkham, Douglas. You knew that didn't you?"

"Of course, I did. Wonder if the Duke will be in."

"I think you will find that he is the Earl of Leicester, Douglas."

"Whatever."

"Do you know him, then?"

"No."

"So, why the interest in him then?"

"No reason."

It took another twenty minutes at a sedate pace before they were nearing Wells-next-the-Sea and turned onto the coast road for the few extra miles to the village of Holkham.

"Let's go down to the sea first, please," said Hilda.

"Did you bring suitable boots? Or your swimming costume?"

"Don't be silly, now. Yes, I've got my good walking shoes."

They turned right into Lady's Drive and saw that there were cars almost the whole long length of it.

"I'll go right down to the disabled parking spaces at the end," he said.

"But Douglas you are *not* disabled."

"But I do have a disabled person's badge that I can put on the dashboard."

"Where in God's name did you get that?"

"It's for me to know."

"Douglas! You are incorrigible."

Georgia Stephens was relieved that her landlord had been up to the mark after the flooded rooms in her home by organising the replacement floor coverings and providing dehumidifiers so that the house was habitable after only a few days.

However, the interim period had been stressful. She and her three children had been housed in a local hotel and the restrictions to the way they had to live their days had caused tensions.

Georgia and Becca shared a room, which wasn't so unusual given the time they had shared a bed in the past when Becca had felt unwell, but Tyler's routine and interests were so difficult to manage without the equipment he used at home, and he became sullen. His own small room in a hotel was not the place for a young and energetic teenaged boy and he constantly moaned about the situation. The hotel was a small one and there were no exercise facilities for him to let off steam.

Nevertheless, they were back home and into their normal habitats, and attitudes returned to normal. At least, normal for them.

Becca, despite the odd day when she felt pains in her lower body, was feeling better and was enjoying being back at school and was circulating amongst her friends, whilst Tyler, having passed his necessary courses to satisfy health and safety issues, was finding casual work on building sites which helped to fund his clothes and to give a bit of money to his mum.

———

DI Tony Lovelace was following up his earlier thoughts and had rung through to Cambridgeshire Police to see if there could be some improved cooperation between the two forces regarding the second missing surveyor and, after a five minute wait was put through to DCI Jacqueline Rickards.

"Good morning, DCI Rickards, I hope you can help. I'm DI Tony Lovelace from Norfolk Police and we are investigating the death of a man who had been buried in an unusual location and may have been on a surveying project when he went missing. I understand from an article in the Peterborough newspaper of about seven years ago that there was a similar case in Cambridgeshire, and we are hoping that you might be able to put some resource into delving a bit further into that case so we can see if there are any connections between the two. Do you think you could help, please?"

Tony's manner was not typical of his often brusque way of dealing with his own team and was putting on the charm.

"Well, Tony," she said in a very clipped tone that didn't bode well for the next statement, "I don't know about your set-up, but we are down to the bone at the moment."

"Oh, very good. Dead bodies and bones."

"It's no joking matter. Honestly, I don't think we can help."

"OK, I understand. What about the chances of us having access to your system and sending one of my officers to come to you and carry out some research. Would that be acceptable?"

"I'll have to talk to my people. I'll call you back." She terminated the call.

"Jesus, Mary and Joseph," blustered Tony, "it's like getting sodding blood out of a stone."

Next, he contacted Dave Wakefield to try and get an idea of the appraisals that planning staff gave to technical reports submitted with planning applications.

Dave replied, "I'm not sure what the process is now, but when I was there and if there were reports that were beyond our understanding, we would either ask someone within the council who may have some expertise or often go to appropriate consultants to give an independent appraisal of the information."

"I bet that cost you!"

"Oh yes it did, but we always budgeted for it! Anyway, would you like me to check the current situation?"

"That would be helpful. Thanks."

"I'll call you."

Dave rang Jane Seabrook at her office and asked if the checking of technical reports on solar farm applications was more robust than when he was there.

"We haven't had any lately, Dave, but in truth I don't think the process has changed. Why do you ask?"

"Well, you know this issue of the missing surveyors? It may be that the reports that they are alleged to have published were bogus, and just said what the developers wanted them to say. It's all a real mystery, and it's messing with my head."

"I'll ask the team, but you'll only get something if I find out something that's different to what you did!"

"Ok, bless you, Jane. Bye for now."

"Bye, Dave. We must have our lunchtime chat sometime."

"Indeed we must. Let me know when you can make it. Bye."

Chapter 19

Georgia and Tyler were at home on a swift lunchtime break and chatting about his day. He had soon got back to his normal self and said that he had to go back to his job working with the dad of one of his mates on a local building site, so time was tight. In his short time working, Tyler had gained many skills in so many practical jobs for such a young lad. No academic was Tyler, but he would turn his hand at anything physical. Manual work was what he enjoyed most.

He was also a popular lad and met up with his mates in an evening, lounging around the town park in the summer, and catching up with the gossip on a Friday evening, often at The Brown Bear. After a few typical teenage years when he had brushed with trouble, Tyler was settling down to be a useful citizen and found himself volunteering for work parties organised to tidy up the town and collect strewn rubbish on a Saturday morning. He was becoming very aware of all around him. He knew who to trust and who to get on his side, and was becoming a leader in the Friday evening gatherings.

From a difficult start in his life and the odd hard talking to from a number of people in authority, Georgia was immensely proud of her son.

———

Myra Plater had much on her mind. The news from the Goldcrest Home confirmed that her mother had indeed suffered from a severe urinary infection that had messed with her mind, and Myra knew she ought to take a return trip to try and salve her conscience. However, she didn't relish the thought and managed to put the idea to the back of her mind for the time being.

The *'Leave well alone'* note she had received was troubling. Was someone trying to steer her away from the Thompson Common body, from making life difficult for the developers in Easthoe, or something else?

She walked around her garden deadheading the tulips and trying to work it out.

"I can't see why anyone would want to say that to me about the body at Thompson Common. There's no reason to. It can't be that. Can it?" she muttered to herself. "Must be something to do with the housing proposal. I wonder who would do such a thing."

A walk around the village might help to free her mind, and so she went indoors and to her bedroom where she changed into her tweed skirt and a pink silk blouse. She checked that her hair was in place and then went down the stairs and put on her best brogues. She donned a pair of sunglasses to reduce the glare from the sun and set out to the Market Square where she entered the butcher's shop and bought herself a piece of pork tenderloin that she would dry roast with some spices and cook some egg noodles and stir fried vegetables. With, of course a good glass of wine, and perhaps a small glass of port.

"Morning Mrs Plater!"

Myra turned and saw Sir James Parker, one of the Parish Councillors who lived in the Manor House.

"Good morning to you, Sir James. Not seen you for a while. How are you doing."

"I'm well, thank you, but I am afraid that Ellen, my wife is not."

"Oh dear, I am sorry to hear that. What is the matter with her?

"It's not good, I'm afraid. She has been diagnosed with lung cancer that appears to have spread elsewhere, and they are not sure what the prospects are. It's awful for her, and it's not as if she had ever smoked."

"Oh my, that's awful for you both. Is there anything I can do. Should I pop round and see her?"

"That would be very kind of you, but one never knows what state she will be in at any one time."

"Should I ring you before I set out then?"

"Most kind."

He tipped the hat that would have been there if he had worn one, and they went their separate ways.

Something else for Myra to ponder. It was curious, she thought to herself how so many different people suffered from foul diseases whilst other stayed so relatively healthy. She was sure that it must be in the genes.

Myra knew

―

Having placed the disabled driver card on his dashboard, Sir Douglas and Lady Hilda discovered that the trek through the pines towards the sea was further than they remembered. After they moved into the open area of the bay, they noticed that the tide was out, and it was a soft and sandy trudge on the west side of the bay up to the dunes. Hilda was thrilled once they reached the ridge to look upon the open North Sea and the distant wind farms, so much so that she squealed with delight, "Oh, Douglas, I do so love the sea."

"Bloody good job there isn't one of those biting north-easterlies hurtling towards us," thought the Vice-Admiral with memories of times when his ship was bouncing its way through the choppy seas in the South Atlantic Ocean.

Once onto the firmer sand, they walked west with only a few souls and their dogs for distant company. The width of the huge blue sky, the few puffy white clouds, the wheeling of the seagulls and the calls of the oystercatchers should have calmed any soul, but Douglas was feeling the stretch of his calves after the walk in the soft sand and he was getting back to his irritable self.

"Look, Douglas, there's one of those motorised kite things with someone slung underneath it."

"Bloody racket. Noise pollution in what should be a peaceful part of the world."

"Oh, do stop it."

"Let's take that path back through the woods."

"Why, have you had enough?"

"I'm not feeling that fit at the moment, thank you, Hilda."

"Do you want to sit down? Have a drink of water?"

"I'd rather have a drop of whisky."

"I don't have any Douglas. Didn't you bring your hip flask?"

"I don't take it everywhere, and you know it."

"All right, don't get tetchy. I'm only trying to help."

"Look, let's get back to the car."

On their way they found a bird hide looking over the marshes and they sat for a while on the benches looking out towards the Holkham estate and the fields of geese.

It took another twenty minutes of gentle walking before they returned to the Bentley, where they sat and chewed on cereal bars and sipped from bottles of apple juice. Hilda kept a close eye on her husband in case he felt worse, but after a while he perked up and said he felt better.

"Maybe you needed a bit of help to lift your blood sugar level," she mused.

"Maybe."

"Are you OK to drive, or shall I take the wheel?"

"Not on your life, Hilda. I'm fine now."

———

Murray Flanagan was on holiday. No energetic walking in the hills but lounging on a Caribbean beach with his latest woman, Gail and her three daughters. The girls were eighteen, nineteen and twenty one, all in extraordinary physical shape. All had employed fillers to their lips, one of which had gone wrong and rather than 'trout pout' it was more 'pike like'. Poor girl was distraught and spent her time under a shelter. Murray cast a leering glance at the other two and despite his partner's grimace, kept his eyes on the girls.

Murray was now working in the Bristol area of the country and told his new friends that he was earning in excess of a hundred thousand pounds a year, holidaying in exotic places every few months and completely under the spell of Gail.

No longer was he a man to go pubbing three or four times a week with a decent punch-up at the end of an evening and a night in the cells, no longer a man who enjoyed the highs of a drug fuelled night, but more into cocktails and working his way into what he saw as a higher form of society.

The form where people who knew people who would do the unpleasant jobs for the right amount of cash.

Cash, and particularly the cash of her previous three husbands and now of Murray was the major attraction for Gail. It was clear to her friends, but certainly not to Murray that she was the complete control freak, and she ensured that most of their money was funnelled into offshore accounts where the tax burden didn't bite so hard but made sure that she had enough for her to go shopping.

The girls were also a burden on his wallet and needed their weekly 'allowances' despite their ages and abilities to earn good money for themselves.

But Murray was besotted and so under her spell that he barely noticed what Gail was doing to him.

He had managed to forget – or at least managed to put them well to the back of his thoughts - two main things; firstly, that his past life of anger and violence had not truly left his new self and, secondly, that he had not given any money to support his own children with Harriet for a least two years.

He would carry on as he had done, completely under the spell of Gail.

Pete Evans from the Cold Case team had been successful in tracking down the right person at Interpol's headquarters in Lyon and sent pictures of the facial reconstruction of the pingo body to the Missing Persons Division, together with the team's information regarding the discovered burial and the suspected East European origin of the man, as well as the understood timeframe.

Pete was married to Maria a stocky five foot two brunette with slim legs, a pert backside and small breasts. She showed no sign of having borne him two sons who were top grade students at the local High School. Whilst shorter in stature than Pete, it was she who constantly won their battles on the badminton court.

Pete had been in the Police for nearly twenty years and was considered the 'go to' man in the Cold Case team. At five foot nine and stocky with sandy hair and light blue eyes he was totally committed to his work.

His allocated contact at Interpol was one Marianne Auguste who was particularly intrigued by the case and said that her colleagues would interrogate their databases. Her voice was calm and seductive, and Pete hoped that there might be a case for him to go to southern France for a one to one meeting.

Some hope.

Johnny McNeil had a haggard look about him. Sunken eyes and drawn cheeks, he was wearing a light grey hooded track suit and a pair of worn white Nike trainers he had bought from a charity shop. No bling and fancy clothes at this end of the drug chain.

He had been pacing about and waiting for over an hour at the usual location on the rough land at the rear of the railway station, and there had been no sign of the black Ford Kuga. He didn't want to irritate the man, but was getting well and truly pissed off, not least because there was a chance that the police would be about.

"Fucking hurry up," he muttered and looked at his phone for the umpteenth time.

Ten minutes later the car turned the corner and drove into the open area near to where where Johnnie was waiting.

"Where the fuck have you been," he spluttered as Fat Robbie wound down a window.

"Steady on lad, do you want the goods or not? It's no good you screaming blue murder at me. I'm just the delivery boy."

"Where the hell have you been? I've been standing here like a spare prick for over an hour. I need to be able to trust you, otherwise I'm in danger of being nicked."

"I got held up in Suffolk, mate and there were so many bloody roadworks it isn't true."

"Well, let's get on with it. What you got for me today?"

Fat Robbie passed him a carrier bag and said there were mixed packets inside with codes written on them.

"How do I know what the codes are. Is this a new sort of trick?"

"I will send you a text with the answers. Give us the money, you little rat."

Johnnie passed him an envelope and said, "Don't you bother to count it, it's what we agreed."

"Good. Right. Better be off. I'll be late for the next drop."

"See yer."

Fat Robbie sped off into the Norfolk countryside heading for the coast.

Johnny McNeil shuffled off to his bedroom in a scruffy three storied semi-detached house with basement rooms that was converted into a set of bed-sits. There he tipped out the bag onto his bed and checked that he had been given the required numbers of packages for his customers.

He would await the message with the details of the codes so he could make his deliveries.

Chapter 20

The following week, Jack Chambers arranged to call round to see his daughter, Harriet whilst the children were out. He took her to a local park where they sat quietly on one of the many commemorative benches for few minutes before Jack broke the ice.

"My dear girl," he said in his most compassionate voice, "We need to get all the crap out of your head. Let's talk openly. Can I suggest we chat about the kids first, and then I want you to be honest with me about your financial situation, and any other issues that are clogging up your mind."

"Dad, I'm not sure I'm ready for that yet. Everything is still in a whirl, and I can't focus on any one issue."

"I completely understand that, so let's just talk about Oliver. I love that boy, and I guess he has got into the wrong crowd."

"I suppose so. I can't keep him on a lead you know."

"Of course not. It's only another fifteen months or so and he will be an adult. Eligible to go and fight for his country. He is learning tough lessons, but maybe not quickly enough."

"I don't know if I've given him enough time. I feel guilty about the trouble he gets himself into."

"I remember some twenty odd years ago when a certain young lady was out all night at gigs and parties, where drugs were passed around, and your mother and I waited all night, not sleeping, waiting for that girl to come home."

"Yes, I know, but I think the world is a much more dangerous place nowadays. I'm scared, Dad."

"Do you think this latest problem will have shaken it out of him?"

"I don't know. I hadn't told you before, but it's not the first time he has been pulled in by the cops. Not for drugs, but for fighting. He has such a rage inside him," Harriet said, her eyes visibly wet with tears.

"Do you know what the cause of that is?"

"Not really, but I suspect it's something to do with his father. He barely calls the kids. Either of them. I think they, and Oliver, in particular is reacting to that feeling of rejection."

"Quite likely. Do you ever talk about Murray to them?"

"No way. That bastard has ruined my life, just like he said he would. He's stopped paying maintenance some while ago, as well as making little contact with his children."

"Has he indeed. What have you been doing about that?"

"I've been to Citizens' Advice, and had a free half hour with a lawyer, but that's not got us very far."

"Is Murray out of work then, or is there something else that's stopped him paying you?"

"I don't know."

"I think we need some decent evidence about his lifestyle, his workplace, his income, and anything else that would help. Are you up for trying to find more information?"

"I have wondered about it. I've tracked down his Facebook pages, and I think I should spend more time on searching."

The next two weeks she did just that.

―――

Georgia Stephens had befriended one of the waiters at the local Portuguese restaurant. Bruno was tall and dark haired with the expected olive skin, gleaming teeth and a stunning smile.

She had popped in where he worked and took a seat by the window overlooking the market place and ordered a hot chocolate and a sweet pastry called a *'jesuita'*. Bruno had taken her order with a smile that said, "I think I can like you."

Silently Georgia swooned and promised herself that she would try and have an evening with him.

Life might be getting better.

―――

Lady Hilda had been buttonholed in the Post Office in the general store by a friend called Peg Halford - well, actually more of an unwelcome acquaintance – who regularly confided in her about her health. Mind you, most people of Hilda's generation were now mainly focussed on ailments and pills.

She had put up with the Vice-Admiral's gripes about the number of pills he had to take each day and had merely grunted when Hilda told him in no uncertain terms that he would be 'a damn site worse off without them'. Even so she begrudged the time it took each month to fill up his container of daily pill boxes.

Peg who had lost her husband a good while back was one of those women who always thought that whoever she bumped into had to know all her particular current story. Spoke to anyone and everyone, did Peg. This time, she told Hilda that she had been particularly concerned about her recent onset of pain in her stomach – even though she didn't know exactly where her stomach was.

Hilda told her that she ought to go to the doctor and see what the outcome was, and to report back. Peg was staggered. "I've not been to see him since I had my troubles with my women's bits when I was going through the '*Minnipaws*.'

"Well, I think you ought to get referred to the hospital and be examined properly."

"Do you really think so, Myra?"

"Well, I suppose it depends on whether or not you want to feel better."

It took some time for Peg to get round to see her GP, and as a result she was sent for a series of tests which she said 'involved having tubes down and up me to look at whatever was going on.'

"Don't half make yer fart," she complained when she reported back to Hilda.

"Have they reported back to your doctor, yet?"

"I got a phone call to say I needed to go in and see him."

"And did you do that, Peggy, dear?"

"I did and they say its summat called Krohnas disease."

"Ah, I think it's the one called Crohn's. I knew a friend of Douglas who had it. I think they carved a bit of his gut out and sewed it back up again. Think he got over it all right."

"Did they, now?"

"I'm sure they did. I'll ask him if you like."

"No, don't bother him. I've got the message."

"OK, then Peg. Sorry, dear, I must get on. Busy day."

"I meant to ask you, Hilda dear, Sir Douglas was in the Navy wasn't he?"

"Yes, dear he was. For over thirty years. On the high seas you know."

"He did well for himself, I imagine. Lord High Executioner or summat like that?"

"No, Peg. He became a Vice-Admiral."

"Aha! What was it that a friend told me the other day. Oh yes, she said that the Duke of York was a Vice-Admiral."

"Yes, dear."

Site inspections by the Paston District's Planning Committee were always a nightmare to organise. Councillors had other meetings to attend, avoiding public holidays and half terms for the parents who needed to be with their children, avoidance of days when horse racing was taking place at either Great Yarmouth or Fakenham, and various other excuses.

Eventually a date and time was agreed and seven of the Committee of fifteen members assembled at the car park of Ballington Village Hall, just a five minute walk to the best spot to see the proposed location of the battery storage building. Councillor Mrs Carter-Green, who was unable to walk far was already there in her car, parked at a field entrance and was talking with the District Councillor for Ballington, Frank Porter.

When all were gathered, Evie Beecham, one of the senior planning officers and who was dealing with this proposal, reminded the councillors that this was just an inspection of the site and surroundings so that they could visualise the proposal and the issues involved. No decisions were to be made at that time. She then indicated the site proposed for the development, described the size of the proposed building as well as pointing out the houses and cottages from where objections had been submitted.

Frank Porter told the meeting that there was open hostility to the proposal, and that whilst he supported sustainable energy production there had to be less intrusive ways of getting electricity from offshore wind farms to the National Grid in the most efficient way.

The storage building was to be clad in a light grey metal and would contain the equivalent of thirty shipping containers of equipment to store the lithium batteries.

Members' views ranged from 'the principle is a good one, but it's a bit big for here' to 'Would it look better if it was clad in timber?' to 'I heard that these batteries are likely to explode!' and to 'it's absolutely preposterous. Isn't there better technology to deal with this?'

Having looked, talked, and listened, the meeting dispersed, and Evie Beecham who had taken notes of the comments knew she had more research to do before the application would be discussed at the next full meeting of the Committee.

Chapter 21

Jack Chambers called his daughter, but her phone was engaged, so he left a message, "Harriet, give me a call back when you're free, please," and he went into his garden and started tending to his roses and fading daffodils. When his mobile rang an hour later, Harriet said, "Hi Dad, guess what I've found!"

"A pot of gold?"

"Not quite, but I'm building up a pretty picture."

"Go on.... Or would you rather that we meet for a coffee somewhere?"

"Good idea. You know the café run by the Portuguese people in the Market Place?"

"I know it."

"Say forty minutes?"

"Fine. See you there."

Jack changed out of his gardening clothes and put on a navy blue polo shirt and a fresh pair of jeans and drove into town. Parked the Nissan and walked to the café where he found that his daughter was already there, clutching a white mug of hot chocolate in one hand and a cloth covered notebook in the other. As he walked in, Harriet got up, gave him a hug, and asked what he wanted to drink. "I think I'll have an Americano today. I'll get it."

"My treat. I've got some news that might be useful."

She went and ordered his coffee, turned and sat down.

"Great. Let's have it."

"I did a bit more digging on Facebook and managed to find that Murray has hooked up with a woman from somewhere west of Swindon. I thought that he was in Cambridge or somewhere like that, but he obviously found work in the South-West of the Country. Plenty of new construction around there. She looks like a proper madam. Been divorced three times, and she's only forty-six. Still, she seems to have come out of those with plenty of money.

He's bound to find some attraction in that! All boobs and pouty lips and a bit up her own arse. Seems that she has three grown up daughters as well. Looks like they might be living is a swanky detached house with lots of trees around it. That is if you believe all you see and read on Facebook."

"OK, so we know roughly where he is and who he is with, but what about his financial situation. Have you managed to find anything, apart from her?"

"Not really, but Citizens Advice suggested I spoke with the Child Maintenance Service. They are really hard to get through to, but I've got an appointment with them next week."

"Good girl. That sounds like a sound idea, and it will be interesting to see if they are able to help. Another drink?"

"No thanks Dad. What have you been up to?"

"Pottering in the garden, general tidy up, trying to decide the things I've got and don't use or need. Doing a bit of reading, wondering about getting some decorating done, but you know, I just can't get the enthusiasm for it. It can wait!"

"Perhaps I should suggest to Ollie that he gives you a hand with it. It would do him good and be a 'thank you' for the help you gave him when you went to help and pick him and Jimmy up from Norwich."

"It would be good to see him, and I'm happy to pay. See if he is up for it."

"I will. Good to have the chat, Dad, I must be off. See you soon."

With that she helped him to his feet and gave him a special hug. As she left, Jack sat down and ordered another coffee, found a copy of a local paper, and started to do the crossword.

———

Sally Parmenter and 'Dolly' Parting were hunched over his computer screen looking at some video footage from a private security system taken by a local resident who had seen some suspicious activity from the attic room of their home near to the railway station and had emailed it to the police station.

"See what I found this morning Sarge," said 'Dolly'. "It looks as though there is something interesting taking place on that spare land at the back of the railway station. There's this black car and I think there is a hooded figure standing nearby. Want me to go and have a look?"

"Not yet, 'Dolly'. I know that there are homes and a converted warehouse in that area. It might be worth finding out what other uses are going on around there."

"I had a look on the maps on the computer system, and yes, it seems that there is access to a row of houses, and some warehouses converted into flats. I reckon it's worth putting on some scruffies and taking a stroll."

"I think it might be best to talk to the person who took the video first and see if he or she would try and keep a continuous look out. If this is what I think it is, like a drug drop, it would be useful to find out how regular this takes place. Don't suppose we can see that car registration number, can we? Maybe see if it's local or not?"

'Dolly' tried to zoom in on the picture, but it would only go so far, and the fuzziness made it impossible.

"Right," continued Sally, "let's get the techie guys at HQ to see what they can do. Have you got a contact there?"

"I think I know how to find one," he replied with a large grin on his face.

―――

The police's profiler, Reuban Blanche had visited the Thompson Common site a couple of times, trying to figure out the type of individual who would be likely to bury his – or her victim in a rural site that attracted visitors to see this unusual landscape and those who supported the work of the Wildlife Trust.

After a number of discussions with the Trust's staff he realised that the area where many of the 'ghost' pingos were situated was on an area of land that the Trust had bought only a matter of four years ago. The site of the burial therefore was likely to have been out of the public view at the time the person involved undertook the grim task.

Reuban had tracked down the previous landowner who was a local farmer and had not spent much time in that part of his land, and certainly hadn't noticed any suspicious activity there.

He came to the simple conclusion that it had to be someone with a special knowledge of the area, and whilst the person who carried out the burial might not have been the killer, he or she certainly knew who had ordered this gruesome work.

Reuban would need to carry out more research.

He was at home in their Victorian villa on the outskirts of Coventry, going through his files in his study after a filling meal and a glass of lager with his wife Melanie when he felt unwell and went upstairs to their bedroom to rest.

Within half an hour he felt sick and went to the bathroom and sat on the toilet with his head bent over the wash basin, not sure which end would explode first. Nothing happened apart from a fierce thumping pressure around his breast bone. He called out, "Mel, come here please. Mel!"

Mel paused the latest edition of Coronation Street on the television and rushed upstairs and found Reuban clutching at his chest and looking very grey and sweaty. "Oh, my Lord, I know what this is," she said. "Hang on in there, my love. I'm going to ring for an ambulance."

A paramedic arrived before the ambulance, and after

carrying out an ECG, confirmed that Reuban had suffered an intense heart attack and she had administered some sedative drug to ease the pain. The ambulance was only ten minutes behind, and the police profiler was placed in a specialised wheelchair and carried downstairs to the vehicle where he was transferred to the couch, checked for his vital signs and rushed to the nearest hospital. Melanie was following in her car, and arrived five minutes later, and found the Emergency department where sad faces told her what she had dreaded.

It was too late. Reuban had passed away en route.

———

Dave and Michelle Wakefield had driven up to the coast and decided on a visit to the Cley and Salthouse Marshes. They parked at the visitor centre with its spectacular panoramic window overlooking the nature reserve, and went in and showed their membership cards whilst chatting to the reception staff. Before setting off for their walk they talked to the staff about the particular birds they were most likely to see, and then took the boardwalk to one of the hides which just had space for them to look over the scrapes where avocets and spoonbills were the highlights amongst the waders. And then Michelle nudged Dave and pointed in the sky as about thirty brent geese flew in, and beyond them a marsh harrier glided over the reeds looking for lunch.

A thoroughly enjoyable hour was spent before they went back to the centre and took an well earned cup of coffee and a large slice of carrot cake as they looked out over the marsh where the harrier looked as though he had been successful.

The walk and the birds did them both a world of good and they spoke of it on the way home, and into the evening,

Despite that diversion, Michelle knew that Dave wanted to see if Sam had picked up any gossip about the surveyors.

That evening Dave said he wanted to check on Sam's state of mind and gave him a call in the evening.

"Hi Sam, I do hope you are feeling a bit happier after our chat".

"Yes thanks, Dave, I think it got me out of my stupid mindset, so many thanks for that."

"Excellent, Now, did you get any feedback about the dodgy side of life round here from your guys or from the Golf Club?"

"Not much. Certainly nothing about the Thompson case, but there is lots of gossip about drugs. There's a guy in town who apparently is known as 'Scottish', who picks up supplies for the users around here."

"OK, thanks for that Sam. That's rather what I expected you to say about the Thompson body.

Chapter 22

Late on a Thursday afternoon the phone rang in the office that held the Cold Case team and Hayley called out, "Pete, it's for you. Some sexy voice!"

Sure enough it was Marianne from Interpol to tell him that they had managed to find a couple of possibilities as a match to the information he had sent regarding the body found in Thompson Common. She said she would email the details to him, but it appeared that there was a likelihood of a match to a couple of brothers from Albania who had been on a list of surveyors who worked across Europe.

"Albania, eh? That country had been the centre of many a bad reputation," he said.

Marianne agreed. "But Pete, you should be sure that

you only need a few bad apples to ruin the barrel."

"You're right, of course, Marianne. Is there any way of finding out more about the list of surveyors? My boss is wondering if this is not really a set of surveyors but maybe a group of criminals either in drug or people smuggling."

"We are very busy at the moment, Pete, but I will see what I can do for you."

"Tres bien, Marianne. Merci. Au revoir."

"Au revoir, Pete."

Pete looked forward to the next debrief session with the DI.

The Easthoe Parish Council had organised a meeting in the Village Hall to listen to the developers explain their proposals for a housing development at the edge of the village, and for the parishioners to ask questions and express their opinions. The mood was hostile when the Parish Clerk called the meeting to order and introduced Sir James Parker who would chair the meeting in the absence of the Parish Council Chairman who was isolating after testing positive to Covid-19.

"Ladies and Gentlemen," Sir James stood to all of his six foot three, head back, and looked the senior soldier that he was not. "It is my pleasure to chair this meeting of the Parish Council together with members of the public who are very welcome indeed, and I am sure that you would want to wish our long standing chairman Harold a speedy recovery."

There were a series of 'here heres' and some wag saying rather too loudly that he'd bet that Harold wasn't 'standing long' at present.

"This meeting is solely to listen to a presentation of the details of the housing development that we have all heard about. Mr. David Johns is here from the developers, and after he has told us about his proposals, I will ask you to raise your hands so I can take questions from you to him.

After all the questions have been answered I will ask for comments from you. Similarly, if you wish to speak, please raise your hand and we will take these in turn. I hope that is clear, and I would ask that you listen to Mr. Johns with courtesy. Thank you indeed. Right, Mr Johns, over to you."

"I thank you Mr Chairman and am pleased to present our ideas for the site to you all. I have some slides to show and suggest that the people at the top table move to a suitable location so they can see the screen.

David Johns showed slides of both aerial views and all pictures of the site, some sketches of preliminary ideas of the layout and house types, landscaping, and access details. He went on to explain how the drainage of the site would be dealt with, that the houses would be heavily insulated and have solar panels and air source heating systems. It all looked very well thought out.

After he finished speaking, Sir James asked for questions from the floor, and hands shot up. Sir James chose those first who he thought would be calm in their questioning.

"How many of the houses would be for local people, and what guarantee will you give to that?"

David Johns said, "Of the twenty shown on the sketch, five would be for affordable homes. We will talk with the District Council's planning officers about the best way we can ensure this happens. I expect there will be a need for a formal agreement between my clients and the Council."

"Mr Johns, have you carried out a traffic analysis to ascertain what the effect of the increased traffic would be, particularly in the narrow lanes?"

We have employed traffic engineers to examine this, and we will provide these details with the planning application."

"So, you don't know then."

"As I say, we will detail this, and you will have a copy when the District Council send a copy of the application to the Parish Council."

A young lady asked, "What happens to the old grain store next to the site?"

"That building is not in our ownership."

"Have you tried to buy it?" she continued.

"Well, yes. It was one of the first things we did when we started looking at the site."

"Why didn't you?"

"The owner was asking too much money for it, and we couldn't make the figures work for the overall site."

A young man sitting with her said, "You say that the grain store is not in your ownership. So, we can assume that you've already bought the site you want to develop. Is that right? There's no permission, is there? So, what happens if you don't get approval?"

David Johns replied, "My understanding is that the developers would hold on to it and lease it back to the farmer until such time as the need for new dwellings was at a level that it would be likely to get approval. After all, the site is indicated for residential development in the Council's Local Plan."

Cynical groans around the Hall.

"What proportion of the total expenditure will be on environmental improvement?" asked a lanky long haired man who wore rings through his ear lobes and his nose.

"I don't have that figure with me, but I can let you have it. See me afterwards and I will give you my card. However, I can assure you all that we will be planting trees and hedgerows."

Sir James could feel that the atmosphere was becoming uncomfortable and suggested that he would like to take comments and suggestions at this stage. He informed the meeting that the Parish Clerk would be taking notes.

One young man raised his hand and was asked to speak.

"I have lived here all my life. I work on one of the local farms, and one of the affordable buildings would be very welcome to me and my fiancée."

Another older woman thought that "the whole idea was wrong. That the village couldn't take any more development and that the traffic situation was bad enough now without another fifty vehicles and all the extra deliveries that are bound to follow."

There was much applause.

Another said, "I think it would be a better scheme if it included the grain store site. What on earth will happen to it otherwise. It would be surrounded with no access."

Murmurs of appreciation of a sensible comment rolled around the Hall.

There followed a number of comments about the loss of people's view of the countryside, the noise and dust caused by the construction, the use of decent agricultural land, the destruction of hedgerows and the mutilation of the character of the village.

David Johns kept himself busy by writing notes but was content that these were comments he had expected.

They always were.

Sir James brought the meeting to a close, thanked everyone for coming and thanked David Johns for his clear explanations. He then invited all and sundry to enjoy a cup of tea and some biscuits. There was a muted round of applause.

Six people stayed behind, all from the Parish Council.

And Darren Prescott who had taken copious notes.

Myra, who unusually for her had said nothing all evening slipped quietly away.

Peg Halford was spending her Friday morning catching up with her shopping in Easthoe, and she was having to be careful with her spending. A widow for a dozen years, she was well into her late seventies, very small and hunched over. She wore her grey hair in a tight old fashioned perm often with a knotted headscarf. That day she wore a plain blue blouse with an orange cardigan and a dark green skirt that went well below her knees, together with what her mother would have called 'sensible shoes'. Those poor knees were well bandaged after several recent falls and her near neighbours felt some concern for her health and her state of mind.

She had settled into widowhood reasonably well, but recent years had indicated a noticeable decline.

Soon after her husband's funeral she had been perfectly open and honest and had told her friends that her dear Fred had died from *prostrate* cancer. She had said, "It was such a *mizerble* time, but I had to keep going, di'nt I? Poor old dear, there were times when he was in such *scrutinatin'* pain."

She had bought enough potatoes and carrots together with a small piece of beef shin from the local butcher who had wrapped it in a piece of brown paper, just like her mother had liked it wrapped, and would make a small stew which she expected to last a couple of days.

As she left the butcher's she slipped on the doorstep and was held up by Alfie, the butcher's lad who quietly said to her, "Morning, Mrs Halford, you ought to take more water with it!"

"Cheeky little bugger. But thanks for your support."

"I'll always wear it, Missus, but you are very welcome. You go steady now."

"I will boy," she smiled. "You know where to come if you want to catch me again!"

And with that Peg carefully walked back to her cottage, made a cup of cocoa, and gazed over her unkempt garden, with a chocolate digestive in her left hand, and a fly swatter in the right.

She cared little about new housing developments. She was in a world of her own.

Chapter 23

Myra Plater was considering her options and her opinions. "That meeting was very interesting. Great to see the Hall packed out. Good to hear honest voices. But was that man, whatsisname? Johns, that's it, was he being honest?" she mumbled to herself. "I need to do something to try and find out."

She made herself a cafetiere of decaffeinated coffee and sat in the wicker chair on the patio with a pen and notebook. "Try and remember what he said," she cajoled herself. The coffee was hot and smooth, and the chocolate Hob-nob went down with it rather well. "It was that thing that he pretended he didn't know the answer to, what was it?" She looked down the garden to spot anything that needed deadheading or tidying up, and then it came to her. "Traffic, that was it. Well now, we can tell him a few things about that can't we?" She jotted that down and got to her feet to rid an offending rose bush of its dead flowers. "Good old Arthur, this one was always his favourite."

On her way round the garden, she thought of the battery storage building that she had heard about through her 'connections'. "I really must find out if this is true or not. Can't let that one slip through the net," she told herself.

She went back to her seat on the patio deep in thought. "Ah, that thing about the grain store; that was interesting. I thought it was in the same ownership as the field. How could it not be? Patrick Baines, he's the farmer. Must make it my business to bump into him soon."

It was something that she needed to know.

———

Murray Flanagan had continued to make little contact with his children.

Daisy, despite her physical difficulties was academically very bright and a very clear thinker on many fronts. She had certainly suffered from the earlier acrimony in the household and had days where she had withdrawn into herself. These episodes resulted in her struggling to keep up at college where she was studying design and fashion.

Oliver was a practical one and as such had much in common with his father. It was he who Murray would ring, albeit irregularly, normally only to share his gossip and to brag how well he was doing in business. After a while Oliver caught on to what was happening and refused any invitations to go and join his father in the west of the

Country.

There was rarely a birthday wish and promises of money rarely materialised.

Harriet was convinced that this woman, who she had found out was called Gail had total control over who Murray saw and what he could do with his money.

She thought, "That bitch has a lot to answer for. Cow!"

Murray had changed his children's' lives for the worse, and not for the first time in his life was seen by some as an extremely unpleasant and dangerous individual.

———

Avril Danes had asked Darren to attend that Easthoe Parish Council meeting and to report back next day, ready to submit a piece into the next copy of the Broad Norfolk Post.

"How did the meeting go, then Darren," she asked when he arrived a half hour later that his usual arrival time.

"Sorry I'm a bit late, but it went on for ages. Finished about ten, and I managed a word with the meeting's chairman, got blocked in the car park and when I did get out, and found I had a flat tyre. Managed to change it and got home on the fifty miles an hour tyre at eleven fifteen. I needed an hour to wind down with a couple of cans of Guinness!"

"Bloody hell, Darren, that's a load of bad luck. You sure you didn't pick up some little lady and had a late night?"

"Chance would be a fine thing. Can I put in a claim for the cost of tyre repair?"

"Jenny's in charge of that. You'll have to be sweet to her."

"I always am, but she's got a fella, and I daren't push it too far!"

"Ok, spill the beans about the meeting. Anything worth reporting?"

"I felt that the interesting thing was that there is an old grain store next to the site and there was a question as to why that site wasn't being included into the layout as it would create a link to existing houses. I think I want to chase up more about that part of the scheme and see what other local people think of that."

"Ok, that's good. Deadline in two days. All right?"

"Sure. I'll give it my best shot."

———

DI Tony Lovelace had called his Cold Case team together for a briefing following Pete's work with Interpol.

"We have some sort of a breakthrough, and I understand that the suggestion is that the two missing surveyors were from Albania. In my view there may be more to this than we realise," he said, "I want to find out whether they were involved in any other sort of activities. It's an unfortunate fact but the reputation of some of their countrymen suggests that we would be wrong to close the book now. Any thoughts Pete?"

Pete Evans still had a self-satisfied smile on his face, drew a deep breath and said, "Well, I was delighted that Interpol came up with this information, though I'd have guessed Lithuania, but it makes you wonder if in fact there was some form of gangland involvement, perhaps drugs, perhaps human trafficking. There's more to this, I bet. I've asked Marianne at Interpol if her people can find out more"

"Fine, anything else?" asked Tony.

"Well, yes. I was wondering that if we think these guys might be bogus and part of a gang – or maybe they were in two gangs - is there a link to our body from Thompson Common? Might he have been just at the wrong end of a dispute? Like some sort of revenge killing?"

"Thanks Pete, that's an interesting thought. Well, I know there's plenty of other work we have to deal with, but I agree with Pete. So, I want you, Pete and one other – you can choose your partner in this – to do some background on these two men. Maybe use Interpol again. You have a contact now, Pete. Get on it."

"Thank you, Boss, I will, and I suggest that Debbie works with me on this."

"Very well. Thank you everyone."

Chapter 24

Georgia Stephens had not slept well and had got up before the sun rose. She sat in her kitchen with an early cup of coffee thinking about the day ahead. She was wearing a vest and a pair of shorts as the weather had become increasingly hot. The floorboards upstairs creaked, and she recognised the sounds of Tyler's footsteps as he got himself ready to shower. "Early bird too," she thought. "A son rises before the sun rises."

Ten minutes later he was dressed and downstairs, hair in place and a good splash of one of his many lotions.

"Morning," he said and gave his mum his customary hug.

"Y'oright?" Man of few words.

"What are you doing today, Tyler?"

"Seein' a mate about a job."

"That's good. Any idea where?"

"Nah. I'll just see what turns up. You look sad. What's up?"

"Sorry, I know. I'm just going through a rough time. You having any breakfast?"

"Nah thanks. I'll get something in the City."

"Got your phone?"

"Course."

"Have a good day. I love you, Tyler."

"Love yah."

And with that he was gone and a minute later a navy blue BMW drove up and Tyler slid into the passenger seat.

Georgia finished her coffee and thought about Bruno. Perhaps another visit to the restaurant where he worked would be in order after she left off work at the estate agents office.

At a quarter to five she slipped out, saying "have a good evening, all" and made her way to see if Bruno was working.

He was.

She took her normal seat by the window, and there he was, all smiles. At this time of day, the restaurant was filling up with people who had also just finished their day's work gossiping about the traffic situation in town, and the continuing mystery of the body found at Thompson. It was still hot news.

Georgia decided that she would just have a quick glass of their special lemonade and ask Bruno if he would like to go for a drink after he had finished his shift. He was rushed off his feet and said that he was working until late but would be free at mid-morning the next day.

———

Harriet's efforts to speak to someone in the Child Maintenance Service were frustrated by having to leave messages for them to ring her back. They rarely did, and in her more charitable moods she guessed they were understaffed and overworked, like most public services. Eventually she had got through to a secretary and was able to arrange a meeting at their offices in Norwich for two weeks hence.

She had registered online and obtained a Reference Number which she used to confirm the appointment. On the day she drove to the Child Maintenance Service's offices on one of the Business Parks on the edge of the City and was ushered into a modern meeting room where she waited for ten minutes enjoying a strong cup of coffee that the receptionist had arranged for her.

Eventually the door opened and a dark haired, six foot man, probably in his early thirties wearing red open necked short sleeved button-down shirt and beige trousers entered, shook her hand and introduced himself as Dougie Ferguson. He sat putting his notebook and laptop on the desk alongside his mug of tea.

"Good to meet you, Harriet. Is Ok that I use your first name?"

She said it was and that it was good to meet someone in person and be able to put a face to a name.

"Now then," Dougie started, clearly emphasising his Scottish accent, "we have logged the details of your claim on our system, and you gave us the gist of the story, so I think we should start by you expanding on that. Is that OK?"

"Sure, thanks." She shuffled her papers out of her pocket file, and told him the detail of Daisy's situation, showed him her bank statements, and gave the full details of her account. She gave him details of Murray's address, the companies he had worked for and told Dougie that Murray had bragged to her son, Oliver that he had earned over a hundred thousand pounds during the previous year. She answered a few questions regarding her own income and the educational status of Daisy and suggested that he could ring her with any other questions.

After a few minutes of general chat, Dougie said, "That's fine for now Harriet and it's good to have met you. It will be a few days before we can press ahead, but you can get in touch if you think of anything else," as he handed her his business card, opened the door and escorted her to the exit of the building.

As she was about to leave, she turned to Dougie and said, "I am so grateful for you seeing me. Do you know if this is a waste of time?"

"No claim that is genuine, and it seems that yours is Harriet, will be a waste of time, and it doesn't look as though this one is either. Good luck."

She sat in her car and heaved a sigh.

———

Darren was determined to try and talk with the farmer at Easthoe who had owned the land for the housing development in order to compose his article for the Post, and he eventually found a phone number for Patrick Baines with whom he arranged to meet on the following morning in the Easthoe Market Square.

"Very good of you to see me, Mr Baines."

"You too. Darren, didn't you say? Please call me Patrick, or Pat if you like."

"Thanks Pat. What a lovely day. Do you think we might walk to the site and have a look round?"

"Just what I was going to suggest. Come on, it's this way."

They walked across the road and through New Cut and were behind a row of cottages when Patrick stopped and pointed out the field ahead of them.

"Here we are. It's this field over to the hedgerow over to your right. Pretty flat and the ground drains well."

"I was at the meeting the other night, as I said on the phone," Darren told him, "and I thought there were some really good points made by the public. What did you think?"

"Aye, I thought the same, in the main."

Darren pointed to the dwellings that were close to the site.

"I suppose those homes will be affected, won't they? Would you show me where the access to the road from here will be, please."

Patrick took him across the field to a gap at the end of the cottages and pointed out the main roadway and the vehicles passing by at the end of the gap.

"That gap is a bit tight Pat, isn't it?"

"Well, we think we can make it work, but if push comes to shove, I own the cottages, so the end one might have to be sacrificed."

"Do your workers live in them, then?"

"Only one at the other end. We don't employ much

workforce these days."

"So, the others are let to local people?"

"Mostly. The two at in the middle are holiday lets."

"OK, now there was mention of the use of your old grain store. Is that it there?" Darren pointed to an asbestos clad bulky building. "What do you use it for?"

"Oh, you know, general storage for the farm. Odd bits and pieces."

"But the site would be a better shape if it wasn't there, wouldn't it?"

"I suppose so, but the developers have said that they aren't interested. I think that's because they would have to carry out decontamination work, and removal of asbestos is difficult and costly."

"Ah well that makes some sense, but mighten they get another home or two on the site?" Darren asked.

"I don't know. It's up to them. I just hope they would arrange for some local people to get a home."

"Yes, that certainly was a point made at the meeting. Well, thank you so much for your time, Pat and it certainly looks as though you are open to more discussion. However, as you have sold the site, have you retained any influence over the resultant scheme?"

"Yes, Darren, I have a final say of how it would affect the rest of my property."

"Most interesting. Many thanks for your time. We'll keep in touch."

With that they walked back to the Market Square, shook hands, and got into their cars to drive home.

Just as Myra walked into the Square.

―――

'Dolly' Parting was on the ball. He had developed a growing relationship with DC Penny Topping who worked at Police Headquarters. Penny was an IT specialist and was in her mid-twenties with a blonde pixie haircut that suited her blue eyes and petite body. They had met in a pub often frequented by their colleagues on a quiz night when Penny's team were runaway winners and 'Dolly''s team were in second last place. Much banter and throwing rolled up question papers at each other. 'Dolly' had risked a single pint of Wherry whilst Penny was clearly one for the cocktails.

After the quiz they had chatted, and he asked if he could walk her home. They had gone a few hundred yards from the pub when it happened.

It was up the passage beside the undertakers when she had pulled him towards her and kissed him forcibly full on the lips. He was a bit embarrassed and said he thought he should get her home, but she was craving more thanks to the cocktails. A bit of fumbling later and her phone went off, and she appeared somewhat flustered, and said, "Oh, all right then," in a very sharp tone and rang off.

"Problem?" asked 'Dolly'.

"Just a bit."

"Another boyfriend?"

"Er, well yes. Not happy that I've not got home yet."

"Oh bugger. You're in a steady relationship, eh?"

"Yes, sorry. My fault."

"Not to fret. Let's get you home."

It was the contact that 'Dolly' needed to try and get the enhancement to the CCTV pictures. And it worked a treat.

Chapter 25

The day after Darren's meeting with Patrick Baines he drafted a piece for the next edition of the Broad Norfolk Post and shared it with Avril, who was struggling for time as she was trying to put together a useful article about the way the town centre of West Kelling was changing, and was it for the better, or was it inevitable?

They chewed the fat for a few minutes and with a few small adjustments, the article was ready. Avril was pleased with the way Darren had settled into Norfolk life and that his work was reaching a very acceptable standard. She was quick to tell him so and was pleased to see that he almost blushed.

The article finished, Darren sent it off to the editorial

team, and he went to see if he could make any progress on the matter of drugs in the district.

Uncertainty over new development in Easthoe

A public meeting in the Village Hall in Easthoe was attended by Mr David Johns, a representative of the developers who were proposing a new housing development on the edge of the village.

After showing slides of the site and explaining its physical boundaries, Mr Johns gave a detailed explanation of the company's intentions, and whilst there were only sketch details at this stage, the idea was to hear the views of the local population and work up the details thereafter.

After Mr Johns' presentation, he answered questions, and the Chairman Sir James Parker asked for comments from those present.

There were the expected expressions of opposition to any more development, the traffic problems that the development would exacerbate; the effect on the environment; the need to maintain good agricultural land in food production and the detrimental effect the new houses would have on the existing residents.

On a positive note, there was support for new dwellings for the local people, especially the youngsters who would struggle to find a roof over their heads in their quests to start their own family lives.

An interesting question was raised about the old asbestos clad grain store which was situated on the village side of the site, and why wasn't the site of it integrated into the development, where it would provide a better layout and environment for the new residents.

We interviewed Mr Patrick Baines the previous owner of the site now acquired by the potential developers, and the owner of the grain store. He told us that he was keen to make an arrangement for half of the new houses, estimated to total between sixteen and twenty to be for local people.

This was more than Mr Johns had indicated at the meeting.

We look forward to seeing how the situation evolves.

———

Myra Plater was in her kitchen, finishing her second slice of Seville Orange marmalade on wholemeal toast when her copy of the Broad Norfolk Post was pushed through the letterbox and fell on the floor. She cursed her sciatica as she bent to pick it up and went back to her seat and cup of coffee. She flipped through the pages, hunted through the 'Hatches, Matches and Dispatches' to see who she might know, until she noticed the particular article she was looking for.

"Well, blow me down. How did they manage to talk with him before I did?" she mused. "I must be slipping," she said out loud to anyone who would hear.

No-one did.

———

Georgia was excited to have time alone with Bruno, and had planned the meeting down to the last inch.

She had managed to swing a half hour break mid-morning the following day, and they popped into a nearby pub for a coffee. She was anxious to see if he was up for an evening together, but his mind was on the various discussions that had been whirring around the restaurant.

"Georgia, do you know anything about that guy who they found on that Common?" he asked.

"Not much, only what's been in the paper and online. Why?"

"Well, one of our delivery drivers said that he was sure he had heard that someone in the warehouse knew that it wasn't the killer who buried the body."

"How would he know that, Bruno?"

"I don't know, that was what I heard."

"Did he say who had done the burying, then?"

"Not that I heard, but I guess it must have been someone local, eh?"

"Why?"

"Well, people say that it was done in a place where you had to know the area."

"Has anyone told the police about this?"

"Not me."

"I'll have a word with my son, Tyler and see what he

knows."

"That's good. You know, I've wanted to tell this to someone, and I'm glad it was you."

"That's nice. When do you have an evening when you are not working, Bruno?"

"Not this week. Let me have your mobile number and I will let you know."

"That would be nice."

And with that, Georgia went back to the office, excited in more ways than one.

———

Pleased with his work and the friendly relationships with Avril and Jenny, Darren left the office at six o'clock and went for a well-earned pint at The Brown Bear where he got chatting to a few locals about the weather, the current state of the town's football club and the problems in the cost of living.

After half an hour or so, Darren spotted 'Dolly' Parting chatting to some youngsters who were studying their phones and drinking what looked like soft drinks. This pub was popular with the younger part of the population and the music reflected it.

When 'Dolly' spotted Darren, he walked over to him and greeted him like a long lost friend.

"Darren, my friend how are you doing. Not seen you for a few days."

"I'm fine George," he said, remembering to use his Christian name, "how about you? What's the latest?"

"We are making a bit of progress on the drugs issue, and I like keeping an eye on these kids in here. Generally they are a good bunch, and I think it is useful if we keep on good terms with them, and vice-versa.

Otherwise, I think there may be some news regarding the Thompson body soon."

"Is there nothing you can tell me now? I thought I heard something about Interpol being involved."

"Sorry, not yet, but I'll certainly call you when I can."

"Good man, George. How's your fitness? Not ready for rugby yet?"

"My early morning running is enough for the moment, thanks Darren."

It was over a week before Harriet got a call from Dougie Ferguson, but the news was good. At least it sounded like a step forward. Dougie told her that they had allocated one of their financial investigators to the case and that they would be writing to Murray to establish his working situation and to start the investigation into his finances. It would certainly take some time, and from what she had told them about him, it was entirely possible that Murray would not respond to their request. If that was the case, and the chance of that was well known to them, they would use other methods to examine his accounts.

"How long do you think this will take then?" she asked

Dougie replied, "Honestly it will depend on his willingness to cooperate. As you have said, this is unlikely, so it may take many months. Once our man had completed his report it will be delivered to the Court. Murray will get a copy, and he has the right to appeal against its findings. In that case a Judge will order a Hearing at which you should appear."

"Oh, God," she stumbled, "I do not want to be in a room

with that man. Not ever."

"As the Court will sit in the West Country, I guess that you will probably appear on a video link."

Harriet shook. The possibility of having to travel away to the court was terrifying, and she couldn't contemplate leaving Daisy, who may or may not be having a good day.

"But I have a sick daughter who may need me at any time. I can't go to all that way."

"As I say, we will submit your case, but it is likely that the chairperson of the Hearing, quite possibly a Judge, will want to seek some clarification from you. However, it can be done on Zoom, or Teams or some other system."

"OK, I understand. But thanks for the information, Dougie. I appreciate your calling."

"OK. That's good. Have a good day."

"It's never a good day. Thanks anyway."

DS Pete Evans had spent time working through his jobs list to share with Debbie Lang the DC who would be helping him in the search for links between the Albanian surveyors and their killers. It was assumed that the one who had worked in Cambridgeshire was dead, but there was no confirmation of that, and it was possible that the Thompson body was not one of them either.

They chatted around their thoughts until late in the afternoon. The first thing Pete wanted to do was to try and find the background to the assumed bank of surveyors within Europe and again he would see how far Marianne Auguste at the Interpol had been able to progress.

Was it true? Did the bank exist? If so, who organised it? What was their remit? Who can we talk to about it? Where was it based?

These all questions to ask Marianne again.

Debbie agreed that she would send the agreed set of questions to confirm the conversation that Pete would have with Marianne the following morning, and she worked well into the evening on the preparation of the document that they would send, before she went back to her husband Fran in their small home in Hethersett.

Lady Hilda had felt poorly and hoped that she hadn't caught Covid. She had a stock of test kits that the Vice-Admiral would have nothing to do with and she was relieved when the red line was where it should be. Nevertheless, it didn't help her feeling ill.

She went upstairs to the bathroom and was sick. Initially, Douglas heard nothing but did when she banged on the floor with the handle of the toilet brush.

"What's the matter, Hilda?"

More sounds of vomit, which he did hear.

"Hang old thing, I'll be up as soon as I can."

He struggled up the stairs, pulling himself up on the handrail and saw Hilda on her knees.

"Do you want me to get the Doctor?"

"I'll be all right in a minute. Just get me a glass of water please."

Having taken a few sips and wiped her face with the cold flannel that Douglas handed her, she sat on the floor, looking washed out and pale.

"I think we should get you into your bed, Hilda."

"I'll just lay on top of it for a while," she said, and he managed to lift her by going round to her back and putting his arms under her armpits. In this manner he led her to her bed.

Once she was settled, Douglas left her to sleep and went downstairs to the lounge and poured himself a soothing glass of Navy Rum.

He was dozing when he woke with a start having subconsciously heard a heavy lumping sound from upstairs and a wailing sound.

"Oh, Christ, what now?" he muttered to himself, rose, and made his way up the stairs again. Hilda was on the floor beside her bed with blood coming from her face.

"Oh, come on now. What happened?"

She just groaned the groan of someone who had been knocked out. Douglas picked up the flannel he had given her before, went to the bathroom and ran it under the cold tap and returned to try and clean up the wound.

"Oh, no Hilda. Come on, old thing," he said as tenderly as he ever had. She squawked a guttural sound and emptied her bowels.

"Bloody hell. I better call the Doctor, but before I do that, I had better clear up this mess."

He was about to get to the phone when Hilda opened her eyes, and said, "What happened?"

"You must have rolled out of bed and hit your head on the cabinet. You've a bit of a lump on the forehead. Probably suffered from shock as well, I should think."

"What's that awful smell, Douglas?"

"It's you dear."

He explained what had happened to her as best he could and did his best to clear up the excrement from the floor. Once that was completed, he supported her to her wobbly legs, and they performed a sort of three-legged race to the bathroom where she sat on the side of the bath, regained some form of composure and a bit of colour to her cheeks.

"Might be a good idea if you took a bath, Hilda," he said and started to run the taps. "Shall I help you out of the rest of your clothes, or can you manage?"

"I think I'll be OK now, thank you." She said and bent forward and kissed his cheek.

"First time for everything," he thought.

Chapter 26

Jane and Jim took themselves off for the weekend and chose a hotel in Suffolk on the fringe of the town of Woodbridge and which had a nice spa and an excellent reputation. One thing Jane needed after a hectic week at work, was a good sauna and a sports massage. Jim, however, was happy to sit on the terrace with a book and a pint of locally brewed ale.

Their relationship over the last couple of years had developed into one of friendly companionship rather than the rampant randiness of earlier times, although Jane was sure she would welcome a long gentle session later in the evening.

Having booked into the hotel they drove into the town

and walked the streets, past the railway station and to the riverside with the shrieking gulls and the clanking of stays against the metal masts of the many boats that were perched on the shoreline. They watched those who were sailing their boats on the Deben. testing themselves against the breeze and the currents of the tidal river.

It was beautiful and they felt the warmth of each other's company.

They were sitting on a bench eating ice creams, watching the scenery and the people walking by, when Jim asked if Jane had been involved in any discussions regarding the Thompson Common body.

"Not one bit. It's a lovely part of the District, but not with dead bodies in it. I'm not sure what any of us can do."

"I was wondering if the Council would get involved in funding some of the excavation work on the ghost pingos. It is such a fascinating bit of ancient geography."

"It is fascinating how they were formed, isn't it? I've no idea which budget would bear that cost, though. Why not offer some volunteers from school to help them?"

"Mmm, good idea that."

They got up from the bench and walked along the raised footpath beside the shoreline for a mile with a stiff breeze in their faces, stopped to enjoy the view for a few minutes and decided to retrace their footsteps. They headed towards the old Tide Mill where they were shown the workings and the machinery that operated the milling stones as the tide rose and fell.

Back at the hotel, Jane changed into a swimming costume and went to the spa for her sauna and then for a strong massage to ease her neck and shoulders, whilst Jim wandered around the hotel spotting memorabilia from people who had stayed there. He found the bar where he ordered his pint and sat on the terrace in the sunshine enjoying his thoughts of the day. It had been good for his soul.

Jane was revived and glistening when she returned to their room, rang Jim to say that she was back. He read to the end of the chapter of his book, finished his beer, and made his way to the room.

"Have you looked at the menu yet, Jim? she asked, thumbing through the brochure in the room."

"I'm just looking at you!" he said and moved towards her to give her a hug.

They laid on the bed in a strong embrace and Jim took in the scents from her massage oils and felt the familiar stirring in his loins but knew from Jane's body language that she just wanted the comfort of their embrace and would wait for later.

Over their dinner and a bottle of rich Burgundy, Jane asked if he had been contacted by any other Councillor about the battery storage facility or the Easthoe housing proposal.

"Not work this weekend, my lovely. It's so peaceful here," he replied.

"I know. Sorry I must unwind my mind."

After the meal and a glass of Speyside malt in one of the hotel lounges and then a quick stroll around the gardens, they returned to their room and watched the tv for a while. Jim went to the mini-bar and poured them a whisky with just a splash of water. It reminded him of an old, now dead Scottish friend who use to say, 'just irritate it, please'.

After a few sips Jane said she was going to have a hot

shower and Jim reminded himself of the times they had shared a shower but felt content to sit and enjoy sipping his drink.

He heard the shower stop and within a couple of minutes a slightly damp but naked Jane walked back into the room and slid into bed.

Jim smiled, finished his drink, undressed and joined her.

It wasn't long before Jane unwound.

———

Pete Evans had a great morning. He had managed to chat to the alluring Marianne at Interpol HQ and had used his most appealing voice to ask what progress was being made with her team to see if this bank of surveyors ever existed and was it OK if he sent a series of questions by email for her team to check out.

Marianne was enthusiastic and promised to try to get the resources to assist the search.

"Fabulous, Marianne. Very many thanks for that. We'll keep in touch."

"Pas de problem, Pete. Au revoir."

"Au revoir, Marianne."

As he put the phone down, he realised that his armpits had developed a glowing moist warmth.

"All good, then?" asked Debbie with a smirk.

"Deffo, Let's get that paperwork sent off to her pronto."

———

DC Penny Topping at Norfolk Police HQ's IT Department had overcome her guilt from the late evening encounter with 'Dolly' Parting and had worked in her lunch hour on enhancing the video that 'Dolly' had sent over to her. It transpired that the car was a black Ford Kuga, and the enhancement was good enough to show the number plate clearly enough for her to do a search through the vehicle recognition system. She found that it was owned by a Robert Sylvester from Upminster in Essex.

She sent that information to 'Dolly's' email.

His response was immediate and delighted and he emailed his thanks to her, saying he hoped they would meet on a quiz night again soon.

―――

Two days after her fall, Lady Hilda was still feeling groggy, and had phoned the doctors surgery to get an appointment to review her situation. She had eventually spoken to the receptionist after being 'number twenty-two in the queue' and was told that if she suspected any form of concussion she should go to the A&E department of the Norfolk and Norwich University Hospital.

"Douglas, I have to go to A&E, dear. Will you come with me?"

"Bugger," he thought to himself as he had promised that he would go and meet some friends for lunch.

"Did you hear me, dear?"

"Yes, I did. I'll get changed out of these scruffy clothes. Are you going to drive?"

"Better not, if I've got something wrong."

"Ok, we'd better go in the Land Rover then. Might seem a bit off to arrive in the Bentley."

Forty minutes later Douglas drove into the car park for the A&E and couldn't find a parking space, so Hilda said she would get out and go to the reception area whilst Douglas took the Land Rover round in circles trying and failing to find somewhere close to park. Having spent twenty minutes of frustrating driving, he eventually took himself to the new multi-storey car park where he managed to find a spot on the ground floor. It seemed a long walk back to the A&E main doors and found Hilda waiting for the triage team to decide what to do.

Douglas was not permitted to stay with her, and he grumbled noisily, walked to the little café, found a seat and stared at the people passing by. He used his ancient Nokia phone to keep in touch with his wife by sending text messages that took him an extraordinary time to create. He saw walking sticks, Hi-Viz jackets, ripped knees in jeans, worried faces, chatting nursing staff strutting swiftly, a man in a wheelchair smoking, a fat woman eating doughnuts, and he tut-tutted at the state of the world.

Hilda was eventually directed to what was euphemistically called 'Ambulatory Majors' where all and sundry were sitting, standing, and walking aimlessly wondering where the staff were to help them through the system. She messaged Douglas and he trudged his way back from the café to the area she had described, found her, and they sat together waiting.

Waiting. Watching.

Patients with their heads in their hands, crying with pain, staff pushing trolleys with cardboard boxes and blue plastic bags, others with an array of bedpans and cardboard sick trays. Such a lovely way to spend a day.

There was no obviously visible reception desk, but Hilda, being Hilda marched around, through corridors and asked what she was meant to do. Just wait, she was told.

After an hour her name was called and she followed a nurse to a bay along another corridor, and Douglas felt a measure of relief that they would be home soon. Five minutes later, Hilda returned to her seat.

"It was just a blood test," she said. "They will need to see the results of that before we can go home."

"And how long will that take?"

"No idea."

"Bloody hell, what a nightmare." he grumbled.

"Don't get cross with me, I don't like it any more than you do."

"I know."

Another hour and she was called to see a doctor and explained that she had bumped her head and wondered if she had been concussed and needed a scan.

"Tell me what happened in detail, please," said the doctor, a dark haired Scottish woman, looking quizzically at her assistant.

Hilda went through what she remembered again, and the doctor said she wanted Hilda's husband to come and join them, and when Douglas was called, he rose stiffly from his seat and walked to the consulting room where, after introductions he told the doctor his version of events.

"I think you've just had a nasty bump and I'm not certain if it's necessary or not, but I think you should have a scan to see if there are any problems we need to deal with," the doctor told Hilda, and so they went back to wait another three quarters of an hour an hour before a porter came with a wheelchair to take her to the scanner.

Fifteen minutes later she was wheeled back, and a after another hour's wait Douglas was sufficiently agitated that he went to the doctor's room and asked if the results were back. They were, and Hilda was asked to go the consultation room where the doctor told her that there was no sign of concussion.

The Land Rover took them home after a six hour adventure they didn't want, but at least Hilda had been passed fit but advised to rest for a couple of days.

The Vice-Admiral was convinced that this advice would not be taken.

Chapter 27

'Dolly' Parting had discussed the news regarding Robert Sylvester with Sally and agreed that it would be best to do some background checks on him. She would ask the Essex Police to confirm details of his address and to carry out some covert coverage of his movements and contacts. It would be a major breakthrough if this indeed was the same Fat Robbie.

Progress would also be made if they could find out who it was that Robert Sylvester had met, as the video footage only had a back view of the individual. Black jeans, black hoodie, black Nike trainers on a slim figure of about five foot nine height, was all they could see.

'Dolly' was clear that he would be able to track this

person down given enough time, and he and Sally worked their way through different approaches to that end. Should he put on some jeans and a hoodie and take a walk on the rough ground to the rear of the railway, or might that spook the suspects? Should they try and find someone in the group of youngsters that he had met in The Brown Bear and see if they could extract any useful information from them? Should they use the Post to highlight the issue again and see if any useful response came forward?

In the back of Sally's mind was the devastation the drugs were having on so many families, and the medical and psychological problems to the users that were bound to ensue if the supply was suddenly removed. She thought that an early conversation with anti-drug charities, public health bodies and social services would help especially if they were able to arrange a coordinated approach.

It would be a sensible idea to share this with Tony Lovelace first and to agree that someone from the Drug Squad and County Lines should be involved. 'Dolly' said he would go quietly around the town and wait for Sally's decision to allow him a more proactive way forward.

―――

The Broad Norfolk Post had received a number of responses to the article regarding the proposed housing development at Easthoe. Inevitably the usual respondents to the earlier reports of the same issue had sent in their comments, and there were a few others who were new to the letters pages.

Jenny had received these mainly in the form of emails, as well as the inevitable handwritten note by the Vice-Admiral, and had printed the emails and passed the whole package to Avril for a decision as to which ones to print.

In the end she chose the following: -

> *Dear Sir*
> *I was at the public meeting regarding the new housing proposal at Easthoe and was surprised that more people didn't suggest that if the houses and bungalows were what the villagers needed, that there could hardly be a reasonable objection. If the developers were to hold a meeting with those villagers and agree the types of property that were required, I for one would support it.*
> *No-one has a right to a view.*
> *Local people would be helped, and both the farmer and the developer would gain financially, so long as the prices were affordable for those in need.*
> *The properties have to be both for sale and to let.*
> *Yours faithfully*
> *Brian Collins*
> *(Address withheld)*
> *P.S. Regarding earlier letters re this, must you print the offensive comments by Sir Douglas Ewart-Robinson?*
>
> *Dear Editor*
> *As I said in my previous letter on the subject, the infrastructure in the village is not robust enough to accept any more*

development.

Unless people who make the decisions come here and see the traffic problems at certain times of the day, they will not appreciate the difficulties that the village suffers.

Until someone shows they understand this and do something about it then no more development should be permitted. Full stop.

Yours faithfully
Myra Plater.
Easthoe

Sir

Again, I see that the village of Easthoe is threatened with vandalism by the greed of landowners and developers so that they can line their pockets once more.

Again, it is all about money, and one has to wonder where this will end. I recall the phrase in the Great Book saying that 'the love of money is the root of all evil'.

I suggest that someone knows more than they are saying, and I will say nothing about local councillors or the planners.

This proposal is abhorrent.

Yours
Sir Douglas Ewart-Robinson (Vice-Admiral Rtd.)
Snetterbrook Hall

The District Councillor for the ward that included Easthoe was fifty-six year old Carol Hansen, a history teacher at one of the High Schools in South Bardon. Tall at five foot eleven and slim as a beanpole, long blonde hair and sparkling blue eyes that showed her Scandinavian heritage, she bore a striking presence and was one who argued from the strength of her extensive knowledge. She had been a member of the Council's Planning Committee for the past four years and had also been involved in waste disposal issues affecting a nearby parish during her discussions with the County Council. She was as knowledgeable a councillor as any. She knew her way around the system. She knew who to talk to.

She arranged to meet Jane at the Planning Office and told her that she wanted clear guidance regarding the housing proposal in the village. Jane had told her that she had set aside a day for meetings with councillors to discuss issues on their patches, so the Thursday of that week at ten o'clock was the time for Carol and Jane to meet.

"Thank you so much for arranging this, Jane."

"Not at all. More than happy to discuss issues that are of concern. Do you want to give me your take on the situation or would you rather that I tell you what we know?"

"I think it would be good to hear your side first please."

"OK, well first of all there is no formal application yet, and we have only had a brief chat with the agent acting for the developers, so there's been only a preliminary view been taken so far. As you know, the village is one that we have planned to take a bit more development because it has more facilities than many, the school has capacity for more children, the local shops provide a decent service, so in principle there is scope for a few more dwellings. I think we will need to do more work on the appropriateness of this particular site, once we get a formal approach, and we will also need to look at the scale of development. There may be other physical infrastructure issue like drainage and the road safety concerns, but we've not looked into those yet. We will see how much work the agent produces for us."

"I rather thought that is what you would say. Is there anything I can really say to those who are clearly opposed to anything there?"

"Frankly, just tell them what you know. We are at the beginning of what might be a long debate!"

"Frustrating, isn't it. It would be much better if we had a hard and fast proposal to get our teeth into."

"Putting up with frustration is what we have to do, to be honest!" said Jane with a cynical smile. "Good to talk with you."

"Thanks very much for your time, Jane."

"You're very welcome. You know how to get in touch with me. Bye."

At three o'clock Jane had agreed to meet with Frank Porter the Councillor who represented the parish where the proposal for the battery storage building was located. Frank was a big strong man, dairy farmer and rugby forward. Spoke in a loud and deep voice as though he was calling his cattle in for milking.

"Mr Porter, it's good to see you. We've not had contact with you for a while. Things go quiet for a long time and then we get a big idea like this come up. What would you and your constituents think about this enterprise?"

They shook hands and Jane felt the pain from his grip.

"Well, Mrs Seabrook, I think the whole parish is up in arms. I mean why the hell does it have to be there? Why not nearer the coast? I don't understand it. Can't you tell them that they should look elsewhere?"

"That's a very fair question and one we will need to test. We will ask to see their analysis of all the sites they have looked at, and, if necessary, we will ask consultant engineers to assess their calculations."

"Well, that's encouraging. But I don't see how they even started to decide on this particular site."

"Do you know the owner of the land, Mr Porter?"

"Oh yes. Bit of a shady sort if you ask me. I did wonder if there's some sort of deal going on."

"It might be worth you doing a bit more digging," Jane said with a knowing smile. "Not that fraud or anything like that is a planning issue, but it might bring certain things out into the light."

"Thanks, I will see what I can find out and let you know. So, thanks for seeing me. Can we keep in touch on this, please?"

"Certainly. You have my email address here. Any time. Good to see you."

With that, Frank Porter left the building feeling better than he did when he arrived.

Sergeant Sally Parmenter had taken their information regarding Robert Sylvester to DI Tony Lovelace who had arranged for the Drug Squad and County Lines teams to lead the next part of the discussions, and had been persuaded by Sally to involve representatives of the agencies that were interested in trying to solve the problems of drug taking in West Kelling as well as the rest of the County.

The County Lines team was keen to press ahead as soon as possible, but there was support for the idea that those who were users of the drugs might well need help once their supply was cut off, or at least reduced until another supplier filled the gap.

There was an eventual agreement that the social services, anti-drug charities and the healthcare agencies should meet as a matter of urgency, prepare a plan and report back to the group within two weeks.

In the meantime, Sally's team would keep a covert eye on the land at the rear of the railway station and Tony was asked to obtain sufficient resources in the IT sections to check on messages which were probably encrypted on Robert Sylvester's social media accounts.

Chapter 28

Murray Flanagan was late getting out of bed in his luxurious home on a Saturday morning, recovering from Gail's insistence on an early session of sexual activity, after which he had rolled over and slept for another couple of hours.

In the meantime, Gail got up, showered herself clean of his sweat, donned a silk housecoat and went to make herself a round of toast and a bowl of fruit with some natural yoghurt, which she ate on the patio, reading the post that had just arrived and was addressed to her.

There was also a formal looking envelope addressed to Murray and she was tempted to steam it open and see what it was about. She resisted, determined to see his face when he opened it.

She had gathered herself a great tan on a skin that took the sun easily, and their recent break on the island of Guadeloupe, where they had become married with just her three girls as witnesses, had boosted the skin tones as well as her feeling of certainty.

Now, she knew that she had some control over Murray and his money.

Eventually he got up, showered, and left his stubble, put on a pair of jeans and a silk short sleeved shirt and padded downstairs to try and get Gail to make him some breakfast.

"Murray, I'm busy on the phone," she said, "make yourself what you want," and made conversation to nobody on the other end of her mobile.

"But I want one of your special scrambled eggs."

She put her hand over her phone, and mouthed, "Do it yourself. You're a big boy now."

"What the fuck is that all about?" he murmured to himself, with his blood pressure rising, and did the simple thing of making a couple of pieces of toast and a strong cup of coffee into which he added a decent slug of whisky.

After a quarter of an hour, Gail came into the kitchen and handed him his post.

"There were two bills addressed to me and this one for you," she said glaring at him. "What's this one about?"

"How the fuck do I know, I haven't opened it."

"Alright, alright. No need to get snotty. Well, let's see what you've got. Maybe you've won the lottery."

"Don't try and be funny," he snapped, opening the envelope with a knife that still had traces of honey on it.

It was a formal letter, and Murray was not happy.

"What the fuck is this?" he shouted, eyes wide open. "That fucking woman. I'll see she gets nothing."

"What is it now, Murray?" asked Gail, keeping any amusement clearly hidden.

"She's set the Child Maintenance Service on me. They want to know all about my earnings."

"Well, I expect they do. I'm surprised it's taken this long."

"Oh, thanks for your help."

"Oh, pull yourself together for God's sake. You'll use your usual contacts, lawyers and accountants. We know where the money is. She and her contacts don't."

"It's all right for you, they're not dragging you through the hoops. I know what these bastards can do, and from what I've heard they can find anything. I've had mates who have been through this. It's not nice."

"I don't expect it is, but you don't have to reply. What can happen if you don't?"

"They'll probably use some legal crowbar to get to us."

"So, cross that bridge when you get to that point. Just leave it."

Murray went upstairs to his study and placed the letter in the right hand drawer of his desk.

———

Pete Evans was out of the office when Marianne Auguste rang and after no one answered she left a voicemail message to say she had an update on Interpol's investigation into the Albanian missing persons.

Pete returned from a visit to a Norwich boxing club where he had talked to a potential witness to a serious disturbance some eight years ago that led to an unsolved death of a potential junior champion boxer. This witness thought that a revenge killing might have been what happened and that, whilst – because it was so long ago - he couldn't remember the full name of the other person involved, he did recall someone calling the killer 'Ruby' and had some memory of an Irish sounding name. Pete would need to carry out more research.

Back at Police HQ he smiled when he checked his voicemail, made himself a coffee and settled down for a chat with his favourite French lady.

"Marianne, many thanks for your message that you left earlier. What have you got for me?"

"Bonjour Pete, I thank you for ringing me back. Our best efforts tell us that there probably was no established bank of surveyors who do the sort of work we spoke about. We think that there may have been some informal collaboration, but as far as we can see, the chances are that these men were more likely involved in either trafficking young girls across the continent for the pleasure of men who could afford them, or they might well have been involved in the drug trade, or maybe both."

"So, the stories of the surveyors who disappeared are maybe nothing but a fraud, nothing to do with surveying. Is that right?"

"Oui, we think so."

"Pity, but we are used to chasing dead ends, Marianne. So, it has been good to work with you, and we thank your team for their work. I hope we shall meet some day. Au revoir."

"Au revoir, Pete."

When Pete reported back to Tony and the Cold Case

team it was clear that the chances were that the disappearances of surveyors on solar farm sites was a different issue altogether to the body found on Thompson Common.

"So, it seems to me," he said, "that we have here two quite separate matters that require resolution. Clearly, as long as the Interpol theory is correct, the body that is believed to be an Albanian man might have been part of human trafficking gang and was probably disposed of because he was a threat to other gangs. Certainly a cold case."

Most of the team nodded in agreement.

"However," Pete continued, "the missing surveyors are just that. Missing. Maybe one for the Press to see if readers and viewers can cast any light on the two matters."

"Good work, Pete," said Tony. It seems the correct next step, and as the Thompson body was found in this patch, we should ask the Broad Norfolk Post to lead on this and use the Press Association for a wider circulation.

Next morning Avril took a call from DI Lovelace and was thrilled to lead the stories and prepared her copy for circulation.

Human trafficking possible link to Pingo Body

Investigations by Norfolk Constabulary's Cold Case team and with the help of Interpol have revealed information regarding the body discovered buried in a 'ghost pingo' in one of the County's most unusual wildlife sites. These features are relics of the ice age when water below the surface froze to form small mounds which sunk during the summer thaw to form shallow bowls. These fill with water in the wet seasons and often dry out in summer. Some of the mounds were covered in windblown soil and sand and therefore retained their mounded shape. These are the 'ghost pingos'.

During the work to try and restore some of these to the shallow pools, a volunteer worker with the County Wildlife Trust which owns the site, hit upon a hard object which was later to be revealed as part of a body of a man. That body was carefully extracted from the site and given the full experience of the county specialist forensic scientists.

The Cold Case team organised a facial reconstruction which was circulated through the media and Police Forces throughout the Country, and eventually to Interpol. The analysis of all this work identified the body as probably being of Albanian extract who, it is thought may have been involved in significant trafficking of girls and women from Eastern Europe into this Country.

If that proves to be the case, and however dreadful that trade is, it seems that this man fell foul of other people.

Our previous information linking this body to the disappearance of surveyors who were connected to proposals for new solar farms appears to be incorrect. Nevertheless, the police are still interested in learning more about those missing men. The Police will continue their investigations and anyone who may have information may contact the Norfolk Police Cold Case team or through Crimestoppers.

Friday night and the boys are out on the town. And the girls. Not that West Kelling could hold a candle to the City for nights out, and there were plenty of older people who had said hurrah for that.

But the boys were out. There was always the chance of a bit of a fight somewhere; always the risk of a few who couldn't hold their drink, staggering the pavements; always the possibility of some poor girl having her drink spiked, passing out and leaving her friends to call an ambulance.

After a busy afternoon in the patrol car, 'Dolly' Parting was on the alert. This time acting as Community Cop, trying to act as peacemaker, trying to help some poor lost soul. Chatting and trying to gain the trust those who were naturally suspicious of him and his colleagues.

At ten thirty things were getting lively in the pubs and clubs. So far, the streets were relatively quiet, with a few late night kebab shops serving the after-drink strollers, people coming out of curry houses, and a few chain coffee shops reminding some older folk of youth clubs of their own teenaged days.

'Dolly' drifted into The Brown Bear, and chatted to the landlord who had nurtured the community spirit in the pub. He drank a small glass of Diet Coke and looked around the room at the tables full of chatting youngsters mostly staring at their phones, giggling about something filthy, or cuddling the girl next to them. Mostly in their late teens or early twenties, some raised a hand to acknowledge his presence; some turned their backs, hoods up; but some even came over and said "Hi", or "Y'orrite?"

One such was Tyler Martin.

"It's Tyler, isn't it?" asked 'Dolly'.

"Yep. Busy day?"

"It has been, Tyler. I hope this evening's not going to be too bad."

"Yeah."

"You're the one who got into a bit of bother some time ago, yes? How are you getting on now?"

"Yeah. No trouble for years, man. I'm good. Got a job now. Groundworks."

Good for you Tyler. Decent hard work, eh? Enjoy your evening."

"Cheers, man."

And back Tyler went to his mates who all gave him a loud cheer.

Chapter 29

A Saturday morning, and Murray Flanagan was brooding.

Again.

"Fuck that woman," he snapped.

Gail thought for a moment and said, with some sharpness in her voice, "You did, Murray. Often. You did tell me once that you told her that you would make her life Hell. Well, you probably did, and now she's getting her own back."

"Oh, that's a great help. Thank you *very* much," he said with a sullen look.

"But it might be the truth." She said flicking her blonde ponytail onto her right shoulder. Her eyes were like daggers and the enormous false eyelashes fluttered like a flock of blackbirds.

"It's not the point."

"Then what is the point? Why are they chasing you about child maintenance anyway? You sorted the divorce settlement; you pay your way for the kids. What is it that she is after?"

"That's part of the problem. I've not paid her for months."

"What?" she screamed. "For Christ's sake man. Are you off you mind? What the hell do you think you're doing?"

"You know that you wanted control of our money. Didn't you notice?"

"So, if you have stopped paying what you should be for your kids' upbringing, what do you expect? And what have you been doing with that money?"

"Letting you spend it, that's what."

"So, what happens now? How much do you owe her?"

"I don't know. I expect a few thousand."

"Thousands? What the fuck happens to us then? What happens to my girls?"

"What about them? They're fully grown adults. They should be standing on their own feet."

"Don't be so bloody cruel. Have you always had this evil streak? There are times, Murray when you really are objectionable."

"I need to think," he mumbled and slunk off to the summerhouse at the bottom of the garden where the fridge held some of his favourite beers.

"You bloody well should go and fucking think. About time too."

Dave Wakefield read the Broad Norfolk Post and noticed the latest news regarding the body in the pingo. He creased his forehead wondering how his thoughts had become so scrambled.

"Mich, are you about?" he called to his wife, and Michelle appeared from the utility room still wearing her Marigolds.

"What is it, Dave?"

"Just have a look at this piece in the paper, will you?" He pointed to the article, and she leant forward peering over his shoulder.

"Oh, wow. That's a bit different."

"Exactly. So, if it's not one of the missing surveyors, what the Hell happened to them?"

"I remember you saying that they were employed by that awful Chinese company you worked with. Did you ever meet the one who worked on the project that you did?"

"No, I don't think I did." He thought for a moment and then asserted, "No, I never did, so I've no idea if he was a local or where he came from. He was there to give the solar farm company the technical information about the best layout for the rows of panels and the likely output from them. Obviously if the output didn't make the scheme profitable the company needed to know that as soon as possible, so they wouldn't proceed."

"Didn't they do that before they got you and Frank involved?"

"They should have done. Even a desk exercise should show up any real problems."

"Strange. Very strange people," agreed Dave, "but

surely if the surveyor had been well known in Britain there would be a record of him."

"Do you reckon that they must have been employed directly by the Chinese, then."

"I suppose so. I guess I better go and chat with the Police Sergeant and see what she has to say."

Myra Plater was totting up the various issues that she had to deal with.

There was the church and her churchwardenly duties; the housing issue in the village; amazement at the latest revelation about the body on Thompson Common; and then the state of her mother.

And, what else? Oh, yes then there was the '*Leave well alone*' message. She was confused by that.

It was a case where Myra didn't know.

"What to do first, today," she wondered as she paced around her kitchen with a glass of grapefruit juice and a Rich Tea biscuit. "I suppose I should really be in touch with the vicar. I've not had a chance to talk to him about things lately. I wonder what he thinks about the housing. Oh, and I'd better ring the Home and hope Mum is all right."

First things first.

She rang the vicar.

"Morning Vicar," she said as brightly as she could.

"Myra, good of you to call. I was only thinking yesterday that I'd not seen you since last Sunday's service. Did you like the sermon? Did I go on too long about the Godliness of looking after the poorest in society?"

"Not at all, Vicar, it was exactly what was required. Too many people these days worrying about their next ten thousand rather than offering help to those that have little."

"Quite. Are you involved in this housing debate, Myra? I thought I saw you mentioned in the Post."

"Well. Yes. I do think that the village really can't take any more. The traffic will be awful."

"But, Myra, whilst that is one area of interest, are you not concerned about the youngsters who can't get onto the housing ladder? You know what? I was speaking to a lad the other day, and he would be happy to rent so long as he can get a roof over his head. We can't have our young people having no hope, can we?"

"But is it right to spoil the village like that, Vicar?"

"But, dear lady, we haven't seen the final details yet, have we? Maybe there is a case for a smaller development than everyone fears. Compromise. Find the right path. We must help to give the youngsters some hope of being able to continue living in the village."

"Oh, Vicar, you do have such a way with words! Oh, sorry but there's someone at the door. Must go. Bye for now."

"See you later, Myra."

Myra checked to make sure that there had not been anybody at the door. walked into the garden and sat on her favourite chair. It was a Lloyd Loom which had been her mother's before she was moved to the Goldcrest Home, and Myra had retrieved it before any other of the relatives had laid claim. "Nice and comfortable this is, Mum," she thought, and realised that she had promised to ring the Home and see how the old dear was getting on.

She decided to make a cup of Lady Gray tea and read the paper before she did that. Whilst the tea was cooling, she made sure her hair was as she liked it, as if her mother would be able to see her.

"Oh, good morning, Myra," said the receptionist once Myra had eventually raked up the will to ring, how are you doing? We've not seen you lately."

Myra felt the barbs of the comment but put on a brave face and asked how her mother was getting on.

"I'll pass you over to Sharon who will know the latest," continued the receptionist, and Myra heard a few clicks as various buttons were being pressed.

"Oh, hello, Myra," said Sharon, "we were only talking about you yesterday, and wondering when you might be coming to see Elsie next."

"I really am sorry, Sharon. Life here has been so terribly busy. You know that I am a churchwarden, and the poor Vicar has had a rough time with Covid in the Vicarage, and then the choirboys had contracted it, so I've been chasing around doing the necessary admin that the vicar usually does. How is Mum now?"

"To be honest, she has taken a turn for the worse lately. I think a visit from you would lift her spirits."

"Has she been ill, then, Sharon?"

"Only lonely, I think."

"Well, Sharon, I will aim to make time next week. Thank you for all you do for her. Oh, must go there's someone at the door. Bye Sharon."

She looked up to the ceiling hoping that her Lord would forgive the little white lies.

Chapter 30

Georgia Stephens had dressed in her best peacock blue dress with its low neckline that revealed much of her comely bosom and was hoping for a fulfilling end to the evening out with Bruno.

It had taken a lot of preparation to get him to take her out, and she was nervous as to the likely outcome.

Bruno was certainly attractive, but she wasn't certain of his intentions. Was he looking for a real relationship or was he the sort who was in it just for a 'one-off'?

They met outside the Kashmir Kitchen and during the lamb vindaloo she asked him where he lived, and it transpired that he rented a flat in a set of converted retail units on the fringe of the town centre. It was convenient to his workplace and wasn't very expensive.

Bruno was ten years younger than Georgia and he had been in the UK for five years, moving from London to West Kelling in the past eighteen months to join a thriving Portuguese community in the town.

She told him about her children and about the situation regarding Kyle, to which he said he was sorry for her and hoped her life would be happier.

Bruno had no family nearby and said he was happy being a bit of a loner.

Georgia smiled.

Over a coffee Bruno asked if she had heard anymore about the Thompson body, as customers in his restaurant were still talking and gossiping about it, but Georgia said that she had heard no more since she passed on Bruno's thoughts to Tyler.

"So what's the new gossip, then, Bruno?"

"I only know what I hear, and someone said it was a business disagreement that got out of hand."

"Interesting, what people say, though. Do you think there is any truth in that?"

"I dunno. Maybe."

"Well, it's been a lovely evening. Thank you for coming out with me. Might we do this again?" Georgia asked, hoping for another chance to plan where they might go that wasn't his flat, or her home with the children about!

―――

Fat Robbie could smell danger. He had noticed strangers standing on the pavement near his flat in Upminster, and there had been cars that he had not seen before parked in nearby streets. He needed to get in touch with TAB to warn him that he might be under surveillance but didn't want to appear to be frightened. He relied on the trade he had in East Anglia and needed the income to satisfy his own needs. What to do?

Best to act normally. He peeked between the curtains of the room facing the road and saw nothing to worry him, so he popped out and went to the corner shop for a pack of beers and a new zippo lighter. His store of drugs for his own use was secreted and well stacked under a couple of floorboards beneath the kitchen sink, and he was due to pick up his major supplies to take to his punters in the morning. He didn't want to be followed to see TAB.

His car was always parked in a different spot each evening, and he knew he could use the back alley from the flat so he was not spotted from the pavement at the front of the building. His plan for the next day was being hatched. He would check with TAB by encrypted text message to confirm the pick-up point and was happy when he got an immediate reply and noted from it that it was a different place from the previous week.

Chances of being followed minimised.

Down in Snetterbrook Hall, Lady Hilda was recovering from her fall and the traumatic visit to the hospital, and had busied herself pottering round the garden and getting her man, Dibber to turn the compost heap and to hoe through the rows of carrots and beetroot on the vegetable patch.

"Have you seen the state of that outhouse roof, Dibber? It's definitely leaking. Do you think you can do anything with it, or do I need to get another tradesman in?"

The Thompson Body

she asked.

"Dew I'll hev a look later on, Lady."

"Thank you, Dibber. You are such a good friend."

"Tha's noice of you, Lady."

She went indoors to pour themselves glasses of her homemade lemonade and entered through the back door into the lobby where the wet coats and wellies stayed, as well as Douglas' walking sticks – or canes as he preferred to call them – and past the gun room and the roughly plastered lavatory where the door was properly latched, and into her kitchen. She called out, "Douglas, dear, are you about?" There was a barking cough that emanated from the lavatory, the sound of the cistern chain being pulled, and he stomped out with the Broad Norfolk Post under his arm.

"I tell you something, Hilda, there's strange goings on about that body they found at Thompson Common. I don't like the sound of it."

"Have they found something new? Something interesting?" she asked.

"They reckon the bugger was an Albanian human trafficker. Involved in bringing young girls and single women to the Country to work in the sex trade. What do you make of that, eh?"

"Oh, good Lord. That is horrible. Not that I wish anyone ill, but if it's true I suppose that means there's one less of his type."

"That won't stop them. There's always demand for women who allow their bodies to be traded for much needed money. I've seen it across the world. Never an end to it."

"Your sailors were at it too, I expect," she said with a lopsided smirk.

"Course they were. Six months away from home, testosterone bursting to come out. They had to get relief somewhere."

"They should have had more self-control, Douglas. Did you not warn them of the dangers before you set out, about what diseases they might catch, and what they might be doing to the girls?"

"The Padre on board would have a word now and then, but when the boys get together for a night ashore, all hell lets loose."

"What about you, then. What was your level of self-control like?"

"Perfect, Hilda. Perfect."

"I bet."

"Think what you like. It was a long time ago, anyway."

"Mmm." A long pause before she said, "But someone didn't like that Albanian then, did they?"

"Must have been either someone after his takings or didn't like him treading on their patch. That's my guess. Bastards, all of them."

"I'm sure you are right dear."

She picked up the glasses of lemonade and strolled into the garden where Dibber was leaning on his hoe, looking satisfied with his morning's work.

———

Myra was putting off the necessary visit to her mother and had made it her business to go and talk to farmer Patrick Baines.

Despite the summer weather, she put on her best tweed skirt, white cotton blouse and her favourite brown brogues. She had found Patrick's phone number and arranged to meet for a drink at the '*Tea For You*' shop which had recently opened and which had linen table cloths. Myra thought that was a classy touch.

On her way she bumped into Sir James Parker who she thought she had not seen since the public meeting.

"Sir James, how nice to see you. I must say I thought you handled that meeting so very well. I had an inclination that it might have got out of control, such were the feelings in the Hall."

"Very kind of you, Mrs Plater. It wasn't the easiest evening of my life, but one does what one can, you know."

"Indeed, but I was very impressed how you moved the meeting along. You must have a lot of experience at that sort of thing."

"Well, yes. I did have some difficult meetings when I was involved in my work at the Home Office. Can't say more, Official Secrets Act and all that."

"Of course. I understand. Oh, by the way," she hesitated, but aware of her recent chat with the Vicar she ploughed on, "Haven't seen you at Church, Sir James."

"I know, it's not really my thing, you know. My dear old grandfather used to say, '*church is for sinners*'."

Myra took a while to get the meaning of what he had said and thought it better not to pursue the matter. Thus, she bade Sir James farewell.

Patrick Baines was nursing a mug of strong tea, sitting at a table by the window of '*Tea For You*' looking out across the Market Square and when Myra arrived, he stood up to shake her hand.

"Good morning to you, Mrs Plater. What may I get you to drink?"

"That's nice of you, thank you. I think I'd like a cup of

cappuccino."

Patrick ordered the coffee and returned to his seat.

"So, I assume you wanted to talk to me, like so many in the village have, about the housing proposals."

"Indeed, yes. You know that I wrote to the paper and opposed the idea."

"Yes, I did read that."

Myra waited for the waitress to deliver her coffee before continuing.

"Well, I have discussed it with some close friends, and I think I may be persuaded to withdraw my objection so long as the plan is changed to a smaller scheme that was specifically targeted to the young folk in the village. Do you think that is possible?"

"From my point of view, I'd be completely happy to look at that. In fact I have already spoken to the developers, and they are giving some thought to the idea."

Myra sipped at her coffee and Patrick couldn't help noticing the froth and chocolate clinging to her fine moustache.

"Oh, that's good. How is the farm doing this year, Mr Baines?"

The spring was wet, and this summer is very dry, so we are not doing as well as I would hope."

"That's farming for you, I suppose. Always reliant on the weather," said Myra as she drained her coffee.

"Exactly that, Mrs Plater. That is one thing we can't control. Can I get you another coffee?"

"That's very kind, but no thank you. I have a meeting with the Vicar.

Another of the little white ones!

"Oh, by the way, I'd love to hear how you get on with

your talks with the developers."

"I'll certainly do that, Mrs Plater. Nice to have talked with you. Goodbye."

"Good day to you Mr Baines. Thank you for your time."

She walked home for a quiet lunch on the patio, smiling at her success.

Chapter 31

At the District Council's Planning Office, Evie Beecham was talking through her cases with Jane to agree those applications that would be ready to go on the agenda for the next meeting of the Planning Committee.

They acknowledged that they were still waiting for a detailed proposal for the housing scheme at Easthoe and that it would be some time before they saw a formal application. It would be ages before anything close to an agreeable solution was to be found.

Evie suggested that they should prepare the ground for a report about the battery store at Ballington, and Jane told her that she had discussed this one with the Chief and with Councillor Frank Porter. She said that whilst the need to support the requirements of sustainable energy production was a priority, this proposal was so detrimental to the appearance of the area. There had been no analysis carried out as to why this site was right for the industry, and that a recommendation for refusal should be prepared.

By happy coincidence, it was at this point when Jane received an email from Councillor Porter to say that he believed that the application would be likely to be withdrawn, and would she contact him as soon as possible.

She rang him straight away. "Mr Porter, a good afternoon to you, Thanks so much for your message."

"I thought you should know this as soon I did," he said, sounding as though he was on the last few yards of the East Anglian marathon. "I managed to get into the pub with the owner of the land, and he told me that he had been offered such a crazy amount of money for the developers to buy the site that he could hardly refuse. It would mean that he didn't have to struggle with a farming life any more."

"Are you sure he was being truthful? I mean, he might have spawned the idea himself, in order to achieve that end."

"I hadn't put him down as anyone quite as corrupt as that, but as a farmer myself, I know the pressures he might have been under."

"So, it is possible, then, eh?" asked Jane.

"I guess it is."

"Do you know who the people behind the application are, Mr Porter?"

"He told me that it was his uncle."

"Aahhh! So, we might have a nice little family

conspiracy going on here."

"Indeed, and that's when I put the pressure on a bit, and suggested he made sure that the application should be withdrawn."

"Good. Do you know when that will be done, as it would be nice to know soon, so we don't have to put it on the agenda for the next meeting. It would be helpful if we could know before the weekend."

"No, I'm not sure of the timing, but he suggested it would be soon. I will let you know as soon as I hear."

"Excellent. Many thanks for what you have done."

"No, it's thank you for what you are doing for the District."

"Very kind, Bye for now."

Evie and Jane spoke further and suggested that the application should be on the agenda, if only to give the matter some publicity, and Jane said she would email Frank Porter to give him the lowdown.

Evie shrugged, somewhat disappointed that here was another report she had to write.

———

The County Police Cold Case team were still trying to find out more about the Albanian found at Thompson Common and Tony had secured the authority of his bosses and had brought in their specialist team and those of neighbouring counties to focus on the Serious Crime of human trafficking, together with asking for the help of the National Crime Agency.

They knew that these poor victims, mostly women and girls were placed in degrading housing conditions. They were either employed in low paid work, often having their wages taken in return for their transport and housing or had been forced into the sex trade.

The fact that one man from, it was assumed, one of the gangs dealing with the latter had met his end did not in itself cause much anxiety within the Agency, it was one less such individual to worry about, but it did suggest that there were gangs at each other's throats.

The question was 'which ones?'

Pete Evans though, was convinced it was highly likely to be more complex than this. Whilst the body's geographic origins were reasonably clear, the dubious work he had probably been involved in was not yet proved.

"OK," he thought, "it might have been in trafficking people or drugs, but it might have been neither. There was no evidence of what he was involved in. He might have been a regular migrant worker, either in the fields, perhaps on a building site, a delivery driver, anything."

There was no clue at all.

They would have to keep working on different theories.

———

Dave Wakefield still felt slightly guilty and told Michelle that he ought to talk with Sgt. Sally Parmenter.

"If it will clear your mind, then it must be the right thing to do," she replied, and the following morning Dave felt much easier in his mind as he had a plan.

He rang the police station and asked to speak with Sgt. Parmenter.

"I'm sorry, Sir, but she is at a meeting at HQ today, and may not be back until tomorrow. PC Parting is here if you would care to speak with him."

"Thank you, but it is about the body at Thompson Common. I discussed my thoughts with her some while ago, and feel I owe her an apology."

"OK, I understand. Would it be helpful if I asked her to ring you in the morning."

"Yes please, that is kind of you, thank you."

"I'll do than then, Sir. Thank you for calling."

Dave felt some relief and went into the garden where Michelle was filling the bird baths with fresh water.

"She's not there today, but should ring me tomorrow," he said and walked up behind her and put his arms round her waist. She leant her head back and kissed him. "That's good, my love."

"Have you heard anything from Annie lately, Mich?"

"Nothing for ages. I expect they would call if there was anything wrong. Why do you ask?"

"I've not heard from Sam either. I hope they are OK. Perhaps I'll ring them tonight."

"Don't worry about them, Dave, they are grown up and can sort their own problems out. If they've got any."

"I just hope that he has sorted his mind out about his sister's family."

"I know, but you don't have to have such regular contact. They have their own lives to live. They will always call us if they have a major problem."

"She's still my Babe."

"Oh, don't be so soppy. Remember, the phone has two ends."

"I fancy a coffee. You?"

"Please."

In the afternoon they drove out to a plant nursery and

poked around with no special purchase in mind, took a trolley and spent seventy pounds on plants that they knew would need watering every day in the hot summer that was upon them, and, once they got home they spent time putting the pots where they thought they would fit into the borders, moved them about to the agreed locations, planted them and watered them well.

"That was a good job done," Michelle said with a big smile, and gave Dave a hug.

"Yes, it is. I really enjoyed that."

"Good."

In the following morning, about eight thirty the phone rang. Dave picked it up quickly and was pleased to hear that it was Sally Parmenter on the other end.

"Morning Dave. Sorry I wasn't available yesterday. I gather you wanted to talk about the Thompson issue."

"Absolutely. Many thanks for calling back. I feel so foolish pushing you towards a cul-de-sac of no use. However, now you know more about that body, have you any information about the missing surveyors?"

"Don't be sorry, please. We'd much rather have leads that may go in the wrong direction than have people hiding what might be useful. No need to feel badly; none at all. But, no, we have no leads at all about the missing men. Nothing further I can tell you."

"Well, many thanks for the chat. Oh, by the way, Sally – and I'm sorry to ask - would you mind messaging Tony Lovelace to say that it seems his suspicion about the bogus reports from the surveyors is probably right. That would be most helpful. Thanks. Bye."

"I'll arrange for that to happen. Bye, Dave. Have a nice

day."

He did.

Fat Robbie prepared himself for the trip to meet TAB, as Tariq Browne was known, and collect his consignment of drugs to take on his trip to East Anglia. He looked between the curtains onto the roadside and saw nothing suspicious, made sure he had his phone, wallet and envelope with the cash from the last trip and crept out of the back door, through the alley and onto the street where the Kuga was parked.

He did not see a member of the Essex Drug Squad hiding in the hedgerow of the park opposite.

He looked around and slid into the driver's seat, checked that his Glock and knife were still under the seat, and drove towards London. He put his radio on to check for the traffic information and then switched to the auxiliary mode where his own compilation of rap music thumped out the rhythm with which he kept time with his fingers on the black leather steering wheel. The pickup point on an old dockland site was easy to find and he saw TAB's white Mercedes beside a white container and drove towards it as smoothly as he could.

Windows were opened so they could speak to each other.

"Robbie. You OK?"

"Fine."

Got your contacts sorted?"

"All done. Did 'em last night. All encrypted texts."

"Good. Where's my money, then from the last package?"

Fat Robbie showed him the brown envelope. "I got it."

"Do I need to count it?"

"Have I ever let you down, TAB?"

"Not yet. Let's have it."

One envelope passed over. One cloth bag containing many plastic packages of 'the products' passed the other way.

Fat Robbie nodded to the boss, closed his window, and drove, very gently away and towards the A12.

Suffolk first.

As he left the old dockyard, a man in a twelve year old navy blue Ford Focus made a note and five minutes later circulated a message to colleagues.

Chapter 32

It was late in the afternoon and Sgt. Sally Parmenter was at her desk, munching her way through a cereal bar and nursing a hot mug of very ordinary coffee in her left hand. She had hit a number of dead ends as she ploughed her way through her caseload, and the bloody administrative tasks that helped the bean-counters tick all their boxes. This was nothing new, but it frustrated her to hell.

There had to be some means to make a bit of headway in the confusion that surrounded the body in the pingo and these blasted missing surveyors. Was it really her worry? Why was she so concerned about these cases? Surely it was for Tony Lovelace's team, not hers, but she still felt a responsibility because Thompson was in her patch.

She had rung through to her husband, Ed who was hardly surprised when she said that would be late home. Again.

Earlier she had rung Tony to ask if his Cold Case team would be good enough to go through their old notebooks and see if they could find some clues as to any potential contacts with the cases of any dead and missing bodies, and Tony had promised to raise it on emails to the team and discuss any progress at the next briefing session in the morning. She was also concerned that she had heard nothing from Reuban Blanche, the consultant profiler that Tony had engaged. The suggestion that the burial at Thompson had probably been carried out by a local contact of the killer had been a strong one, but no further information or theory had been forwarded, and she asked if Tony would find out the latest from Reuban.

It was a shock when, a week later they heard that Reuban had suffered a fatal heart attack.

They would get no more help from him.

Avril Danes was at her desk in the office of the broad Norfolk Post and had received a call from the editor of one of the Sunday broadsheets asking if she would do an interview for their Magazine regarding the Thompson Common case, as the location and the nature of the police investigation was so unusual.

She was completely taken aback, not because of the nature of her story, but that she didn't see herself as one seeking any publicity. She enjoyed the work for a provincial paper that was relatively low key and, more particularly, local. The fact that it was important to spread the story of the pingo body in order to raise the profile of the awful issue of human trafficking was good enough, but she said that she would think about it and let them know within twenty four hours.

Avril sent an email to the editor to seek his advice and had a quick reply suggesting that it would be great publicity for the paper, but to leave the decision to her. She decided that she would talk it over with husband Jake that evening.

Meanwhile, the office of the Broad Norfolk Post was inundated with emails, tweets, and letters about the recent article regarding the body at Thompson Common, and Jenny was sifting through them to provide the folder of this new material for Avril and Darren.

They included:-

> *To the Editor*
> *What an absolute disgrace for our wonderful Broad Norfolk Post to publish such disgusting material as that story of the body found at Thompson Common. This is one of the most delightful spots in East Anglia with a wonderful history that will be forever sullied by this foul tale.*
> *Publicising it so widely casts very black clouds over our beautiful County, and it is bound to bring hordes of ghoulish sightseers, plugging up the highways and littering the place with their detritus.*
> *We need better than this, and I suggest that you buck up your ideas of decent*

journalism.
I am truly appalled.
Yours
Mrs Margot Fortescue
Norwich

Dear Sir
It was good to see the fine work of our Police investigatory teams together with their European colleagues in reaching conclusions regarding the identification of the body discovered at Thompson Common.
Congratulations too on the way the Broad Norfolk Post has kept us informed of progress in this case.
Well done everyone.
Yours faithfully
Pavel Tankowski
Thetford

Sir
So, this saga rolls on and those who revel in the sordid world we live in will have enjoyed your recent article about the body found on the Common at Thompson. The evil that this man was allegedly involved in has found him out.
I say this rarely, but may the Good Lord ensure that his soul does not rest.
Publicising this repulsive activity may encourage others, and I urge you to

ensure that you retract the emphasis on this reprehensible behaviour.
Your faithfully
Michael Pratt-Browne
Bury St Edmunds

Hello
My grandad said a rude word when he was reading the paper and I asked him why he said that rude word. He said that people who hurt children should be strung up by their nuts. I didn't know what he meant. I love nuts specially peanuts and peanut butter. I love my grandad.
Love from
Marcus
Aged 6

Myra Plater was humming along to the radio in her car as she drove to see her mother at the Goldcrest Home in Bury St. Edmunds. She took the A11 south west and crossed the delightful Nuns Bridges in Thetford, across the heathland and onwards towards the Suffolk town.

On reaching the entrance to the Home, she took a deep breath in anticipation of what might be another difficult encounter.

On a business footing, Myra was always confident, but the personal side of difficult discussions always gave her nervous system a bit of a tweak.

As she entered the front porch the smell of what she thought was like roast pork made her smile. It was one of her mother's special meals when she was growing up. All that lovely crackling, golden brown glistening on the top of the joint, but now making her giggle at the thought of the number of dentures that would struggle with it when lunch was served here.

She went to the office where Sharon was busy organising the staff's shift patterns, knocked on the door and once Sharon looked up, said, "Good morning, Sharon. I think I should have rung through first to let you know I was coming today, but it slipped my mind. I do hope it's not a problem for your team, or indeed, for Mum."

"It's no problem for us, Myra. You are always welcome to visit. I'm not sure if Elsie is dressed and ready for you to see her. I'll check."

"Thanks, I'll go and sit in the visitors room, shall I?"

"Good idea. I'll get someone to let you know."

It was a while before one of the nurses, Paulina came to collect Myra and told her that she was sorry it took so long, but Elsie had been sick in the bathroom, and Paulina had taken time to freshen her up, help her into clean clothes and settled in her armchair.

"That is so kind of you. What made her sick, do you think?"

"I really don't know. She was fine when she woke today. Perhaps something stuck in her throat."

"Might have been the thought of me," thought Myra, but kept a faint smile on her face as she followed Paulina to the Mum's room.

"Hello, Mum. This lovely nurse tells me that you have been sick this morning. Are you feeling better, now?"

"I'm all right, aren't I Paulie?"

"You are now, dear. Enjoy the chat with your daughter,

Elsie. I will see you later."

"OK."

"Are you sure you feel all right now, Mum? What have you been doing lately. Made anything nice? Any knitting? You were always so good at that."

"I've no-one to knit for, have I?"

"Well, I'm sure that some of the nurses have children who would love to have a jumper or a scarf."

"I don't know."

"That Paulina seems very kind, does she look after you all the time?"

"Sometimes."

Myra took a second to wonder why her Mum was talking in such a sharp short way. "What's the matter, Mum? You're not you normal chatty self, today."

"I've been a bit fed up for a while."

"Anything in particular that's upsetting you?"

"I don't see you very often."

"Oh, I am so sorry. How often would you like me to come here, then?"

"It's lonely here. I'm on my own and I don't like anyone here."

"Oh heavens. But you used to get on with a lot of the residents, didn't you?"

"They're all dead."

Myra took a long breath and thought that something must be wrong. "Mum, I'm going to have a chat with Sharon and see what she says about it. OK?"

"OK."

Myra left the room with damp eyes and went to the office where Sharon was in conversation with another member of staff.

"Sorry to interrupt," said Myra, "but Mum is saying she has no friends here. Is that right?"

"I don't think so, Myra, what else did she say?"

"She said that they are all dead."

"Did she, now. I wonder what's brought that on."

"I think I should make more effort to come down, say once a week. Would that be sensible?"

"I do think that would help Myra, but we need to get to the bottom of this latest thinking."

"I'll just go and say goodbye, and I'll be off. Do let me know what you discover. Please."

She went back to Elsie's room where the old dear had taken to her bed and was either asleep, or more likely pretending to.

Myra left with a very muddled mind. Whatever was going on?

Myra didn't know.

———

Fat Robbie had made deliveries in Essex and Suffolk dropping off packages in a village outside Chelmsford, Sudbury and Ipswich, grabbing a sandwich in a suburban line of shops from where he had sent his encrypted confirmations of his next stops before heading north. He had planned his journey to avoid his competition in Norwich, so he travelled cross country from Long Stratton, through Attleborough and onto West Kelling where he had arranged to meet up with Johnnie McNeil at the usual drop off point behind the railway station.

Johnnie had been waiting long beyond the agreed meeting time and felt conspicuous. He was getting irritated again but had learned that these trips for Robbie were subject to unexpected stops. So, he held his tongue when the black Kuga eventually turned up and he handed over the cash to the big man in the driving seat before he picked up the bag that was thrown out of the car. Robbie barely stopped saying he was late for his next drop.

Further down the disused yard in the doorway of an old railway shed was a man wearing black jeans and a navy hoodie who was operating a long night vision lens on his camera.

"Gotcha."

Chapter 33

Deep into the hottest summer on record and with East Anglia having had barely a drop of rain in months, people's garden lawns were light brown and plants withered. Early harvests had brought poor yields and forecasts for rising food prices, exacerbated by Russia's dirty work in Ukraine were putting stresses on households.

Stubble fields caught light when sparks which were created by machinery contacting flints on the surface of the land, led to some huge field fires. Despite the best efforts of the exhausted Fire Services the fires raged such that they were uncontrollable, and a number of cottages around the County were engulfed in the flames.

Avril Danes had been busy with this latest news and

had abandoned her planned time away with Jake and the boys in order to deal with reporting the devastation.

She had interviewed villagers and members of the emergency services who had been involved, and she wrote the following in the Broad Norfolk Post:-

Horror and Devastation

My last few hours are ones I never want to visit again.

Those much older than me will recall the horrors of the Blitz and the fear that brought, but this is the worst disaster I have ever witnessed. And not just in this area. Random field fires sprang up across the County. Gardens, their buildings and equipment destroyed, even houses and cottages in the rural areas, burnt.

All possessions destroyed; memories obliterated.

"This must be what Hell is like," one resident of Oakhill, a small village south-west of West Kelling told me.

Jack Moore said, "There I was, walking my dog across the Green when this great sound, a sort of very loud 'Whoosh' seemed to shake the ground, and when I looked back there was this vast cloud of black smoke, and I saw that the field was alight. Right across it, it was. The wind was really strong and blowing towards the village, the flames were higher than I have ever seen, and all of a sudden, they seemed to fly across the gardens and onto the cottages. It was awful. I suppose everything was so dry, all the timbers in the roofs, and in no time at all the flames were shooting out of the roofs. Those poor people. I know a couple of them real well. Lovely folk, so kind, nothing fancy about them, just wonderful countryfolk, good company, always got a story to tell. I tell you what, they've got the biggest story of their lives now. I think they lost all their belongings but managed to save the cat. Terrible. Really terrible."

Jack Moore tells of the event from first hand, and he tells it so very well.

At The Broad Norfolk Post we will continue to report on the progress being made by all the emergency services but we must praise the local people who have come to the immediate aid of those who have lost so much, by offering shelter, food and friendship.

The savagery of the field fires had stunned the affected villages and their surrounding hamlets. Children screamed in the night; parents barely slept hoping that their properties would not be hit by another flare up.

Those whose houses were burned came back to try and retrieve belongings, but there was barely anything to find.

All possessions gone. Pictures of the children as they were growing up, wedding pictures, precious mementoes of time spent together.

The only fortunate thing was that no-one in Oakhill had lost their life.

The local community quickly found the energy and hospitality to give the displaced neighbours a roof and shelter whilst longer term arrangements were made, but everyone knew it would take many months to carry out the necessary forensic work, for insurances to be settled and for reconstruction to take place.

In the course of their various investigations, the Fire Service and the Police combined to carry out surveys with drones collecting video evidence of the paths of the fires, and in the village of Coney Temple an anomaly was shown up in a ditch adjoining rarely used rural lane.

A body.

Darren had also been rushed off his feet chasing stories of the fires, and his notebook was struggling to keep up. He had interviewed the folk who had lost all they had, the publicans who had fed and watered the fire officers, the police and the volunteer helpers.

He had just picked up the reports of the recently found body at Coney Temple and tried to find one of the police officers to see what the latest information was. No-one was able to tell him anything helpful.

One evening that week he came across his friend 'Dolly' Parting. They had shared a pint or three one evening in the Rat and Rabbit after 'Dolly' had finished his shift, and who told Darren that little could be said about that new body at that moment.

It was a fresh discovery, and because of the remote

position of the road, which in truth was little more than a narrow lane with tufts of grass running up its middle, it was possible that the body had been there long before the fires. It would of course be referred to the forensic team.

Chapter 34

In suburban Gloucestershire, the post arrived early that morning and Murray Flanagan was having his breakfast in preparation for a busy day when Gail, who was padding about in her silk PJs, cleavage well to the fore and with her false eyelashes in place picked up the letters and passed one to Murray.

She opened hers and squealed with delight as she saw she had won a thousand pounds in the PostCode Lottery.

Murray opened his.

No cheque.

What he had was a further demand from the Child Maintenance Service for information about his salary and bonuses.

"What have you got today, Murray?"

"Those bastards are still chasing for my financial information."

"Who are?"

"That fucking Child Maintenance Service."

"So, you never did reply to the previous one, then?"

"You told me not to."

Gail gave him one of her 'you are a sorry boy' looks and smiled sweetly.

"Advice only, Murray. You are a big boy. You made your own decisions about this, not me."

"Thanks very much for your help, Gail."

"Look, you have to take responsibility. Your problem. Sort it out for God's sake."

"This time they say they will speak to my employers, current and past, and undergo a full financial investigation. Apparently, I have a right of appeal against what they come up with. Dependant on what they suggest and what I say, the matter may end up in the Court."

"Oh dear," she said and flounced out of the kitchen to indulge herself in an early morning bath.

"It's more than fucking 'Oh dear'."

———

David Johns, the agent for the housing project at Easthoe had prepared a revised scheme showing fewer houses than the previous proposal. It included four two-bedroomed houses in two pairs of semi-detached buildings, two three-bedroomed detached houses, a four-bedroomed house together with a two bedroomed bungalow and a pair of three-bedroomed bungalows. He had also prepared a 'Statement of Intent' which indicated that the smaller houses would be for sale or rent to local people, as would be the bungalows, which would allow for local folk in bigger properties to downsize.

The principle appeared to meet many of the ideals of those villagers, including Myra Plater, who had previously opposed the original scheme. He felt he was in with a chance.

The dilemma he had was this: - should he speak to the planners first or try and arrange to meet the Parish Council to gain their support?

He chose the latter and agreed to attend their next meeting.

Harold Carpenter had recovered from his thankfully mild effects of Covid and was in the Chair for the public meeting of Easthoe Parish Council and, once the audience had quietened down from the normal hubble-bubble of a general gathering. He welcomed members of the public and introduced David Johns. He proposed that after the taking of apologies for absence, and the consideration of the minutes of the previous meeting he would allow Mr Johns to present his new scheme and take comments on it before going on to the other matters on the agenda. This would allow for Mr. Johns and any other members of the public who didn't wish to stay for the rest of the meeting, to leave.

David Johns thanked the Chairman for his introduction, and said, "My clients and I have had some interesting conversations with some of you that are here tonight, and I thank you for your views. I have taken on board many of the comments made when I was last in discussion with the Parish Council and the public at your previous meeting, as well as those further discussions that

I have enjoyed separately with members of the village community."

He then gave a presentation indicating the detail of the revised scheme.

The general consensus was that this was a much better proposal, and whilst there were some who still wanted nothing to be built, there was a significant number in favour. However, there was still no traffic or engineering report about the access and the additional amount of traffic, and no clarity concerning the future of the Grain Store.

There were also those who queried the 'Statement of Intent', how it could be enforced or what happened if the developers reneged on it. Basically, everyone thought this was a matter of trust, and many of the residents didn't trust developers or landowners where profit normally was more important than the needs of the community.

David Johns would have to work on this. A discussion with the planners at Paston District Council would be the next step.

———

The following Friday evening 'Dolly' Parting was doing the rounds and finished up in The Brown Bear where the usual bunch of lads were at their normal tables chewing the fat, checking their phones, and enjoying whatever drinks they were permitted to enjoy. They were lifting their glasses and singing 'Happy Birthday' to one of their number who 'Dolly' couldn't see properly. It didn't take long before he recognised Tyler Martin and was glad that the lad, now a man, was having a good evening of it.

It was rowdy, but there was no real trouble, and he

was finishing his Diet Coke when Darren entered the pub, saw him, and came over offering to buy him another drink as he ordered his own pint of Guinness.

"George, how are you? Not seen you for a few days. How's this heat suiting you?"

"Not enjoying it to be truthful. Too hot outside and there's no air-con in the office, so it's a rock and a hard place."

"Me too, and I went down to Oakhill and saw the awful outcome of that fire. It's truly amazing how the village has pulled together and helped those that lost their homes."

"I just hope that the heat keeps the troublemakers at home and not gearing up for a fight."

"These lads in here seem unlikely to cause you too much bother, eh?"

"Generally, they're a good bunch, and one or two are pretty friendly with us."

"That's great. Anything you can tell me about the investigations regarding the drug problem?" asked Darren.

"I can't at the moment mate, but we have had some excellent cooperation with the Essex Force. I hope we shall make some real progress next week. I'll let you know."

"Thanks for that George. I'll look forward to it."

"You're very welcome. Can I get you another beer?"

"Kind of you but I've just popped out for a quick one and better get back to the desk. I'm on the late shift!"

"OK. See you later."

"Yep, see you."

Once Darren had left, 'Dolly' was finishing his drink and thinking of an early night, but knew he had to be on duty for another couple of hours. He yawned and made his way to the door, hoping to find a cooling breeze, when he was tapped on the shoulder.

He turned and there was Tyler, pint pot in his hand, large smile and slurring speech.

"Cheers, man. Oh, by the way I heard that the guy who buried that body down at Thompson must have been a local."

"We have wondered if that was so. How did you find this out?"

"Someone heard someone else saying it. Who else would know about the place anyway?"

"But you've not heard who that was, or whether he was the killer?"

"Nah. Don't know any more."

"OK, thanks anyway. Tell me, do you recognise this chap?" 'Dolly' showed him the photograph he had taken the other evening from near the railway station.

"Oh him. Smackhead. Idiot."

"Do you know his name?"

"I just know him as 'Scottish'."

"Is that his name or is he from Scotland?"

"Don't know, man."

"Ok, thanks anyway. You have a good evening, Tyler. And ... stay out of trouble."

"Yep. I've been out of trouble for years, man."

Chapter 35

It was after a good lunch, and the Vice-Admiral was drifting into a snooze following his mid-day glass of Oban Malt and a smoked salmon sandwich when Lady Hilda came into the lounge.

"You threw that new shirt I bought you last week straight into the laundry basket."

"Did I really?"

"You did."

"Are you sure it was the new one, because you know I already have one with the same pattern? Or did you forget that when you bought the new one?"

"Oh, Douglas, don't be so churlish. When was the last time you bought any decent clothes?"

"Why should I? I've plenty enough clothes for what I want to do. I'm not a bloody woman, Hilda. You with your wardrobes full of clothes. I bet you don't wear half of them. Bloody waste of money, I'd say."

"What about all the bottles of spirits you buy? I note they don't last as long as my clothes!"

"That's a stupid argument. You can't wear a decent bottle of malt. And I bet I get more pleasure out of it than your fancy blouses give you."

"Oh, all right. That's enough. I've got a ladies evening to arrange".

"What again? You did one last week."

"That was a month ago, Douglas."

"Time flies," Douglas muttered and sloped off to the downstairs lavatory for a happy half hour with the Broad Norfolk Post.

"If you are going where I think you are, I don't want you leaving a bad smell in there!"

"Least of my worries," he mumbled as he slid his braces off his shoulders.

He had been reading for ten minutes or so when he came across Avril's detailed piece about the fires in the village of Oakhill.

"Good Gorleston Cliffs," he spluttered. It was an expression that one of their cleaners had used.

"Hilda!"

"Oh, what is it now? Are you stuck in there?" she said as she walked to the lavatory door.

"Have you read the Post?"

"No. Why?"

"I saw a bit about those fires on the news but didn't realise it was so bad. Half a bloody village burnt down, and not that far from here. It's terrible."

She had her mind on the upcoming bridge evening and hesitated.

Then, "Oh Heavens. I wonder what Johanna will have to say about that!"

"Plenty, I would expect."

It was another twenty minutes before the Vice-Admiral lifted himself off the seat, hitched up his trousers, buttoned up his flies, adjusted his braces and pulled the chain.

For the benefit of Hilda, he opened the little window.

———

DI Tony Lovelace called his Cold Case team together for a general debriefing session to check progress on cases. He told the team that the National Crime Agency had made no progress with the matter of the Albanian found at Thompson Common, and that the team should leave the matter to them. There were other matters to progress.

The body found at Coney Temple had been recovered and was being examined by the forensic pathologist. Once that examination was complete and he had received the report, the team would focus on that.

"What about the missing surveyors, Guv?" asked Pete Evans. "I was thinking that if they were truly experts in their field of surveying they must be operating somewhere."

"I've been thinking the same thing, Pete. It looks as though we ought to be finding out which companies are operating in the County, any Chinese connections, any cases where Councils are querying the evidence. However, I still think there's something dodgy about them. However, if they are outside the County, do we still need to be chasing this? I think not. And are we assuming they are still alive? So, probably no cold case. Back burner, I think.

Now, anything for Sally Parmenter at West Kelling?"

Pete Evans said, "I've been looking into that old case of the death of a young boxer in Norwich, and out of the blue I got a contact name for a witness who was nearby at the time and told me the possibility of someone with an Irish name, probably called 'Ruby'. Not sure if it's helpful at all."

Tony asked him to contact Sally directly and pass on the information.

Meanwhile, 'Dolly' Parting had been intrigued by Tyler Martin's reference to the man in the photograph as being 'Scottish' and he shared his thoughts with Sally Parmenter.

"Guv, I think we need to go through the records of tenants of private landlords and Housing Associations. I can't see him being a homeowner. Unless you can think of another way we can find out."

"I agree it's a starting point," said Sally. "Then there is the Electoral Register, but I bet it's unlikely he had put his name on it. I don't think we should publicise any of this yet. No pictures posted anywhere, as it would only scare him off. It's important that we establish the identity of this individual, and people he deals with. We know that in the City the teenagers fly around on the electric scooters to their customers, but we've not identified the way our man is getting the product to the customers."

"How are the HQ team getting on with tracking the supplier?" asked 'Dolly'.

"I understand that an operation is in place, and surveillance is proving useful. Again, it's being kept quiet until all those involved are tracked down."

"I'll try and have another quiet word with Tyler and see if he has said anything to his mates. See if they know who the lad might be.

My guess he has a Scottish accent. People here would surely notice that."

"Or, he has a Scottish name."

"Aye."

David Johns rang the Planning Office and found that Jane was away on holiday with her two daughters in the Loire Valley, but that Evie Beecham, who was part of the team that dealt with proposals in the south of the District would be happy to meet him.

Evie, in her thirties with blue streaks in her auburn hair which went with her blue eyes stood a good five foot nine and had a strong physique. Clearly, she gave out an aura of one who was not going to be messed about.

She met David in the reception area and directed him along a short corridor to an interview room with no character, block walls painted in magnolia and with a table and four chairs. There was a panic button on the wall within the white plastic conduit that ran round the wall and contained power plugs and a couple of USB ports.

After the introductions and no offer of coffee they sat side by side and David told her the history of the scheme and the discussions at the first public meeting as well as at the recent Parish Council meeting.

Evie knew some of this background through the press and the general gossip that always filtered back to the department. She was well aware that the village was well equipped with a school, shops and a doctor's surgery, that there were good bus services and access to the main highway network all of which had made the village suitable for some new development as shown in the approved Local Plan for the District.

She listened to David's explanation of the latest revision, and he asked her opinion of the possibility of a legal agreement regarding the sale or lease to local people.

"We have done this is the past, but it is difficult to monitor and enforce."

"So, you don't like the idea?"

"No, we don't. Once bitten… you know."

"What then is the best way that you prefer to deal with this, please?" he asked, suspecting that he knew the answer.

"I would say that you get a Housing Association involved. They can control the occupancy where we can't."

"I think I should have thought that through more clearly," thought David, but just said, "I wondered if that was what you would say. Now, do you see any problems with the scale of the development and the layout?"

Evie took some time before saying, "I think it probably fits into the pattern of the homes nearby, but I do think the matter of the grain store needs to be clarified. I really do think it is going to be an eyesore amongst the dwellings, and how on earth would it be of any use on its own?"

"Yes, I know that is a real problem, and I think I'm going to have to have another conversation with my clients. Anyway, it was good to meet you. Thank you for your time."

"You're welcome. Is there anything else? I mean how are you dealing with the traffic issue?"

"Our engineers are working on it as we speak."

"OK. It will be interesting to see what they come up with."

"Thanks again."

On reaching his car he realised that he was sweating profusely. Partly because of the heat, partly because the tension of sorting these things out usually affected him this way, and partly due to Evie's perfume.

Chapter 36

Darren Prescott had again returned to the village of Oakhill so devastated by the fire. This time he had spoken to the Chairman of the Parish Council, the publicans, the manager of the Care Home, the District Councillor and the civil emergency team that coordinated the help across the District and County Councils, police, charities and the NHS. He was overwhelmed by the efforts of all concerned, particularly those who opened their homes to those who had lost theirs.

At the primary school he had talked with the Headteacher who had asked a number of the year four children who were more forthcoming than many, to come and tell him how they had felt.

The simplicity and honesty of the responses had

nearly brought Darren to tears.

The next edition of the Broad Norfolk post included this:-

Human Suffering and Human Generosity

The Broad Norfolk Post is proud to celebrate the magnificent fortitude of those who suffered recently in the fires that swept parts of the County, as well as the extraordinary help and generosity shown by individuals and organisations. These people opened their doors and hearts to accommodate families who suffered the devastation of losing their homes.

We spoke with children at the local Primary School who thought the fires had been both exciting but very frightening, and some were clearly suffering from the trauma. Young minds finding it difficult to accept that some of their friends were having nightmares about what might happen to them if the fires came back.

The Chairman of the Oakhill Parish Council, Alan Jackson was full of admiration, but not of surprise at the way the villagers had banded together. He told the Broad Norfolk Post, "I saw such kindness, skill, professionalism, and patience in all those folk who supported the needs of the village. It has been a huge shock to all of us, and we can't imagine the feelings of those who lost their homes. We pray for the swiftest possible resolution to the insurance claims so that the properties can be restored for the benefit of the residents as soon as possible. A big thank you to all those involved in helping our village."

We endorse these comments without hesitation and add our congratulations to those who put others before themselves. The generosity shown by so many can only warm our hearts.

———

Dave Wakefield could still not shake the matter of the missing surveyors out of his mind. It seemed so strange. These were two men, believed to be Eastern European who had worked for the Chinese company and had just disappeared. Were they whisked away, and if so for what reason? Were they truly specialist surveyors? Were they a cover for some other dealings? Did they ever produce any reports? How the Hell could he find out?

Perhaps in the wider context of his life this was of little consequence, but as he said to Michelle, "It's just bloody annoying to not know. It's unsettling."

"Dave, your days of solving other peoples' problems are over, you should let it go. Find some freedom for goodness' sake."

"My problem is that I know you're right, but it still niggles away. If there's been a clear fraud, or something worse, I would feel more settled if I knew what had happened. I even think they might have been behind the killing of that bloke at Thompson Common,"

"I'm sure you would feel better if you knew, but it mustn't eat you up. Is it so important that you can't let it go?"

"But, I do feel that it is important. I guess it's quite inconsequential to everyone else, but I can't shake it off."

"Well, who else can help you, because I can't? Do you think you need some alternative therapy?"

"Good God no. I think I'll try and talk to Frank again and see if anything comes to light."

"OK then, but let's get this out of the way as soon as we can."

"OK. Sorry for being a pain."

"Come on, Dave, we need to get you out for a good walk to clear your mind. Let's go to the Great Wood at North Oakleigh where you met that lovely man who made our coffee table. I wonder if he is still there."

"Good idea. It would be nice to catch up with him again." He stopped for a moment and then said, "You know what? Today, I'd rather just go up to Foxley Wood and see how they are getting on with the work on clearing the scrub."

They set off after lunch for the twenty minute drive and found the car parking areas where a couple of other vehicles had parked, and one family was just returning to make their way home.

They exchanged pleasantries and made their way through the wood which gave a pleasant refuge from the searing heat.

"My, it's different from when we were here last," said Dave looking at the areas where scrub had been cleared to give more light to the understorey.

As they looked across the area, a family of roe deer jumped through the clearing and the sound of woodpeckers thrilled their senses.

Dave was so glad that he had been persuaded to free his mind with the wonders that nature brings.

———

Peg Halford left her tiny cottage which was set in a small group only a hundred yards from the Market Square in Easthoe and made her way to the centre of the village. She wanted to buy her normal provisions and the local paper as well as one of the national tabloids. Peg liked to do the puzzles over a cup of cocoa in the afternoons. Whatever the weather, hot or cold, always a cup of cocoa.

First, she went into the butcher's shop where she bought a couple of beef sausages, a small piece of lamb's liver and four rashes of bacon which would keep her fed for two or three days. She then popped over the road to the general store for some *'vegables'* and a tin of peach slices and a can of evaporated milk.

As she wandered around the shop, she bumped into Myra Plater who was chatting to a very round woman by the hardware shelves, mainly about the weather and the proposed housing scheme.

As she struggled to get past them, Peg looked at a small Teflon coated saucepan and thought that would be better for making her scrambled eggs and decided to use some of her carefully managed pension as a treat to herself.

Mid-sentence in her chat with the other woman Myra turned and said, "Morning, Peg, dear, I haven't seen you about lately, are you keeping OK?"

"Mornin' to yer, Myra. Not too bad. Not too bad for an old'un"

"Just out for a bit of shopping, then?"

"Yis, Jist a foo bits for me dinner."

"Going a bit wild buying yourself a new pan, then?"

"Gotta treat yerself if you've not long to go, yer know."

"You'll go on forever, Peg."

"Wouldn't want to. Times I wish I was with my Fred."

"You've got plenty of life left in you yet, dear. You take care, Peg."

Peg went and paid for her shopping and trudged home feeling very maudlin. She lit the stove and used her new pan to heat the milk for her cocoa.

―――

'Dolly' Parting spent the morning nursing cups of coffee and chocolate digestive biscuits and trawling his way through various web sites and electoral registers. He had spoken to administrators at four of the Housing Associations that operated in the area, and especially in West Kelling, and asked for detailed lists of tenants. He had to explain that this was a criminal investigation and despite the reticence to give out the personal information, he did gain access to all these databases.

But what exactly was he looking for? Scottish names, or just surnames? Apart from the obvious 'Mac' or 'Mc' there had to be the Campbells, Gordons, Wallaces, Fergusons and plenty of others.

"Chances are," he thought as he crunched through another biscuit, "if the lads are calling him 'Scottish' it will be a 'Mac' or 'Mc' It will be a hell of a job otherwise."

The Electoral Register for the West Kelling area was a start. 'Dolly' knew the patch well enough and thought he should start concentrating on the areas where the Housing Association properties existed. He highlighted a couple of large estates, but he knew that many of these dwellings had been sold to the tenants and would probably be able tell which ones by the efforts of the owners at their DIY projects. He assumed that there was a reasonable chance that he should put those properties to one side. But which ones were they?

Perhaps best then to just look for the 'Mac's and 'Mc's and eliminate where there were at least two of the same name at the same address, one male one female as they were likely to be man and wife. The target was unlikely to be living in a family home.

He found himself with a shortlist of nine properties, but knew it was entirely possible that the lad was not on the Register. He was rapidly coming to the conclusion that the lad was not a tenant of any Housing Association but lived in one of the properties that had been bought out of drug dealing profits by one of the Eastern European drug gangs.

How on earth could he find out?

That was one problem to solve, and now there was another. Sally had passed on the message from Pete Evans that there had been someone involved in a murder in Norwich about eight years ago who had an Irish name. and might be called 'Ruby'. He remembered the legendary murder of JFK and that involved someone called, he thought, Jack Ruby. However, the timescale of eight years ago was interesting.

"It's all getting very confusing, and it feels like a cross

between *Countdown* and *Who Do You Think You Are*," he sighed and poured himself another coffee.

Chapter 37

Harriet Chambers was angry. Angry that Murray had still not paid any of his dues in respect of the maintenance of his children for ages. She was getting desperate for cash. She was only able to carry out part time working at the local supermarket because of Daisy's illnesses which cropped up on such an irregular basis, and the wages were only just enough, together with the few pounds of Benefits to make ends meet.

Heavy and increasing bills to put petrol in the car and buy food meant that the prospect of a winter with massively increased fuel costs to heat the home was very scary, although she knew she was not alone. That knowledge made little difference, and she confided in her father, Jack who said he would come round to see her at the weekend and talk through the options.

When they met on the following Saturday morning, Jack asked what the latest situation was regarding the work that the Child Maintenance Service was doing for his daughter. Harriet said that she had heard nothing and was waiting for the results of their challenging Murray for his full financial situation but suspected that he wouldn't cooperate with them.

"So, there's little progress. My God, this is taking ages."

"It's just so bloody frustrating, Dad."

"I can see that. We better sort out how I can help you through this next six months or so."

"I don't want charity, Dad. I don't like it."

"Tell me what happened to the money that was raised for Daisy's treatments. Were they used, or where are they now?"

"Dad, this is so embarrassing. Murray kept at me to do it. I hated the idea when he was earning so much. Much of it was promised and not actual cash, and the rest was put into a trust fund. It's still there, and it's not a huge amount, but it can only be used for Daisy. So, it's no use for our general expenditure."

"OK, that's helpful. At least we know there is a little there if Daisy needs it. Now, you may not like it, but you are where you are. You're doing as much work as the situation with Daisy allows, and there's not much more that you can do. But I can."

"But you still have to live your life. I'm certainly not going to take that from you."

"I know you wouldn't want to. I would rather not have to do it either, but until this situation is resolved you and your kids need to live. Look, I have a decent pension and my monthly outgoings are less than my income. Therefore, I have been able to put a bit away for a rainy day. And you know what? It's pouring, and you need an umbrella!"

"Oh, I don't know. I hate the thought of being in debt, especially to you."

"Look, we can do this one of two, or maybe three ways. I can give you a lump sum to top up what you already get from work and Benefits for, say a period of six months, or I can give you a monthly allowance. Then you can pay me back once that bastard finally has to pay you. Or, and this probably suits best, we can find a lump sum, you get the money now, and I can deduct it from what you would get once I move on upstairs."

"What do you mean? You want to move in here?"

"No, you daft thing, when I am no more. I can adjust my will so that you get less at that stage that your brother. It's easily done."

"But I would lose my inheritance."

"Only part of it. Anyway, why is that a problem? There's still the house which will be for you two to share the proceeds of the sale, and it's so much more sensible that you get money now when you really need it."

"Are you sure you want to do this?"

"As I said, I have enough for me to live the life I choose. The last thing I want is for you and the kids to suffer any more. They've had a rough time of it, and a bit of security would do you all good. And, you never know, that Tribunal just might come up trumps and find some money for you."

"Dad."

"What?"

"I can't thank you enough. I love you so much. I just

wish Mum was here too."

Jack and Harriet stood and hugged as the tears rolled down both their faces.

Jack to the rescue again.

———

The week after the raging fires, there was a call for volunteers to help with trying to sort out the chaos that remained in the village of Oakhill. Whilst much of the clearance work had to wait for the authority of the insurance companies, there was a general wish to do as much as possible to make the village look more like its normal self.

On the Saturday a group of the youngsters who had met up the previous evening at The Brown Bear, had gathered in the car park of the pub at the instigation of Tyler Martin and drove to the village to offer their help.

The workforce included a local Scout group and some soldiers from the army which was stationed at Swinton, a few miles north of West Kelling, and was organised by the Chairman of the Oakhill Parish Council, Alan Jackson.

After a hard morning's work giving help to residents whose gardens needed so much effort, there were free drinks and sandwiches at the local pub before the gang were back at their tasks for the afternoon session, after which they all gathered to the cheers of the villagers and the thanks from Alan.

The Brown Bear lads and lasses said they were knackered but really pleased that they had put in a decent shift and given help to some folk who had been through something that they could only struggle to imagine.

———

Tony Lovelace was anxious to get to grips with the situation regarding the new body found by the drone footage, and which appeared to have been burnt during the fierce field fires. He was pacing around the office expecting the pathologist's report at any time.

He took a few deep breaths to relax and got himself into boring mode doing the necessary drudge work of checking protocols, performance levels, checking off requests for leave, checking his department's expenditure and comparing it with his budget.

That last one was a worry. He knew that the Cold Case team was expensive and dreaded the day when the top brass would seek cuts in their annual expenditure. He had thought that he should be preparing his case for the time when he had to defend his various teams' work against the bean counters.

Eventually, he got a call late one afternoon from the Laboratory to say that the report was on its way by email, and that he would find it interesting. Ten minutes later, the double ping on his laptop proved the point and the document was attached to the email. There was plenty of it, and as it was late in the day, he decided to take the laptop home and read it over a glass of beer.

He had started to go through the index of the report when his wife, Rita said that dinner was ready and that he might enjoy one of his favourites. He walked into the dining room full of anticipation and was not disappointed when Rita produced a liver and bacon casserole with mashed potatoes and spiced red cabbage.

With the excellent meal over, he excused himself and went back to his study with a further bottle of beer. The work produced by the pathologist appeared to be impressive, and Tony did what he always did when going through these reports; he went to the summary pages at the end. "Always go the sports pages first," he said to himself.

The pathologist had concluded that the body was of a man of some thirty years, underweight and had almost certainly been dead before the fire raged over his body. There was no evidence of any other injury, no sign of strangulation, no stab wounds, no sign of gunshots. However, the tests that had been carried out indicated that the man had significant amounts of cocaine within his system.

"So," thought Tony, "drugged up to the eyeballs, probably right off his head and fell, comatose into the ditch. But what the hell was he doing there, out in the sticks? Did someone take him there and drop him off?"

Anyway, there was another victim of the drug menace growing in the area.

———

Myra was about to ring the Home to check on the health of her mother after the confusion of her recent visit when her attention was smashed by the sound of a pigeon flying into the closed kitchen window leaving the ghostly impression of an angel on the glass.

It had flown away after a few minutes of wondering what had happened, supposed Myra.

"Stupid birds with little brains," said Myra who normally enjoyed 'all things bright and beautiful' but found herself considering pigeons as the most irritating.

The memory of that *'Leave well alone'* note kept fluttering into her mind, and all thoughts of her mother had flown away with the pigeon. Then, she was wondering if she should tell the Vicar of the latest changes to the housing proposal, and that she had found herself in agreement with him at last. She rang the Vicarage.

"Oh hello, Madeline," she said to the Vicar's wife who had answered the phone, "I was wondering if the Vicar is available for a short chat."

Madeline knew that there was no such thing and that Myra's conversations must have kept the phone company in good annual profits.

"Sorry Myra, but he has gone to see the residents at the Care Home in the village. Should I ask him to call you? What can I tell him it's about?"

"Oh no, don't bother, dear. It was just that I wanted to give him an update on the new housing proposal."

"Oh, I see. Actually, he spoke with Harold Carpenter yesterday, and was given the latest information. So, he is up to date."

"Ahh. OK then, Bye."

"Goodbye Myra."

So, here was another thing that Myra didn't know.

It was then that she remembered she had to find out about her mother.

―――

The social services, anti-drug charities and the healthcare agencies had met, discussed and considered the consequences of cutting off a significant supply of drugs in West Kenning and had reported to Sgt Sally Parmenter.

They had concluded that there was a distinct possibility of that gap in supplies being filled by another operator, but also acknowledged that there was a real chance that some of the addicts may need help in coming off the drugs even if for a temporary period. Whilst many of the users were known to some of those agencies and that they could try and keep an eye on them, it was possible that some others may react badly.

The group had acknowledged that the real lack of sufficient personnel in these organisations meant that there was little chance in being particularly proactive.

There was no optimism that any user would find it as a permanent way to come off their drug of choice.

A bad situation might get worse. However, Sally knew that what had to be done, had to be done. It would be for others to deal with the consequences.

Chapter 38

Vice-Admiral Sir Douglas Ewart-Robinson was spending his lunchtime with some close friends in the back bar of The Lion's Mane, a small hotel in the nearby village of East Hawning. It was a comfortable room with sofas and lounge chairs covered in various fabrics, with hunting and shooting prints in gilded frames upon the walls which themselves were covered in flock wallpaper, maroon being the predominant colour. In the corner of the room was a stuffed bear standing upright with its fore paws stretched forward and holding a plate upon which visitors were expected to place cash for the staff.

Most of the customers left their business cards instead.

With Douglas were Colonel Barry Farquharson, Squadron Leader Johnny Carpenter, and Edward Blanchard, a former Chief Constable of Essex who had retired to the Norfolk coast 'for the benefit of his health'.

They had enjoyed one of the hotel's Specials of Chicken Kiev with triple fried chips and asparagus washed down with a couple of bottles of South African Pinot Noir, in a private dining room, and were now taking their coffees and mints in the small back bar.

"We're in for this long hot summer to last for months," said Johnny, claiming that his meteorologic knowledge was better than most.

"Not too hot, I hope," the Colonel retorted, "my soil won't take too much more of this heat, and the veg hate it."

"Bit of warmth is good for the joints though, old boy."

"Bloody well need something. My knees are letting me down too often,"

"You better get some new ones, then Barry,"

"Bugger that, can't get to see a doctor, let alone get new knees."

Douglas was keeping quiet on the matter, as his hips had been playing up for months. However, he wanted to get in on the chit-chat. "You'll have to go private, Colonel, you must have plenty of your Army pension to use. You can't take it with you, you know."

"I know, I know. Anyway, what about the rising prices of every bloody thing. Can't understand it, meself."

Douglas was warming to the conversation. "I know, I'm struggling to get my weekly packet of shag with any decent change from a tenner. And, I say, have you noticed how ginger nuts have got so much smaller?"

"Mine have too!"

Eddie Blanchard got a word in, "Well, you fellows will all have good military pensions. Bet you could afford anything you wanted."

Douglas was getting agitated, "Anyway, Hilda was worrying about the poor buggers who haven't got a pension at all, just living on the state."

"Bloody parasites," muttered Johnny.

Edward felt that was a bit strong, and said, "Well, hang on, Hilda may have a point. Who's going to look after them? Bet you won't, Johnny."

"Christ," spluttered Johnny, "you're not all getting Lib Dem on us are you?"

Douglas replied, "Not me, old boy, it's Her Ladyship. The real problem is some of the women she is mixing with. Strange company she keeps, you know. Dreadful people."

―――

Murray Flanagan was panicking, he didn't know what he was looking for, but expected to recognise it once it turned up.

After he and Gail had eaten dinner in a glum silence, he said that he had some paperwork to finish and went upstairs to his study on the second floor of their three storied house built in the mid nineteen nineties and which they bought for half a million pounds in 2018.

"There has got to be more than this. I know I filed all the bank statements in that ring binder. Or was it that one, or maybe in one of the box files," he muttered as he went through the bookshelves and the filing cabinet, looking for the important documents that the Tribunal has insisted that he produced.

The house stood amongst a group of a dozen similar

properties in a wooded suburb in an area of Gloucestershire that was 'on the up'. It was an area where neighbours kept themselves to themselves, and Murray was pleased about that.

Gail had stacked the dishwasher and was on her second glass of Beaujolais-Villages, a case of which they had brought back from a holiday in one of the chateaux in the Beaujolais region of France, when she heard a crash from above. She went into the hallway and called up to him, "Murray, are you all right? Have you fallen?"

"I just dropped a drawer full of bloody files."

She went back to the lounge with her glass and the remainder of the bottle to watch the latest version of Love Island, wishing she was there rather than in the gloom that inhabited their house.

Upstairs, Murray found nothing relevant. Plenty of files relating to jobs he worked on twenty years ago and well before he joined the big national company that employed him in a series of roles until he became the Operational Director for the South-West of England.

"Well, if it's not here and I can't find it, then they won't be able to find it either, whatever it is they are after."

Thoroughly dissatisfied, he gave up the search and went down to the den overlooking the back garden, poured himself a large glass of brandy and turned on the television to watch his beloved Chelsea in the Champions League game.

———

Tyler Martin enjoyed the warm summer evenings especially after a hard day of physical work and he had met up with Ben with whom he had been friendly for many years. Ben was a bit of a wild one, had not had a good childhood, had driven himself off the rails a number of times and had even spent a few months behind bars. Now, however he had got rid of much of his aggression and whilst still being on the police radar had kept away from major trouble.

The two of them strolled around the town and went along to the park where they threw skimming stones across what would have been the pond if it hadn't dried up in the weeks of intense heat. At least the ducks and drakes had all gone to find water elsewhere and missed the doubtful enjoyment of dodging the bullets.

"You got anyone in tow, Ben?"

"Nah. Can't be doing with it. What about you?"

"I'm all right," replied Tyler.

"What happened to that girl, what was she called? Ah yes, Viola wasn't it? You saw a lot of her, eh?"

"I saw most of her, mate."

"Not all of it?"

"Well, all right then. She was good but she got a bit too heavy on for me. Wanted us to get tied down. Not ready for that yet, mate," said Tyler with a heavy shrug.

"Good for you. 'Spose you still get your end away now and again, eh?"

"Can't be arsed."

Ben changed the subject. "You still using?"

"Nah, waste of money and time," said Tyler shoving his hands into his jeans' pockets. "Just need to stay clean."

"Still plenty about if you want it."

"You need to go careful, with your history, Ben. You got contacts, then?"

"A couple. I make a few quid."

"For fuck's sake, Ben. You gotta be careful. You selling as well?"

"A bit. Just passing it on for a few mates."

"Shit, mate, you must be fucking crazy. You'll get your comeuppance you will. Anyway, Where do you get it from?"

"There's a bloke they call Albie. I think it's 'cos he's from Albania. Then there's a bloke called 'Scottish'."

"I've heard his name. Is he really Scottish?"

"He don't sound it, but he's got some sort of Scottish name."

"What, like 'Mac' something?"

"Think so."

―――

The reception area at Paston District Council's Planning Department was busy with people wanting to see details of various planning applications, wanting to complain about the way decisions had been made, and wanting to know who were the people blocking the footpaths. These people were told which website to look at and some became particularly irritated and said they didn't have the internet and didn't know how to use it if they were shown a computer.

Twiddling his fingers in the queue was David Johns who wished that he had put the finalised planning application documents in the post. In the end he laid the large envelope on the reception desk and walked out into the sweltering heat.

Three days later, with the registration and early parts of the administration of the application complete and all consultations sent out, it landed, as with all new applications on Jane Seabrook's desk for an immediate perusal. Whilst the majority of the work with these applications was simply delegated to the team leaders to process, she liked to get an overview of what was going on in the district.

Her initial reaction was one of reasonable satisfaction although she took some time to go through the traffic engineer's report to see how he had analysed the increase in traffic and the effect it would have on the village. On the face of it she thought he had covered the issue well.

With the application and all its details being sent out for consultation to see if there were any unresolved matters, the team would await the views of the Highway Authority, the Parish Council, the Water Authority, and the public at large, before making a further assessment of the proposal.

Chapter 39

Myra had written herself a note to ring the Goldcrest Home and check on her mother's health.

"If there was anything wrong, I'm sure they would have rung me," she comforted herself after the feeling of guilt had ebbed away. "Perhaps I'll just have a quick breakfast and drive down to see her, unexpected."

She was only a few miles down the road when her mobile phone rang, and, as she had never learned how to operate the Jeep Cherokee's hands free facility, she pulled into the next layby and opened the phone to see that there was a message from the Home to ask if she would come as soon as she could, as Elsie was not well. She replied immediately to say that she was already on the road.

"Coincidence or a witch's intuition," she wondered to herself, and travelled on using the speed limit as a guide rather than a requirement.

She scrunched and slid to a halt on the Home's gravel drive and dashed as quickly as her little steps would allow into the entrance hall, and poked her nose into the office where Sharon was looking more than a little exasperated.

Rather than disturb her she went straight to her mother's room, tapped on the door, and heard a familiar voice inside. She opened the door and was greeting by the sight of Doctor Polly Grainger and two of the nursing staff round the bed.

"Oh, my Lord," she said. "Hello again, Polly. Please tell me what's wrong."

One of the nurses, whom she had seen before but had forgotten her name said, "Hello Myra, it's good of you to come. Elsie may have had a heart attack. We are waiting for the Ambulance, but you know what the delays are like. Anyway, the doctor has made her comfortable and given her a light sedative. Come and sit with her."

Myra looked at her Mum and saw how grey she appeared. She sat beside the bed as the other nurse left the room, and whispered, "Hello Mum. It's Myra here. You have some wonderful people helping you now."

There was no response, and she didn't expect any. It was clear that Elsie was unaware of what was going on.

"When did you ring for the ambulance, Polly?"

"The girls here rang for it as soon as they suspected something serious, and then got in touch with me. I came as soon as I put the phone down."

"That's very kind of you."

Myra sat and stared at nothing in particular. She felt

numb. This was so unexpected, and yet she should have anticipated that someday her mother would become this unwell.

When the paramedics arrived and unloaded their equipment they checked Elsie's blood pressure, her temperature and oxygen levels, and then gave her an electrocardiogram which confirmed that she had suffered a mild heart attack. Particularly bearing in mind her age, they said that she needed to be taken to the local hospital to check if further action needed to be taken.

Myra was struggling to stay in control of her emotions, but once she had calmed, washed her face in cold water and climbed into the Jeep, she was ready to follow the ambulance to the hospital, where she would wait until the doctors told her the conclusion of their investigations.

Oh, the uncertainty. Myra hated it.

Myra wanted to know.

———

Dave Wakefield had rung his friend Frank Pack and offered to buy lunch at the pub a hundred yards from Frank's office so that they could talk about any progress that was being made in solving the mystery of the missing surveyors.

Dave was seated at a table near the door with a couple of pints of the pub's own brew and was thumbing through the menu when Frank walked in with a young lady. Dave rose to welcome his friend and was introduced to Emma who was apparently a bit of an IT expert within Frank's office.

"Nice to meet you Emma, what can I get you to drink?"

"Vodka and tonic please, Dave," she replied in a very

friendly manner. Dave took to her immediately and guessed that she had been brought along as she might be able to find her way through Frank's filing systems that were more than complex.

Once they were all seated, and glasses raised and chinked together Frank said that Emma had spent a bit of time trying to find out about the surveyors who had worked for the Chinese company in advance of this lunchtime meeting.

"It's been fascinating," she enthused, "and from what I've been able to find out these guys were part of a real fraudulent bunch of people who produced regurgitated reports and just changed the site location, so that the proposed solar farms were always technically in the right orientation and would produce excellent outputs to the National Grid. They appear to have been employed directly by specific companies both Chinese and European".

"We had been wondering if that was the case. Are these men themselves Chinese or European?"

"It looks like European."

"So, part of Mafia style gangs?" asked Dave.

"That's a bit strong, Dave. I can't say yet, but it's certainly possible."

"Well, we shall certainly need good evidence if we are to help the authorities. That will mean more work. So, Frank, are you happy to have Emma spend more time on that?"

"I think so, so long as my mainstream work isn't compromised."

Dave hesitated and then said, "Just going back to the issue of these technical reports, from my contacts not many planners check them. They mainly focus on the effect the panels would have on the environment, the visual appearance, and the traffic impact. Hey, let's order food. What are you having Emma? Frank?"

With chilli and chips for three ordered and much of the drinks downed they settled into general chit-chat about football, social lives, and Frank's workload.

Dave finished his pint and rose to get refills "By the way, I came in on the bus so I would enjoy my beer! I must say a big thank you to both of you for the time you've spent on this. I do realise there is little to be gained for you."

"I'm not sure you are right," said Frank, "I think we can make some gains over other companies by spreading a bit of confusion within the industry. We are not doing much of this solar work now as the Housing Associations' programmes keeps us busy, and that's where our money is. That, mind you is despite the minimal funds coming from Government."

The food arrived in large white bowls, and they tucked in feeling pretty pleased with the result of Emma's work.

Between mouthfuls, Dave said, "I've made some good contacts at the local police station, and they may well be interested in this development. I really am most grateful. I was getting nowhere with it, and I know it's barely a major issue for many people, but I just had a feeling in my water that there was something that smelt wrong."

"I suppose that's the result of too many pints of beer, then Dave?" asked Emma with a smirk.

Dave said, "Good one, Emma. I like that!" and made a mental note to talk with Sergeant Sally Parmenter about this new theory.

At the next briefing session of the Cold Case team DI Tony Lovelace told them the basic detail of the forensic report on the burnt body from the ditch in Coney Temple and suggested that the next steps were to try and find whatever they could from the Missing Persons records. They would need to try and identify any local acquaintances of the man together with links to his drug suppliers.

The group were allocated different tasks, and there were some doubts expressed as to whether or not they were wasting time. A muttered voice at the back of the room said, "He got what he deserved, why do we need to find out anything about him?"

"Shut up, pillock, what if it was your brother?"

"OK, you lot. Stop bickering and get on with it. Reports on progress tomorrow four pm," said Tony and went to his office where his secretary told him that the Chief Superintendent wanted to see him.

Pete Evans took the lead on the missing persons register searches, and his thoughts were wandering.

"Does anyone know if the pathologist took any DNA from the body?"

Nobody replied and Pete hoped that was because they were deep into their own research, so he rang the forensic science laboratory and spoke to what sounded like a young male trainee, gave the reference number of the body and asked if there was any record of DNA having been taken.

"Hang on, I'll look at the records."

Pete hung on for ten minutes and was about to terminate the call when the lad said, "Sorry for the delay. This was the burnt body, wasn't it?"

Pete confirmed that it was.

"OK, it looks as though it wasn't taken at the time, I assume because of the state of it. But it looks as though the boss had second thoughts, and extracted some yesterday and has sent it off asking for a swift response."

"Is there any indication of where the sample was taken from, please?"

"The underside of the body, presumably where it was touching the ground and was not particularly scorched. It was obviously possible to take the sample from the leg and bone. I hope that's helpful."

"It most certainly is. Many thanks for your help."

Having been summoned, Tony went along the corridor, up a flight of stairs to the Chief Super's office where he was told that local County and District Councillors were showing concerns that little or no progress seemed to being made, particularly regarding the Thompson Common body.

Local residents were feeling most uncomfortable that the human trafficking was apparently happening so close to home, and he wanted to know what reassurances he could give them.

Tony responded that the matter had been taken over by the National Crime Agency and that no work on the matter had since been undertaken by his team. He assured the Chief Superintendent that he would check on the Agency's progress and report back.

Chapter 40

Myra was at her wit's end. There was nothing she could do but wait, and wait.

Wait for what? Wait for the worst news possible or wait and twiddle your fingers in the hope that the doctors would do their usual miracles? All she could do was remember the day her beloved Arthur passed away in hospital after his brain haemorrhage.

She had hated hospitals ever since. She knew friends who had relatives who had suffered heart attacks and the doctors had resolved the blocked arteries with drugs or stents. She knew that the doctors and surgeons did wonders.

Myra knew.

An exceptionally long hour had passed before one of the senior nurses came to speak to her and told her that the procedure had been much more difficult than expected. Some blood vessels had proved to be thin and very weak and there had been the need to try and reinforce these.

The nurse said that the surgeon had told her that whilst Elsie would almost certainly make a recovery it was uncertain if it would be robust and complete. She would need a great deal of care and observation and would have to stay in the hospital for some days, and maybe a couple of weeks before the doctors would feel that she was fit enough to go back to the care of the Goldcrest Home.

"Am I able to see her, please."

"In a few moments, yes. You must be prepared to find her asleep as she has been sedated to allow the healing drugs to work without unnecessary movement."

"Oh, I see. Please hold my hand for a moment, would you. This is so awful."

The nurse did just that and sat with Myra for ten minutes or so, allowing her to quietly sob, blow her nose and wipe her eyes and eventually recover her composure.

"I quite understand that this is not what you would have expected, Myra. Do you have someone you would like to call and be with you when you get home?"

Myra had given no thought to the trip home and didn't relish the journey, even less to the idea of having someone to stay with her. Eventually she said, "My closest friend is probably our Vicar. I think I ought to let him know where I am."

"That's a good idea. I'll leave you in peace for a while so you can do that."

"Thank you and thank you for your kindness."

"You are more than welcome."

She rang the vicarage only to get Madeline answering the phone and telling her that the Vicar was at the church with a couple preparing for their wedding.

"Please tell him that I am with my mother at the hospital in Bury St. Edmunds, and I don't know when I shall get home. I would like to talk to him, though."

"Oh, I am so sorry, Myra. Would you like him to come and meet you there?"

"No, I don't think that would be necessary. I'd just like to hear his voice."

"I'll tell him."

"Thank you, Madeline."

———

Dave was keen to pass on his latest findings to the local police thanks to Emma's work and left a message asking Sally to ring him.

It was late in the afternoon when Sally called him back and after the usual pleasantries Dave told her that there was a likelihood that the missing surveyors were part of an Eastern European organised crime unit using their cover of surveying to organise the movement of drugs into the Country. It was also likely that this unit had connections to one of the huge Albanian networks and it was also possible that it may be a strand of one of the enormous Italian mafia organisations.

"Mmm, interesting," said Sally, "I'm going to have to pass this one upstairs, Dave. I guess the Anti-Drug unit will want to follow this up."

"My contact tells me that there is more work needed to delve further, which I'm hoping we can get further information in the next fortnight or so. I will let you know once we make some decent progress."

"OK, I think it's best that I hold this for now and wait until you finish your work, and hopefully produce good evidence that we can work with. Good stuff, though, Dave. Thanks."

"You're very welcome, Sally. This is at least keeping me off the streets! Bye for now."

———

Myra's mobile buzzed its vibration and she saw that it was the Vicar calling her, so she left the visitor's room where a dozen other worried relations and friends were staring at their phones or biting their nails, waiting news of their loved ones.

She found a quiet area in an outside quadrangle which was dimly lit and where a couple of members of the staff were smoking, to which, even in her shocked state, Myra managed a shake of the head

"Thank you so much for ringing, Vicar. I am so worried about Mum. It seems that what they thought would be a simple procedure to open up her heart vessels has turned out to be far more complex."

"My dear Myra, how horrid for you both. Anything I can do to help?"

"To tell the truth, I don't think there is anything. I just needed to hear a friendly voice. Although having said that, the staff and especially the senior nurse have been kindness itself. I suppose I ought to go home, but I don't trust myself at this time of night. I reckon I'll end up having a nap in these horrid chairs. I will text you once I know what's happening."

"Take it steady, Myra. Trust in the Lord."

"I will Vicar. He has been in my thoughts a lot today. Goodnight, and thanks for ringing."

Harriet was more settled after she had accepted her father's offer of funds now on a regular basis and had spent time sorting through her household budget, especially with the rising cost of food, petrol, and the impending increase in the cost of gas and electricity. Her part-time work at the supermarket, and the discount for her food certainly helped a bit. Daisy's disability benefits, albeit small, meant that the young daughter could manage her own finances and save a bit. Ollie, found a few casual jobs and would give his mum a few pounds from his earnings. There wasn't much, but it all helped.

The doorbell rang and the post lady asked for Harriet's signature on a registered letter. She sat at the kitchen table with her coffee and opened the envelope to find a very formal letter from the Child Maintenance Service which told her that they had served notices on Murray for further information. It said that Murray had appealed against the case submitted by the CMS, and that they would be preparing their evidence to go before a Hearing in Court and that she would be required to attend.

"Oh, God, I can't be in the same room as that bloody man," she said to herself, and she felt herself getting hot and sweaty. After a drink of water, she settled and decided to ring her contact at the CMS, Dougie Ferguson.

"Hi, is that Mr Ferguson?"

"No, sorry he has been moved to a different department. My name is Paul Overton. How may I help you today?"

"Oh, that's a shame, as we got on very well. Oh, sorry, I didn't mean it to come out that way! I didn't mean to be rude. I've had a letter from you, and she read out the reference number at the top of the letter."

"OK, wait a mo, please." There was a pause as Paul went to his computer and searched for the reference number. "Right, I have got it. So, please confirm your name."

"I'm Harriet Chambers. Sorry I should have said that first. I am a bit shaken."

"Please don't worry, we're used to it. Now, what are you worried about?"

"The letter says I have to attend court, and I really can't be in the same room as him."

"That's your former husband, is it? Murray Flanagan?"

"Yes. Can you tell me where the Court is anyway?"

"Bearing in mind that this is his appeal that the Court will hear and where he lives, the hearings are almost certainly to be in the South-West possibly in Bristol, Harriet. Is it all right for me to call you by your first name?"

"Yes, that's fine. But, please understand that I don't have the money for that. I can't possibly go there. I do have a daughter who needs care."

"Don't worry. It would have been more difficult for you many years ago, but you can appear by video. By Zoom or something similar. That way you can see and hear what's going on, but from your own home if that's where you want to do it."

"Oh, thank you so much. Sorry, but I remember now, Dougie did tell me that. My brain is so mixed up. I was really winding myself up about it all. Do you know when this will be?"

"Not yet, no. We will keep you informed of progress."

"Thanks. That is comforting. I am very grateful."

"You are most welcome. From what I have seen, I think we have a good case against Mr Flanagan."

"Excellent. Thanks again. Bye."

"Bye. Have a better day!"

"I certainly will."

Chapter 41

Pete Evans was delighted when he got a call from Zac Prentice, the young man in the Forensic Laboratory to say that the DNA test result regarding the burnt body had been received. The pathologist was not available, but Zac said that he was sure that it would be fine for him to let Pete know that the investigation appeared to show the man had Eastern European roots and that there were signs of significant drugs in his system. The full report would be sent through once the boss had checked it and agreed it could be forwarded to him.

"That is very good of you. I guess I haven't had this conversation with you!"

"Good idea. I wish you well with your work."

Pete thanked him again and wondered if this

interesting but not very specific piece of information would be of much help. The drugs factor was already known, but the geographic origin of the man was interesting. However broad it may be, he wondered if there was some sort of link between this body and the Thompson Common man.

Another Friday night and the lads were gathered round the tables at The Brown Bear with the usual banter, moans about the boring night life in West Kelling, and tittle-tattle about the various girlfriends.

Tyler was in good form throwing insults at his mates and repeating jokes he had learned from his gang of workmates. He was part way through a long shaggy dog story about a man who swallowed a glass eye when 'Dolly' Parting came in, closely followed ten minutes later by Darren, notebook in hand.

"Hi Darren, can I get you a drink?"

"That would be good, George, thanks. I see you've got yourself a decent pint!"

"I'm off duty tonight, so I thought I'd have a pint of what you'd be likely to have!"

They raised their couple of pints of Guinness, and stood at the bar checking up on each other's day of work.

"To be honest," said Darren, "we're getting a number of readers ringing us to see what the latest is on the Thompson case, and frankly there's little we can tell them, Any news from your end?"

"Nothing I'm afraid, mate. I think it went over to the National Crime Agency, but I've not heard anything. Want me to check?"

"If we can get something that we can print to soothe the minds of the worrying public, the sooner the better."

"I'll see what the Sarg. says tomorrow."

"Not any more about your lead on the drugs supply issue?"

"Not really. We think the local contact for the big boys is probably a lad with a Scottish surname. Possibly a 'Mac' or 'Mc' something, and I've been trawling through all sorts of databases but not got anywhere yet. We don't think that he's on the electoral register, and I don't believe that he's housed by any of the Housing Associations, so we are just keeping our eyes open. Don't want to scare him off by any publicity yet."

"OK, I get that. Is there anything we can do to help?"

"Not unless you want to go under cover and try to buy some stuff!" George said with a grin.

"Might be an idea. I'll see what Avril has to say."

"I was joking."

"I know, but..."

Tyler was on his way to the toilet and, as he passed the bar, he slipped a piece of paper into 'Dolly's' pocket. It was very subtle for a tall gangly lad who had put on a lot of muscle since starting physical work, and as he walked back to his seat, he said his usual "Yo'rite?"

"We're fine Tyler thanks. How about you?"

"I'm good."

"Great, enjoy your evening."

When 'Dolly' got home and got his keys out of his jacket pocket he found a piece of paper with them which merely said, 'Mc is right'.

The weather was still hot when Dave and Michelle chose to pick up on her idea to go for a walk in North Oakleigh's Great Wood. They parked the car close to the road in a dedicated layby and strode purposefully along the main track with the beech and oak trees providing shelter from the sun.

Dave was remembering the little groups of families who made camp in the wood in previous summers and was keen to see if they had returned, whilst Michelle had said she wanted to see if 'Chuck' Balls was still producing finely crafted furniture from his workshop.

It was clear that the oak trees had been under a lot of stress during the baking hot summer and plenty of acorns were under their feet at this early time for them to drop. As they continued walking, hearing the 'mew' of buzzards in the distance and the chirping and tweeting of sparrows, tits, and finches they took in the distant signs and smells of wood smoke.

"That may be the camp sites," said Dave, "it would be good to see if the same families are there as before."

As they approached the area, they slowed down as the growl of what sounded like a big dog was heard a few feet away. Dave called out, "Hello, please let us know if your dog is on a lead."

"Denis, come here," a deep female voice called.

"Who the hell calls a big dog 'Denis'?" whispered Michelle.

"Someone who lives in the woods, I should think!"

"Are you sure you want to go any further?"

"Yes, I do. I don't think the people will be frightening, even if Denis is."

"You go first then."

The Thompson Body

Dave moved through the bushes that formed the understorey and emerged in a clearing where there were just three shelters, one with a campfire smouldering gently.

"Hello there," Dave called, and a dark pony-tailed woman, he presumed the one who had called the dog, came out of the middle shelter dressed in a pink vest and very short red shorts and wearing a pair of well worn sandals.

"Hi," she said, "Can I help you?"

Dave explained that he had made friends with families here a few summers ago and wondered if the same people were here again.

"I don't think so, dear. From what I heard a couple of the families caught Covid and one of the boys didn't make it. I guess they thought this place was responsible. None of them came back as far as I know."

"Oh no. That's awful," said Michelle. "Are you enjoying your time here?"

"It's wonderfully free. You do miss some of the normal comforts, but it's great if you don't mind the smoke and a few bugs!"

"Where are the others, then?" asked Dave.

"Gathering wood and berries. Amazing in this heat, but there are a few mushrooms coming up already. Most unusual."

"That sounds very early. The seasons aren't what they used to be."

"You're right there."

"Well, good to meet you. Enjoy your time here."

"Thanks. Peace."

They walked away from the camp and after a couple of

hundred yards heard the chug of a generator and headed towards the sound in the hope that it was the power source for 'Chuck's machinery. And sure enough, as soon as they approached the old workshop the sound of a power plane suggested that there was a craftsman happy in his work.

Michelle went first and knocked on the door, quite expecting no reaction as 'Chuck' had a large pair of ear defenders on, but the man had a sort of sixth sense and knew someone was nearby. He turned and with a huge smile came forward and gave Michelle a big hug and shook Dave's hand with his scaly hands from all the manual hard work.

"Oh, my word. Long time, no see. Hello my dear friends. How are you?"

"We're really well, thanks, and still loving that coffee table you made for us."

"It was a pleasure to make, and a pleasure to give. I'll put the kettle on if you'd like a drink."

"Too damned hot, 'Chuck', thanks anyway. We thought we'd like a walk in these woods as we haven't been here for some time, and hoped you were still about and to see how you were getting on. What's on the bench now?"

"I'm in the middle of a four poster bed for a couple in the Midlands. It's amazing how the word gets around. And I'm thankful it does."

"Well deserved, my friend," said Dave, and meant it. "Are you keeping well?"

"Aye, I'm doing OK. The back tweaks a bit. It's all this leaning at a strange angle, but there's no way round that problem. I still love it here and love the work."

"We've just seen that there are less families camped

out in the wood this year. We were sorry to hear of the problems the previous families suffered."

"Great shame that. They were a lovely crowd."

"Well, we won't keep you from the bedstead," said Dave, "Lovely to see you and to know that all is well with you."

"Many thanks for popping by. Great to see you both so well too."

Dave and Michelle walked back to the car, happy to have enjoyed exactly what they had expected.

Apart from Denis.

When they got home, Dave found the landline answerphone had a message waiting for him from Emma. It was disappointing.

"Hi Dave, its Emma from Frank's office. It was good to meet you last week, but I'm afraid I have no good news for you. I wasn't able to make any progress on detecting any more about the so-called surveyors or their employers. My guess is that these were cash-in-hand deals and the companies were happy to pay so long as they got the answers they wanted. Sorry I can't do any more. It might be one for Interpol. Bye for now."

"Not really surprising," he thought to himself, and rang back to say thanks for her efforts.

"Never known the ground here to be so dry," said Dibber Eke, scratching the side of his bulbous nose. "Just look you here, Lady," he said as Lady Hilda walked past for her post-breakfast stroll around the garden. "Can't get much to grow these days. Blast, we don't half need a few nights of steady rain. Carrots aren't doing anything, nor are the beet. Runners are flowerin' but not producing beans. Tha's a really bad year."

"My dear Dibber," said Hilda, "one thing I do know is that we can't do anything about the weather."

"I do know that, Lady, I really do. Even after all the compost we spread on the land. Still, tha's gotta rain sometime."

"It will sort itself out in time, Dibber. Good job though that we avoided those horrid field fires, and that everything here is still intact."

"Y'ore roight enough there, Lady. My cousin lives in Oakhill and says that really has hurt so many folk."

"Count our blessings, eh Dibber?"

"Yes indeed, Lady. Them dahlias don't half need the rain. Never seen 'em so late."

"All in good time, I expect."

Chapter 42

Jane Seabrook was feeling tense after a few rough days with both her hormones and with members of the public who were slinging accusations at the team through a number of social media outlets. They were alleging conspiracies, siding with developers, and not caring enough about those residents who had enjoyed their lives in their particular area for so many years.

This was nothing new, and she kept telling herself that she had a tough skin and could take it. However, she knew that was just all an act and that deep down she struggled to keep her feelings under control. She needed a friend to lean on and rang Jim Prentice to see if he fancied going out for a meal.

He did.

Jim was wearing black chinos and a pink polo shirt when he drove to Jane's house to pick her up. As the front door was unlocked, he knocked and went in to say hello to the girls but found that Jane was on her own. Molly was away at a teaching hospital in London and Lou was having a sleepover with her best friend Aster Green.

"Hi Jim, lovely to see you." She smiled and gave him a hug as she put down her glass of cold white burgundy, which she said, with a smile, was her aperitif.

They were going to walk into town, but a few spots of very welcome rain suggested that it was best to go in Jim's car. They managed to find a parking space in the Market Place and walked to the 'Taste of Italy' where they ordered beers and a plate of spinach tortellini each, together with garlic bread.

"I'm so glad you said you would come along tonight, Jim. I needed some company and there are times when I miss you more than you could know. I've felt that the pressure of work has been bloody awful lately and you are always a wonderful antidote to that!"

"Very pleased to help. You know that you are always at the front of my mind. It's been ages since we did this."

"You are so kind, Jim. How are things at home?"

"Not bad at all. Philly is doing well at College, and Zac found himself a new interest, did some background studying and found himself an apprenticeship at the police path lab. He's loving it."

"That's fab. Good for him. It is wonderful how some of the kids start off as such a worry, but end up finding their feet, growing up all of a sudden and becoming a credit to their parents and friends. It does happen surprisingly often. I'm really pleased for him."

Jim stayed with his first beer, as he was driving, but ordered a large glass of chianti for Jane who, by now had lost the frown lines in her face. She was smiling at him, and her sparkling eyes were brighter than before, although they appeared a little damp.

They finished their meal with a favourite zabaglione, declined the offer of coffee and Jane insisted on paying the bill. "I asked you out, Jim. I pay!" she said firmly. She smiled, took him by the hand, kissed his cheek and said, "Home, James."

Once they got home, Jane made coffee and offered Jim a glass of brandy, saying, "You know you can stay the night, you do know that, don't you?"

He was considering the offer when she sat beside him on the sofa, put her hand under his shirt, pulled him towards her and kissed him firmly on the lips. He moved his free arm around her waist and was about to turn her round so that he could sit astride her legs when they heard a key in the front door, and Lou entered the house in a bright and breezy mood. "Guess what?" she screamed.

Jim shuffled back to a decent position, crossed his legs to avoid the embarrassment of the shape of his trousers, when Jane called out, "we're in here!"

"Oh, sorry, guys," said Lou, "didn't realise you were having an evening together."

"Spur of the moment. We went to the Italian for a meal."

"Good for you. Hi Jim. You OK?"

"I'm fine Lou, thanks. You look happy."

"I am. Had a great evening with Aster, and was going to stay over, but she got a call from her boyfriend and she wanted to go out with him."

"Good to see you looking really well, Lou." Said Jim. "Well Jane, I better get back; it's been a lovely evening. We must do it more often."

"Indeed we must Jim, and thanks for being my sounding board. Your turn next!"

"Of course, and believe me it won't be so long next time. Bye, and bye, Lou." He gave Jane a long goodnight kiss and made his way home.

Lou looked at her mother who seemed as though she had a tear in her eyes, gave her a hug and said, Mum, what's the matter. You look so sad."

"Do you know, Lou I miss that man so much. I haven't asked him lately, but I do wonder if we could live together."

"Mum, I would love that. You would too and you're missing out on so much, and more than just his company, aren't you?"

"I know that more than you can know, my dearest Lou."

Chapter 43

At two o'clock in the morning, Myra was awoken from her lounge chair by a gentle tap on her shoulder. It was the senior nurse who squatted down to Myra's level.

"Oh, what is it?"

"I think you should come and be with your mum, Myra."

"Oh, my God, what's happened?"

"I'm so sorry, Myra, but I think the work that the surgeons have done has not been enough to save her, and that she might be close to the end."

"Surely not. I thought they had sorted it all out," she stuttered, still trying to wake from her sleep.

"She was very weak, and the repair work was

probably too much for her. I am so sorry. Come along. I think it's time to say your farewells."

Myra rose from the chair and held on to its back for a moment as she felt her head swimming, and after a few more seconds she asked the nurse to take her arm and help her to Elsie's room.

She had been moved to a single room so there was total privacy, and other nursing staff were giving the old lady some dabs of water to moisten her lips. She was grey and her lips so pale that Myra thought that she had already passed, but when she told her mother that she was there with her, the eyelids fluttered, and a weak groan suggested that she understood.

"Mum, we had some wonderful times together. Just think of those lovely days we all had at the beach. You always loved the sound of the sea, didn't you?"

A feint movement of her lips as though a smile was not far away suggested she was listening to the waves pounding the shoreline, and with a gentle throaty gurgle she was gone.

Myra fell forward and placed her face on her mother's chest, held her left hand, raised it slightly so she could kiss it, and said, "Bye Mum. I love you. I always have. Thank you for all you gave me."

A tear, a sniffle, and a look up to the nurse who looked so comforting and just nodded gently to her.

Myra lifted her head and looked at the nurse. "Thank you for all your kindness, dear. This was not what I expected when I was called here yesterday, but you have made the matter so much easier to bear."

"Myra, you are so welcome, but this is what we do."

"I suppose I must go home and tell the family. And I

guess I better talk to the Vicar."

"I'm sure there is no need to rush, Myra. Why don't you wait until it is light, and you can have some breakfast, before you take the journey home? Would you like me to organise a cup of tea?"

"Maybe that would be best. And yes, please, I would like that. Thank you so much."

She sent a text to the Vicar, expecting him to pick the message up in the morning. Within five minutes she had received his reply and his prayers for Elsie's soul and for Myra's peace.

The tea was just what Myra needed, and she prepared herself for the coming days. It was bound to be grim.

Myra knew.

Chapter 44

At Police Headquarters DI Tony Lovelace was frustrated and getting more than a little irritated. He had contacted the switchboard at the National Crime Agency to try and speak with whoever was investigating the situation relating to the human trafficking gangs that had been involved in the Thompson Common body.

However, it appeared as though the Agency was in chaotic mode and the person who answered knew nothing about the matter. He was passed to an official who apparently kept a check on all live cases, but with a lack of available staff and an increasing need to monitor all the refugees arriving in the Country, all other work, apart from current serious major crime and drug cases, had barely

The Thompson Body

seen the light of day.

"So, you are telling me that whilst the matter was referred to you over a month ago, and despite a previous apparent commitment to cooperation, nothing has happened since. Is that correct?" asked Tony, only just holding on to his temper.

"I'm afraid it would appear to be so, sir."

"And your team didn't have the decency to tell us?"

"Again, that does appear to be the case, sir."

Tony rang off with a muttered "fuck you for bugger all", and prepared an email to his Chief Superintendent, who rang him immediately, and with clear irritation in his voice, saying "What do you mean Detective Inspector, no progress? None at all?"

"No sir. It seems that this is not on their priority list."

"We're not going to appear very helpful to our public, are we? But, I expect that with all the problems in the Channel and the cuts that we all have had to put up with, they have to put up with the situation, the same as us."

"Absolutely, Sir. It's not helpful at all. Do you think we should work on this ourselves. Would a word to the MP have any effect? Maybe the Press as well?"

There was a muffled noise from the Chief. "Let me think on that, Tony. In the meantime, see if you can work on a possible plan of action for us to deal with it ourselves."

―――

It was evening and Murray was late home after a drinking session with the MD of one of his sub-contracting companies. He said a quick "hi" to Gail and went upstairs to change into a tee shirt and joggers after a quick shower.

He had found a letter addressed to him and took it

upstairs with him. His stomach went cold as he opened it to find it was a further one from the Child Maintenance Service requiring more detail of his income and tax payments, together with notice that his attendance would be required at a formal Tribunal Hearing in front of a Judge probably in Bristol or Cardiff.

"Christ, this is getting fucking stupid. She'll bloody swing for this," he muttered to himself once he had read the letter twice to make sure he understood the words.

He kept it out of Gail's sight as he went downstairs and ploughed his way through a bowl of pasta with prawns in a hot chilli tomato sauce that she had prepared for him earlier in the day.

"Had a hard day again, Murray?"

"Again and again. It never stops," he said spluttering tomato and basil sauce over the tablecloth.

"And do you want to know what my day has been like?"

"Not really. I suppose you've been spending lots of my money again."

"I went to the Club and had a lovely massage, met up with Jilly and we had lunch and put the world to rights."

"That's all right then. Hard day."

"Don't be so bloody sarky, Murray."

He changed his mind and showed Gail the letter.

"Look at this latest letter. It was me that appealed against the case she had cobbled together and look where it got me."

"Well, that was bound to happen. She was never going to let go of this, was she?"

"Bitch. Wait till I get to that courtroom. I'll tell the Judge all about her. Bloody woman."

"I think you'll have to focus on the money, and not what you think of her, Murray. They will want you to answer their questions."

"I'll still tell him."

'Dolly' Parting had arranged to sit down with Sgt. Sally Parmenter to discuss ways they might be able to use in tracking down the man involved in the local distribution of drugs. They gathered their coffees and sat in Sally's office with the windows open, uncertain if it was sensible to let more heat in than was going out. The air conditioning units had been overworking in the intense heat and the maintenance team hadn't yet got round to sorting out the system.

"Right then, 'Dolly' what more have you been able to pick up?"

"Well, as a bit of previous background, I'm pretty certain that the lad is a Mc or a Mac but he's not on the Electoral Register nor is he a tenant of any of the Housing Associations. So, the feeling is that he is probably living in one of the properties owned and run by one of the gangs, but we've not been able to track him down yet."

"So, no real progress then? You must be able to find out where those properties are. What about the estate agents?"

"They're not going to be marketed through the normal channels, Boss, are they? The only thing we've got is that the drugs appear to be brought to the fella on a roughly monthly basis and we know where at least two of the drop-offs have been carried out. There may, of course be other drop off points that we don't know about. By the way, what's the latest info from the Essex Force then, Guv?"

"They know who the courier is and where he lives. It looks as though he goes to the London suburbs at various locations to pick up his supplies and probably passes over the cash to the Big Man. Essex are trailing both of these guys."

"Who's putting all this info together, guv? Is it DI Lovelace's team or the Drug Squad?"

"Should be the latter, I would think. But I need to check."

"Hmm. What about the Comms team? Can they track down the messages between these guys? I mean we're pretty certain that the courier and our Laddo must be in touch, probably by encrypted messaging."

"I'll see what I can find on both accounts."

"Just a thought, guv, what do you think about us trying to put a plant in the group of local drug takers?"

"If we don't know who they are, we're not going to be able to, are we? And, I'm not sure that we would get anywhere by asking social services or the others that looked at the consequences of stopping this particular supply."

"I may have someone who can help, though."

"Not yet, 'Dolly'. Not yet. It's not Tyler Martin is it?"

"No it's not, but I think he knows someone who may know."

"Just hold tight on that, and let's make sure the techies get their teeth into finding more about the connections between all these phones. There are the Essex and London connections, those between our courier and our target, and then the target and the users."

"OK, I'll hang on."

"I'll try and see what Tony Lovelace can tell me."
"Great, thanks guv."

"Douglas!"

"Oh God, what does she want now." The Vice-Admiral muttered as he sat in his favourite chair in the lounge where he was watching a sparrowhawk on the lawn in the middle of pulling at the breast feathers of a collared dove which hadn't been quick enough.

"Douglas! Can you hear me?"

"No," he thought to himself.

"Douglas, she called again as she descended the wide staircase with its threadbare carpet which was held in place by brass brackets and rods. "Oh, there you are. Didn't you hear me?"

"What is it, Hilda?"

"I'm preparing to discard some of my clothes from the second wardrobe and donate them to the poor folk in Ukraine. You must have loads of old jumpers and coats you never wear. Can I take them with me?"

"Certainly you cannot. I will do as I please with my possessions, thank you very much."

"No compassion there, then. That's your trouble, Douglas. Don't you feel some sympathy for those people? Bombed out of their homes by the mad Russian. They have a far better case than those coming here in small boats – or ships I suppose I should call them."

"They are boats, Hilda, rubber bloody boats, and you know it. Bloody people coming here to bleed our welfare system and flood the NHS. I don't know why we don't send out submarines to puncture the bloody things. More taxes for us to pay for it as well. It beggars belief. Governed by a bunch of bloody softies, we are, that's what."

"Thank you for that, Douglas. Very kind hearted. I suppose you'd send them all back to their famine and war torn countries, eh?"

"Well," he was shifting in his chair and winding himself up to one of his infamous rants, "how are we supposed to find money for all of them. Thousands of the buggers. And what benefits do they give us once they're here. That's what I want to know. It's the fault of the bloody Frogs, that's what it is. Why don't they shoot them before they get in their little rubber boats?"

"Douglas, there are times when you are quite offensive."

"But honest, Hilda. Honest."

"Do you want to find some clothes for my donation box, then or not?"

"Why, of course I will, dear. When do you want them?"

"I was going to take them this afternoon. The exercise will do you good."

"What exercise?"

"Up and down the stairs!"

Chapter 45

Georgia had been disappointed, but not surprised when she had heard nothing more from Bruno, despite her occasional visits to his restaurant.

However, this feeling was hugely overridden by the fact that her children were at long last pulling together, maturing enough to recognise the struggles that their mother had endured over so many years. They had agreed amongst themselves that they would do more to help around the house and contribute some funds towards their upkeep.

In particular, Becca was put in charge of organising rotas for the chores and for tidiness of their rooms, as well as having to look out for opportunities to contribute to local community events, whilst Tyler would put his talents to all the DIY repairs that seemed to be always required.

Georgia was both delighted and relieved, and told them so.

Elsewhere, and equally delighted was Jack Chambers when he received a phone call from his grandson, Ollie to ask when he could come round and help with the decorating. It seemed that the lad had turned a corner in his life. Jack invited him round to see what he was best able to do, and they decided on the hallway, as it was the first thing any visitors saw. They agreed that they would strip the walls of the faded and flowery wallpaper and paint them a warm light shade of apricot.

Jack said he would get the paint and the other equipment that they needed and agreed that Ollie could take as long as he needed to help complete the job.

Ollie went home with a huge grin on his face and Jack poured himself a bottle of beer into one of his special tankards, settled into his favourite chair as satisfied as he had been for months.

At the local office of the Broad Norfolk Post, Avril and Darren were discussing the options for the lead article for the next local edition and they ended up with a choice from:- the latest on the burnt cottages; the burnt body; the latest on the drugs issue; the state and future of the town centre or the lack of progress in chasing the gangs involved in human trafficking.

The village of Oakhill was managing its recovery

exceptionally well with the help of the Local Authorities and Charities and the story would be best told once restoration of the cottages was well under way. There was little information about the burnt body, the drug courier issue was under wraps until the police had achieved an arrest and the matter of the future of the town centre would take forever to solve. Therefore, they were left with going on the attack regarding the trafficking gangs involved with the sex trade.

Locals fear over possible further trafficking of sex workers.

The lack of progress in the investigation of gangs involved in human trafficking, often within the sex trade is of major concern to local folk who fear there may be continued dangers to girls and young women in the area. With the influx of refugees and foreign families from Eastern Europe and Africa, the primary concern of the public expressed to our reporters, is one of uncertainty.

Whilst we have no wish to exacerbate that feeling, the Broad Norfolk Post is appalled at the lack of progress. As Detective Inspector Tony Lovelace told us "The National Crime Agency appear to have other priorities and say that their lack of resources has not allowed them time to investigate our concerns."

We will be contacting Members of Parliament representing the County to impress upon them the seriousness of the local concerns, which we wholeheartedly support.

―――

After a morning working at the supermarket where she had been on the tills, Harriet managed to do some careful shopping, and, once back at home she spent more time gathering all the information she could to make sure that the CMS had all the documents they would need, in readiness for the Tribunal Hearing.

She gathered together her bank statements, letters from her solicitor, divorce documents, emails and messages from years back which had involved Murray, the valuation of his property in Gloucestershire, details of his and Gail's holidays abroad, together with documents from the Hospital confirming Becca's continued medical conditions.

She had arranged that copies of these were sent to Paul Overton at the Child Maintenance Service, with a note to say that she suspected that some of them would be duplicates of what they already had on file but hoped the other information would help.

A couple of days' later Paul rang to thank her for the useful documents that would all be useful when the CMS presented a file with full written evidence to the Hearing.

―――

After their work on the scrub clearance at a nearby woodland, the restoration work team finally returned to Thompson Common and there was a high level of understandable excitement at the prospect of other unusual discoveries.

A month into their work, and good progress was being made with two of the ghost pingos looking ready for the autumn rains to fill the pools and for nature to take its course.

Then a surprise. The third site, not far from the original burial location was being excavated by a new young volunteer named Gemma who was studying archaeology at university and was gaining some experience in the field. Having taken away half a metre of topsoil she hit upon something that was not expected to be there.

A black bin bag.

Benny, the supervisor of the work immediately halted all action and invited the police to visit the excavation and examine the contents of the bag.

Within hours an officer from the Cold Case team had arrived, talked with Benny and carefully extracted the bag, taking it to the forensic laboratory for detailed examination.

Myra's next job was to ring her daughters Patricia and Olivia and tell them that she had been called to the hospital where Granny Roe underwent major surgery on her heart which was not able to fix the problem.

"We've lost her, dear," she told Trish.

"Oh Mum. I didn't know she was that ill."

"I don't think anyone did. I must ring Livvy."

"They are away, in Italy, I think. Shall I contact her for you?"

"No, dear. I think I should. I've not spoken to her for a

month or more. She'll have her mobile, I suppose?"

"Bound to, in case there is a lucrative bit of work popping up!"

"Now, now. I know you two have your rather different approaches to life."

"Ah well. That's the way the world goes round, I suppose. What about the boys, Mum?"

"What about them?"

"They ought to be told."

"I haven't heard from them since they rang to wish me Merry Christmas, nearly nine months ago."

"Oh, Mum, they're still part of our family. You could always ring them."

"You can tell them, Trish."

"OK then. By the way, do you need any help with the funeral arrangements?"

"I don't think so, dear. I'm seeing the undertakers tomorrow and I'm with my solicitor this afternoon."

"Keep me in touch, Mum. Would you like me to come up and be with you?"

"Thanks, Trish, but I'm alright."

"Let me know how you get on, please."

"I will. Bye for now, dear. I'm going to ring Livvy."

The connection to Olivia's phone was poor, and so she sent her a text telling her that she couldn't get through to talk to her, but that she ought to know that Grannie Roe had passed away and asked that Livvy should contact her when she got home from her holiday.

Chapter 46

Sally was having an early morning in the office going through her paperwork, the requests for holidays from the staff, and so many emails, before getting her head round the current situation regarding current cases.

She made a list.

Sally loved making lists as it kept her as organised as it was possible.

- Thompson Common body – probably E European - ??sex trafficker? ?Drug trafficker? Prob killed 6-8 years ago - Issue with NCA – no action Check with Tony. Should I try with NCA? What about the profiler, Reuban Blanche? Check his progress.

- Missing surveyors – prob drug traffickers –

disappeared – again poss E Europ, - Fraud – no relevant body of surveyors – need to keep on books? – check Tony

- Burnt body at Coney Temple – full of cocaine – again E Europ. – Poss passed out in ditch – then fires. Any further work for us? Check Tony

- Drugs in the town – waiting on Essex. When to arrest 'Scottish' – Need to identify him.

<u>Action</u>
- Update 'Dolly'
- Check Tony re above.
- Check Tony re IT & encryption of texts – progress?

Having cleared her mind of all the caseload, as well as the minor bits of admin she had to carry out, she took herself away from her desk and made a large mug of black coffee ready for a meeting with 'Dolly'.

As 'Dolly' walked his way to work he was still musing about the message that Pete Evans had passed on to Sally about an Irish name and 'Ruby'.

He was only a few hundred yards away from the police station when he thought, "I hope I'm wrong, but Flanagan must be an Irish name. I must talk to Oliver and see what he knows about his ancestry. But, 'Ruby'?

'*Ruby don't take your love to town*'? '*Ruby Tuesday*'? Hang on!" Then, he stopped in his tracks, "Ruby Murray! Curry. Wooah, fuck me backwards. Not Murray Flanagan, surely? There's another one for the Sarg.

Once they found time to sit together, 'Dolly' was bursting to tell of his suspicion as to who may have been involved in the murder so long ago involving a youngster from the boxing club in Norwich.

After Sally had brought him up to speed with the

issues relating to the bodies, they focussed on the need to track down the contacts in the distribution of drugs around the town and surrounding areas.

It was clear that the Essex connection was critical, and Sally rang Tony Lovelace's office to see if there was any further intelligence both on the programme for catching Robert Sylvester and the progress of the IT team in trying to solve the matter of the encrypted messaging between all those involved in the drug distribution.

'Dolly' tapped his fingers on the table waiting for Sally to finish her call. Once she had put her phone down, she said, "Well blow me down with a feather. Reuban Blanche had a heart attack and is no more."

"Oh no," said 'Dolly', "do we know if the DI will replace him?"

"He didn't say. Everyone's a bit shocked. Anyway, is there anything else for today?"

"A thought" said 'Dolly', "and I don't know where it takes us, but you remember Pete Evans talking about the death a while ago of a youngster at the boxing club in the City? He said there was talk of someone being involved who had an Irish sort of name and was called 'Ruby'."

"Yes, I do remember. So how does that help us?"

"Well, I was thinking after seeing young Oliver Flanagan that he has an Irish name."

"Oh, don't. I thought he was being a good useful citizen."

"I think he is. But it's the 'Ruby' bit. It's slang for a curry, right? Ruby Murray."

"I know that. She was a singer in the fifties."

"So, how about Murray Flanagan."

"OK, I get that, but what evidence do we have that he

was involved. Could have been anyone. Good guess though."

"Yes, but he was a really rough diamond in his younger days. Nasty bugger apparently."

"Well, it's the Cold Case team's job now, not ours, but pass your thoughts on to Pete Evans"

"I will. Thanks, boss."

Paston District Council's Planning Committee met with a long agenda for a day that was going to be tiresome. Crowds of intrigued members of the public crammed into the Council Chamber to hear the arguments over proposals that they had vested interests in.

Chairman, Nathan Bryant called for order, and held the normal formalities regarding the minutes of previous meetings, absences noted and arrangements for the day. The crowd shuffled in anticipation of something exciting, but the first four applications were of little interest until the announcement that the application for the battery store at Ballington had been withdrawn. At this point there were cheers, but some annoyance that no one had told the public before, and seven members of the public stood and walked out grumbling about lousy communication..

The time came for the housing application at Easthoe to be discussed and the details were shown on the big screens at the front of the room behind the top table and on the councillors' laptops. It was Evie Beecham who presented the description of the proposal and the arguments for and against it. The main issues of concern to the revised proposal were the access to the site and the retention of the old grain store. She said that the principle was acceptable subject to certain conditions and was therefore recommended for approval.

David Johns presented the case for the developers, accepted that the grain store would remain, acknowledged the help from local people in leading towards the smaller scheme and from the Planning Department for the suggestions of arranging for a local Housing Association to acquire the dwellings that would be for local residents. He believed that his highway engineers had designed the access to meet the standards required by the County Council.

Murmurs of disapproval came from the public gallery and Chairman Bryant had to bring the gathering back to order, with the bang of his gavel, supported by others making 'sshhh' noises.

Once everyone had settled down, the Parish Council Chairman, Harold Carpenter told the meeting that there was a significant need for new dwellings within the village, especially for local folk, and that the revised scheme was a result of both Mr. Johns' and the landowner's willingness to compromise.

Whilst the access wasn't perfect it connected to the main street in a twenty miles an hour zone and there was no objection from County Highways. He hoped the scheme would be approved.

Two objectors were allowed to speak, one emphasising the impact the scheme would have on existing residents, both from an overlooking point of view and from the uncertainty that existed over the quality of the access to and from the street.

The other felt that the retention of the old grain store would put a blight on the new dwellings and that its site should be incorporated into the site and requested that the application as it was should therefore be refused.

There were cheers from the public gallery, but also cries of 'shame on you' to those protesters from those members of the public that were in favour of the scheme.

These alternative views were also put by members of the Committee, and it appeared that they were heading for a stalemate, until the experienced stalwart member, Jim Prentice summed up by saying he saw the balance of the arguments and was of the view that a further effort should be made to improve the scheme for the benefit of both the village and the new residents by ensuring that the grain store site was included.

He said that there ought to be a financial solution and would happily act as broker in conjunction with the Parish Council, in negotiations between them and the landowner and the developers, together with the planning staff.

Some of the members of the Committee were relieved that they didn't have to make a choice and readily supported Jim's idea. To their delight, the application was deferred for that exploration to take place.

There were groans from some of the public as those interested in the Easthoe project filed out of the room.

———

There had been a diverse set of opinions sent to the Broad Norfolk Post regarding DI Lovelace's comments about the National Crime Agency, and Jenny sorted through them and had sent these two through to Avril for her comments.

"Interesting how different folks see different aspects of the same case", she said, and agreed that they should be inserted into the next edition.

> Dear Editor
> I completely understand the frustrations expressed by DI Lovelace in his comments about the National Crime Agency but would say that the body that was found at Thompson Common was assessed to have been placed there, possibly, up to ten years ago. I believe that the person who placed it there has not been traced. In fact, I have neither seen nor heard any evidence that any effort to trace him or her has been made at all.
> The sort of activity that it is alleged that the dead man was involved in has not been proved, nor has there been any suspicion of similar activity in recent years. I know that dead men tell no secrets, and that there will continue to be some nervousness amongst the local folk.
> However, as far as I can see, this is no time to have to lock up your daughters.
> Yours
> Damien Humberside
> Gt Yarmouth

> Sir
> How dare they? Those who live in or near the Common are so angry at the NCA as that organisation appears to care nothing about sex workers being brought to places

near their homes.
How would those officers like it if it was near their homes?
Sir, this is utterly disgraceful. What do we all pay our taxes for if this is what we get? Nothing, that's what.
I await the views of our MPs.
Faithfully yours
Barry Farquharson (Col. Rtd.)
Home Farm
Easthoe

The Friday evening gatherings at The Brown Bear had seen a number of new faces joining in the celebrations for some at least, of the end of the working week. One of these was Ollie Flanagan who was brought along by his friend Jimmy Patel who had physically recovered from the beating he had taken from the racists, although he still needed to settle from a mental perspective. The two of them were in the same training group at the Swinton Football Club.

They were welcomed with the normal friendly insults and joined in the chit-chat and general gossip, getting the hang of the varied characters and their interests.

Tyler Martin had really become one of the main jokers in the pack and was quick to go to the bar and buy the couple of new lads a glass of lemonade and lime each and a packet of pork scratchings. Ollie was delighted with the way they had been accepted as part of the crowd, and whilst the older lads were getting noisier as their pints of lager slipped down far too quickly, he and Jimmy enjoyed the banter and felt that this might well be a good way to spend an evening.

Approaching half past ten, and in walked 'Dolly' Parting after an evening pounding the streets. He ordered his normal Diet Coke and a packet of cheese and onion crisps whilst leaning against the bar gazing around the room, acknowledging the waves from the lads.

Whilst he had not had any need to contact Ollie, 'Dolly' was aware of the problems that the lad had encountered in the past and was pleased to see that he was amongst this crowd who were always looking after each other's backs and would put right anything that got out of order without any real antagonism.

And the crowd knew that this was partly down to the way that 'Dolly' had reacted to and with them.

Chapter 47

Myra's visit to Mr. Frederick Paine, her solicitor from the firm of Paine and Bottomley in the afternoon was less than satisfactory. It transpired that her mother's solicitor was not at this firm, and thus it was clear that it was not this original family firm that Myra had assumed dealt with all the family affairs.

A rare case.

Myra didn't know.

In order to trace Elsie's will, Myra was advised to talk with someone at the Goldcrest Home in the hope that there was some information there to indicate who the right firm of solicitors might be.

Her subsequent discussion with Sharon at the Home was one of mixed emotion for both of them. Sharon said the staff would all be so sad at Elsie's passing. However, at the same time Myra, somewhat cynically was certain that they would be pleased to have room available for another desperate family, probably at an enhanced rent.

Nevertheless, Myra thanked Sharon and her team for the care they had all given to her Mum and would be pleased to know when she would be able to go and collect her belongings. It was eventually agreed that these would be available the next morning.

Conscious that she had a meeting with the undertakers in the morning, she said she should be able to be at the Home by three o'clock, subject to nothing getting in the way.

The following morning, the undertakers were of the expected efficiency and courteousness, took all the necessary details and advised that further discussions should take place once the death certificate had been issued.

They showed Myra around the showroom to show her the various patterns and materials of coffins, and she thought that Elsie would have been in no state of mind to have had a choice in the matter. In any event they would have to wait until they had laid the body at rest.

Myra was keen to get the whole thing resolved as soon as possible, but was told, as kindly as possible that these things all take time, and proper procedures must take place.

So, little progress there as well.

After an early lunch of a chicken and potato salad and

a cup of Earl Grey, she took the Jeep to Bury St. Edmunds to collect her mother's boxes of belongings and was amazed that she had gathered so many odd things as well as her clothes, books, and notebooks. She piled all these into the Jeep, went back to see Sharon and some of the nursing staff and thanked them again for their constant help and care. She also visited the kitchens and poured much praise on their interesting menus and the quality of their food, not least the steak and kidney puddings.

On leaving, Sharon thrust a set of leaflets in her hand, which Myra took one look at in the car, and threw them on the floor of the passenger side. Begging literature again.

When she got home, she poured herself a cool glass of Pink Prosecco, and opened the boxes.

After an hour when she had had enough of ploughing through all the photograph albums, wedding souvenirs, holiday memories and many trinkets brought back from trips to many parts of the Country, she made herself a quick ham and cheese omelette, had another glass of wine and settled back into the boxes. Clothes, all of which would go to a charity shop, books which she would filter through again at a later date, and then to the personal documents.

There, in a large brown envelope with Myra's name written thereon were a couple of sheets of lined paper with her Mum's handwriting setting out her requested wishes in the case of her demise. The detail of her funeral, specific wishes for donations to certain charities, a large donation to the Goldcrest Home, and the name, address, and phone numbers of solicitors in Bury St. Edmunds.

"Well, blow me down with a feather," said Myra to herself, "She certainly did get herself organised."

In the morning she would ring Miss Antonia Forsythe

at Stills, Hills, and Lake.

"Ought to be Stills, Hills and Wills" she thought, and finished the bottle of fizz.

Chapter 48

The day of the Tribunal Hearing came, and Harriet was excited to get the thing under way, but nervous at the prospect of seeing Murray, probably at his gloating worst, even though she was over a hundred miles away and on a computer screen. She had been given clear instructions regarding the process, that she would be seen by everyone at the Hearing and that she would see the room with the Judge, a financial advisor to the Judge, Murray and anyone advising him.

Harriet had asked her best friend Claire to be with her, and who sat in the living room in sight of the screen, but out of shot to the Hearing.

Claire was thrilled to be asked and guessed her experience in social housing work, with a few court cases behind her might be helpful. She wanted to see Murray squirm. She had never liked the man.

The Judge was Mrs Delores Cohen, and she opened the session by introducing herself and asked all participants to do the same. She indicated that this was a hearing into the appeal by Mr Flanagan against the claims made against him by the Child Maintenance Service on behalf of Ms. Chambers.

Harriet felt encouraged that the Judge was a woman but was surprised and somewhat disappointed that no one from the Child Maintenance Service was in attendance. The Judge felt the same way and said so.

Mrs Justice Cohen told the Hearing, "I have received the case for Ms Chambers through the CMS and have read all their documents, and I understand the basis for her case. I have also received some information from Mr Flanagan following his appeal, but I have to say there is insufficient detail, and I shall want more information from him."

Murray shifted in his seat but made an effort to show no emotion, and was certainly not encouraged that the Judge was a woman.

The Judge continued, "Mr Flanagan, please tell us how many companies you are employed by."

"Well, I am self-employed."

"Is that correct? I ask because I find no evidence of any payment of income tax in the information you have submitted."

"As far as I know, I was being paid nett of tax."

"As far as you know? Surely as a successful businessman shouldn't you be certain?"

Murray flinched and looked blankly at the Judge.

"But you say you were not employed by any company," continued Mrs Justice Cohen. "What is the name of the business that you run?"

"It's merely in my own name."

"Mr Flanagan, we have evidence from the Child Maintenance Service that you earned considerable sums, and yet you seem unable to give us the simple detail of your income."

Murray was showing signs of stress, his face and neck becoming damp and red.

Harriet and Claire in particular were certainly enjoying the encounter.

"I will give you two weeks to provide this Tribunal with bank statements from all your accounts, and your joint accounts, private and business. We have seen the information relating to the companies that you have worked for, from the information recently provided by the Child Maintenance Service, and we shall seek information from them relating to payments made to you over the last seven years. Please ensure that you accede to these instructions. I will also instruct the Child Maintenance Service to be represented in person at the next Hearing."

The Hearing was adjourned to allow that information to be presented to the Judge.

Mrs Justice Cohen told all parties that due to the uncertainty and lack of clarity in Murray's evidence and the potential for other courts to be involved, she would ensure that she would be taking all further sessions of the Tribunal herself in order to satisfy herself that the investigations into Murray's financial affairs were complete.

Harriet was comforted in that thought, and when she

got home, she rang her dad, Jack Chambers and told him what had happened. Jack was delighted and congratulated her on sticking with the case and on her courage in facing the Judge.

He told her that he thought she was winning at half-time.

DI Tony Lovelace was in a small conference room embroiled in a discussion with his Chief Superintendent and a member of the Force's Finance Department. They were talking about the overspend by Tony's Cold Case team, which seemed to him like an inevitability, given the high profile of the recent unusual cases.

"These bodies caused a lot of local concern, and we spent a lot of time with local people, there was more travel and expenses," he had explained.

"But you would have seen that you were exceeding your budget, wouldn't you?" asked the finance man.

"Are you suggesting that the Force should not have got itself involved in this sort of case, then?"

"That's an operational decision, but you should be aware of the costs. Was there any benefit in engaging a profiler as a consultant?"

"On the basis that he has died recently, I'm afraid that we shall never know."

"I'm sorry to hear that. Has he been replaced?"

"Not yet. So, are you saying that once we hit the budget figure, we should stop work? That's plainly stupid."

"Tony, be serious, please," warned the Super.

He was about to explode into a rant about bean counters not understanding that this sort of work cropped up without being planned when his mobile vibrated.

"Excuse me a moment, I need to take this call. It's not about a cold case, by the way."

"Don't be tetchy, Inspector."

Tony left the room and found a quiet spot outside in the fresh air.

"Sally, you've just saved my job."

"That's good news, Tony. What happened?"

"I nearly told the Super what I thought of him and the budget!"

"Glad to have been of help. Can you update me on the techy guys' progress on the phone calls relating to our druggy friends as well as the status of the Essex investigations. We are close to knowing our main local distributor at this end."

"I'll have to check and come back to you. Give me ten."

"OK, thanks."

Tony put his head round the door of the conference room.

"Sorry gentlemen, I have an urgent request for information regarding a current case that ought to lead to arrests. Will you need me anymore? Shouldn't be more than half an hour."

"You carry on, Inspector. I'll wrap this up."

"Thank you, Sir."

Tony heaved a sigh of relief and went to speak to his team to try and get the up to date story for Sally.

Pete Evans' clear thinking was once again to the fore. "I've come to a conclusion that the Thompson body may well not have been gang related, at least not the sort of gangs we have been thinking of," he said as he scratched the back of his neck. "I would put money on the idea of a revenge killing. Maybe the guy was killed for threatening to expose his murderer, for something he had found out about him. Fraud perhaps, money laundering or perhaps he witnessed a confrontation. I don't know for sure, but that's what I'm leaning towards."

"So, not the drug gangs, then?" asked Tony.

"As I say, there's no hard evidence, but that's my best guess, and interestingly what Reuban Blanche had suggested at the start of this."

"Thanks, Pete. So, when we catch the drug gang that's supplying West Kelling and places nearby, we can put some pressure on them for any info. they have about the Thompson case. Is that your view?"

"Yes sir, it is."

Tony would put that in the plan that the Chief Super had asked for.

Within three quarters of an hour he rang Sally back to tell her that there was a belief that there would be an exchange between Robert Sylvester and Tariq Browne in two evening's time and they were pretty certain that they would both be apprehended. It suggested that there was a chance that Robert should be distributing the following day. He suggested that the normal location for the local lad to collect his goods should be watched and staff be ready to apprehend him.

Chapter 49

Time seemed to stand still for Harriet.

It seemed ages since the Hearing when the Judge instructed Murray to present extra information regarding his finances. Four months later she received a letter from the Tribunal's office indicating that the Judge had received information both from Murray and his major employer. It seemed that over a four year period up to 2020, the company had paid him just short of £1m, at well over £200k each year, but his accounts hadn't shown that.

The Judge, Mrs Dolores Cohen had said that she would refer the matter to the Tax Authorities and the Fraud Squad, and from her experience, he could reasonably expect a jail sentence. In the meantime, she had been convinced that Murray had failed to support his children, has caused misery to Harriet and her family, and that she would be considering the payments that Murray should make to her. She would present her final judgement in writing within a month and that it was unlikely that a resumption of the formal Hearing would be required.

The Fraud Squad were quick to act and arrived at Murray's home within a matter of hours. They searched the house and its outbuildings, noted the equipment, furniture, artwork and wine cellar, and took all the computers from his home as well as his office laptop, and his three mobile phones. And the laptops and phones from Gail and her daughters.

Gail was apoplectic with rage, as were the girls, knowing that they had recently upgraded to the latest versions of phones and would have lost access to all their cloud based files. It was the sheer intrusion into their 'Oh So Perfect' lives.

IT experts went through the computers and phones, both the current content and the detail that Murray had assumed he had deleted together with his data held in the cloud. They found some interesting communications with Chelsea Football Club, with a great number of people in the construction industry going back some fifteen years, but more importantly many pornographic files, websites referring to sex workers both in East Anglia and in the South-West of the Country. They needed more time to examine the contacts of his emails to and from Polish, Lithuanian and Albanian individuals.

Eventually it emerged that he had upset some groups of men who had threatened him with financial ruin and attacks on his family.

These particular messages went back nearly ten years, a time when he lived in Norwich with Harriet, and Murray was oblivious to the discovery of all this information, as his arrogance had led him to believe that all the computer's history had been wiped from his records.

Not so.

And somehow, the report of the Hearing and the Fraud Squad's investigations came to the knowledge of Avril Danes at the Broad Norfolk Post, and she felt it worthy of some publicity.

Former Norfolk man failed to support his family

It has come to our notice that a man, once married to a Norfolk woman has failed to support his family despite earning a six figure annual sum. The Child Maintenance Service brought the case against Mr Murray Flanagan, and he was unable to convince a Hearing at a Tribunal held in the South-West which had met to consider his appeal against that case, that his earnings were insufficient for him to be able to support his children. The Judge's examination of his bank accounts indicated that he had not paid income tax for at least four years. Flanagan indicated that he thought his employers were paying the tax.

The Judge's final decisions are awaited, but we publish this information as a

warning to anyone who feels that selfishness and lack of responsibility to the welfare of their children is an acceptable way to go about a civilised life.
It is not, and it does not just apply to those with large salaries.

―――

Myra's visit to her mother's solicitor was quite enlightening. She had expected a room with lots of brown furniture in a former Victorian house on one of Bury St. Edmunds side streets but found herself in a modern suite on a business park. All glowing lights, light ash furniture and modern prints on the walls.

Miss Antonia Forsythe, a red-headed woman in her early thirties, dressed in a dark suit over a cream silk blouse invited her into her office and offered her a cup of coffee and biscuits, which were gratefully received.

"I'm so sorry that we meet for the first time in such difficult circumstance for you, Mrs Plater," she said and opened the file with Elsie's documents inside.

"I didn't know your mother that well, as we only met a couple times, and they were just to sign off her letters of personal wishes."

The coffee arrived on a smart tray with a plate of mixed biscuits and some mints.

"This is very kind of you. It was such a shock to lose Mum so quickly. I've not really got over it yet."

"I'm sure, and it may take a while, I expect."

"So, where do we start, Miss Forsythe?" asked Myra, remembering these sorts of meeting from her time working in a solicitor's office, but giving nothing away.

"Well, your mother's will and her instructions are well defined, but they may be a little difficult for you to understand straight away."

"Oh dear, that sounds ominous."

"Not for you, though. Let's get down to the detail. You were Elsie and Arthur's only child, and you have four surviving children. Is that right?"

"Yes, my youngest daughter passed away some years ago."

"That's right. I'm sorry to have raised it, but it is relevant, as it appears that she may have misunderstood the situation."

"What do you mean?"

"I will get to that in a minute. Firstly, her house was, as you probably remember, settled in trust to you and our senior partner, Mr Hills as trustees. The current tenants should have the option to buy it first, in my opinion, but if you wish to place it on the market, then we suggest that the tenants are given reasonable time to find alternative accommodation. Does that sound acceptable to you?"

"Certainly. As far as I know they have caused no problems."

"Good. We will put these alternatives to them. Now, as far as the remainder of Elsie's estate is concerned, there are a number of investments that we will have to close, and I believe you have retained her other belongings from the Home."

"Yes, that's right."

"Now, here comes the unusual bit. Your mothers will, which has been amended by a codicil and letters of her wishes suggest that whilst the proceeds of the house come to you, the remainder of the estate is to be divided equally between you and your three daughters.

There is no reference to your deceased daughter, and no reference to your sons."

"Oh no. That sounds very messy."

"We will need some time to examine the legal aspect of this, and how we can best advise you. I am sorry that this is not simpler."

"Well," said Myra, "I must admit to being very confused. I suppose I should leave you to do your homework and let me have your advice."

"Thank you for your understanding, Mrs Plater."

Myra's drive home was accompanied by her whirring mind.

Chapter 50

As expected by the Essex Police, a location for the meeting between Fat Robbie, aka Robert Sylvester and TAB Browne had been revealed by the specialists who had tracked their phone messages. As always it was a place they had not used before, and teams were on standby ready to take both vehicles and their occupants out.

Tony had asked if the encrypted messages between Robbie and the Norfolk contacts had been sent to ensure that Sally's team could pick up their man, and that he had not been warned off. The specialists agreed that Sally's team could plan their next move to arrest the local distributor.

She gathered her team to plan the action for the

expected time on the following day.

And, as predicted, Fat Robbie was followed on his way to meet up with TAB, who was also being tailed by unmarked vehicles travelling in front of a couple of police vans occupied by ten armed officers. Radio silence ensured no monitoring of their movements as they made their way to a disused warehouse site near Dagenham.

As both targets' cars approached the meeting site, Fat Robbie was feeling the usual mix of excitement and nervousness. Would TAB be there on time? Was anyone else waiting for them? And yet it was good to be ready for another run into Essex, Suffolk and Norfolk on the following day.

Tariq was as cool as the proverbial cucumber in his well air conditioned six-months old Mercedes and arrived at the agreed location three minutes before Fat Robbie pulled up beside him.

The Police teams had them in their sights and waited to both see and to video the exchange of the goods and cash parcels before moving in at speed, shooting the tyres of both vehicles.

Tariq thought quickly and saw a route where he might make a getaway. He dashed behind some old sheds, but not before one of the marksmen had warned him to stand still or be fired on. He kept running and was shot in the right leg. He limped on but was eventually surrounded by police officers all urging him to lie on the ground. His leg was losing blood and stung, and whilst the pain was tolerable, he had lost the will to fight on.

Fat Robbie, by contrast couldn't even undo his seatbelt quickly enough to contemplate getting away. At his best he was a thirteen second sprinter, but that was over only twenty metres after which he would fall down breathless. He accepted his situation, and very nearly said "It's a fair cop, guv."

But he didn't.

———

On the following day, and back in West Kelling, Sergeant Sally Parmenter rounded up her troop for the stake out, keeping away from the usual pick up point behind the railway station. She instructed the officers, all in plain clothes to be unseen and stationed at the entrance to the rough ground, in the upper floors of the house opposite the station with its video camera, in the entrance to the old warehouse that had been converted to flats.

On the railway tracks with a High-Viz jacket an officer looked as though he was inspecting the tracks, and 'Dolly' was stationed in the shed from where he had taken the photograph of 'Scottish'.

At somewhere near the normal drop off time, a hooded Johnnie McNeil shuffled towards the usual meeting spot, passing two of the watching officers but unaware of them.

Sally gave the word and the team approached Johnnie casually at first, and then in a rush shouting for Johnnie to get down on his knees with his hands on his head.

Johnnie just stood there. Bemused and surprisingly scared, before dropping to his knees.

'Dolly' Parting approached him and spoke gently to him. "Hello, they call you 'Scottish', don't they?"

Johnnie grunted something inaudible.

"You are waiting for the car to arrive with a guy called Fat Robbie, aren't you?"

Johnnie nodded. Slowly.

"You will have a package of money for him, yes?"

Another nod. Just.

A more robust policeman was standing behind Johnnie and lifted him to his feet, pulled his arms behind his back and cuffed his wrists.

Sally was with them now, pleased with the way this had gone.

"Right, Mr 'Scottish', let's start by you telling us your name."

"Don't want to."

"I'm sure you don't, but now is the time to stop being stupid. Otherwise, we shall arrest you for obstructing our enquiries."

"You're arresting me anyway, so what's the difference?"

"OK, let's do it your way." Sally read him his rights and told him he was under arrest for obstructing their enquiries and for being under suspicion of dealing in drugs, contrary to the various laws of the land. She then arranged for him to be taken to the Police HQ for further questioning, where his belongings were taken from him, including the envelope with the cash that was supposed to go to Fat Robbie. He still refused to give his name and was placed in a holding cell after he had been processed by the custody officers and his fingerprints taken.

Within half an hour he was taken to an interview room where the interviewing officer said, "Well, Johnnie McNeil, it didn't take long for our guys to find your fingerprints on our system. You've been a naughty boy before, haven't you?"

Johnnie just grunted.

"Well, we have some of our colleagues ferreting away at your home and I suspect they will find somethings that will put you in more trouble than you are already in. What do you think?"

More grunts.

"You should know that our Essex colleagues have arrested Robert Sylvester and Tariq Browne. What can you tell us about them?"

"Not a grass," Johnnie said in a soft growl.

"That's pointless now, Johnnie. We've got them, and they will tell us their other contacts. They will probably confirm your part in this."

"They won't"

"Now, you sell on these packages of drugs to regular customers, don't you? We need some names, Johnnie."

"I don't know their names."

"But you have their contact numbers on your phone. We have looked at them, so if you won't help us, we can ring them and tell them that they won't be getting any fixes from you and that we will be talking to each of them. That means they are bound to get their fixes from someone else, and that will be your loss, won't it? But, we might be able to help you here, Johnnie if you tell us who these people are. Otherwise, I suspect that your customers might become aggressive towards you."

"I'm not a grass."

"OK, then I guess you are out of business now, Johnnie. We will take you to another cell, where you can think about what we have said."

"Fuck off then," he mumbled as they led him away.

Jack Chambers was in a quiet contented mood, looking back and yet looking forward to his future. He sat in his favourite chair looking out across his beloved garden which had only recently recovered from the effects of the summer's relentless heat and drought, mug of coffee in his hand and just daydreaming and feeling grateful for the time that Ollie had spent helping with the decoration of the most needed parts of the house.

He was, despite occasional loneliness becoming much more settled with his own company and had rid his thoughts of ever settling down with someone else. He was clear that his three bedroomed detached house with its large garden was too big for him, and that he saw benefit in downsizing to a bungalow where the lack of stairs would benefit his knees which were more often than not sending WhatsApp messages about old football injuries.

There were few chances of finding new bungalows at a price he wanted to pay, as builders seemed to want to cram as much floorspace on two or three stories onto as little land as possible, and he had no wish to be in a place that was squeezed between others. A two bedroomed bungalow with a reasonable garden is what he needed.

Maybe the project for next year.

Looking back, he had seen how his son, Sam and his terrific wife Annie had weathered the storm of worrying about Harriet's problems and he realised just how pleased he had been to be able to give support to Harriet, Daisy and Oliver. He just hoped that his daughter would get a happy result from her tireless efforts to get her ex-husband Murray to stump up what he should.

Jack was putting his faith in the Judge.

Chapter 51

The long hot days of the summer were over, and the rains had at last come to relieve the dustbowls and brown lawns in the east of the country. Within a week, the countryside looked refreshed, and even looked as though it enjoyed the remarkable growth of weeds.

It was a relief to residents as well. Dibber Eke and Lady Hilda rejoiced as the plants in the borders seemed to want to thank someone.

"Oh, this dew be good, Lady," Dibber said as they strolled around the grounds.

"Good job I didn't buy that rhubarb to plant, Dibber."

"That that is, Lady, dew that'd shrivelled roight up by now."

"Still, we knew that old Mother Nature would sort herself out sooner or later, eh?"

"She's a good old gal is Ma Nature."

———

Avril was away on a postponed holiday with her family, but Darren was delighted when Jenny passed him a letter for publication in the Broad Norfolk Post.

> *Dear Sir*
>
> *It is not long since I suffered the loss of a treasured mother after an operation to save her heart function and in which all the medical and support team were magnificent but were unfortunately unsuccessful.*
>
> *Their efforts and dedication are beyond praise.*
>
> *I read in a recent edition of this paper that a poor local woman has had to go through a desperate number of years without regular income when she had made countless attempts to make her former husband meet his proper responsibilities and make his due payments for the maintenance of his children.*
>
> *It seems that the Judge who heard the case was sufficiently robust to censure him in the strongest possible terms.*
>
> *Here is the contrast.*
>
> *I know my mother was old and gravely ill. It would not have been long before we had*

> *lost her. But despite that inevitability, I miss her and do not have the support of a parent any longer.*
> *But I am older and can accept my situation.*
> *That man did not give proper parental support. He failed both his former wife and more importantly his children.*
> *No child can or should have to accept that.*
> *(Name and address supplied)*

Myra knew.

Once the black bin bag had been removed from the pingo excavation site, and detectives had given the all clear, the team were allowed to continue the restoration work.

In the Forensic Laboratory, DI Tony Lovelace and DS Pete Evans were present as the technicians opened the black bin bag.

It revealed a pair of jeans, socks, men's underpants, a pair of trainers and a white tee shirt with a number of cuts and what appeared to be blood stains around the cuts.

In a pocket of the jeans was a faux leather wallet containing twenty pounds in five pound notes, a driving licence, and a photograph of a dark haired girl in her twenties on a beach wearing a small scarlet bikini. Also there were a couple of business cards and a CSCS blue card, which showed that the man was certified as a skilled worker to carry out joinery work on construction sites, and that he met the required knowledge of Health and Safety regimes.

Tests would be carried out on the DNA from the clothing of the man to check if these were the clothes of the Thompson body. It was hoped that those tests would also throw up the DNA of the murderer.

It was time for another Police press conference.

Darren Prescott was on duty at the Broad Norfolk Post and attended that conference, and later wrote:-

The Thompson Common victim identified.

Today, Detective Inspector Tony Lovelace told a press conference that a further discovery at the site of the restoration of the ghost pingos at Thompson Common had revealed clothing which, through DNA testing had been shown to be those of the murdered man found buried in one of the pingos there a few months ago.

It appears that he was Aron Marcu, a registered Albanian joiner with a British driving licence.

There is no evidence whatsoever to suggest that he had been involved in any criminal gangs, as had been previously suspected. This should bring relief to those in the area who had feared otherwise.

Further tests on his clothing are being carried out in the hope of finding any evidence regarding his killer.

The Thompson Body

Harriet was more relaxed than she had been in years. The Judge had ordered Murray Flanagan to pay her a lump sum of ten thousand pounds within two months of the order, and six hundred and sixty six pounds per month for the next five years.

Murray was even less happy when the Judge referred his tax arrears to another court, and he was not enjoying awaiting the outcome of that matter. What was going to happen to all his money?

Not surprisingly, Gail was even more concerned and threatened divorce. That would make him her fourth ex-husband, and again make her more money. If there was any left!

Murray hoped that would be the end of the matter.

Really??

After a number of long discussions, Myra's mother's will was resolved by an agreement between her and her daughters following the advice of Antonia, that her house would continue to be leased to the existing tenants with the income going to Myra, whilst the remainder of her investments and estate would be divided into four parts shared between Myra, Patricia, and Olivia, with the fourth part shared between Myra's two sons.

Needless to say, the sons were somewhat miffed and desperately said that this was just not fair, but cooled down a bit when Myra told them that in the original letter penned by her mother, who had clearly been in a state of utter confusion, they were to get nothing.

The amount in Elsie's various accounts amazed both Myra and her daughters. They would need for nothing in the future.

Myra quietly thanked her mother but wondered where on earth it had all come from.

It was such a surprise, and Myra didn't know!

Chapter 52

Life at Snetterbrook Hall meandered along as it had done for many years. Minor bickering continued to be the order of the day, and Dibber continued to develop and improve the garden, sort out the compost bins and drink plenty of Hilda's lemonade.

Lady Hilda enhanced her reputation for hosting her bridge evenings with her lady friends, and the Vice-Admiral maintained a resolute fondness for his various choices of spirits and for his half hours in the confines of the peeling plaster in the downstairs lavatory.

With the window open.

―――

Following lengthy discussions with her boss Jane

Seabrook, senior planner Evie Beecham briefed and accompanied Councillor Jim Prentice to meet with David Johns and the developers as well as the Easthoe Parish Chairman and Clerk to try and find a solution to the housing proposal in the village.

Jim had also discussed preferences with individual colleagues from the Planning Committee privately and had agreed the way forward with Evie and Jane.

At that meeting, Evie suggested to the developers that a proposal that involved the removal of the old asbestos clad grain store, and the inclusion of its site within the development area, with a couple of additional dwellings thereon, might be successful subject to the inclusion of the previous agreements for the same number of properties to be acquired by a Housing Association. This would provide much needed accommodation for local folk and would preserve the general form of the village without swamping it and overstretching the infrastructure of the community.

There was some reluctance from the developers to explore this as they considered the removal of the asbestos and the decontamination of the site might be prohibitively expensive. However, after a quiet chat with David Johns, who had suggested that this idea was probably better than the time and money they would need to find to get their current proposal refused and have to take the case to an appeal, they agreed that they would put effort into achieving a solution that would be agreeable to the District Council and the Parish.

Jane and Jim managed a further weekend away this time in Aldeburgh, and the time was well spent, as it always was with them. They talked seriously about the possibility of living together again and agreed that they would make the effort for this to succeed this time.

———

A fortnight later the revised proposal for twelve new houses and bungalows and which included the site of the old grain store was submitted with a letter of intent from two of the local Housing Associations who were prepared to cooperate so long as they had the funding to do so.

After a further six weeks the revised application was approved by the Planning Committee conditional upon legal agreements being concluded to ensure the occupation of six of the dwellings being offered to local people through a Housing Association.

Soon after the permission had been granted, most of the people in the village were pleased with the result.

One particular villager must have been particularly pleased with her own efforts.

Myra Plater was gazing through her kitchen window, turned and spotted another piece of paper near the door. It was a folded piece of plain A4 and the only thing written on it was. *"Good result. Well left."*

———

The officers at the Norfolk Constabulary were delighted to have broken the back of just one of the County Lines but knew there were plenty of others. A useful if a small victory.

Whilst it was still the initial suspicions of some of the officers, there was no proof that TAB's organisation, such as it was, had been involved in either the death of the burnt body or of the Thompson Common body, and the interrogations of Fat Robbie and of TAB gave no hint that either had been involved in anything other than the importing and distribution of drugs.

Each had been sent to jail for considerable time, where no doubt they would cultivate even better connections for the future, and probably enhance their business dealings whilst there.

Johnnie McNeil was sentenced to six months in jail, suspended on condition that he committed to going under a rehabilitation programme.

The disappearance of the alleged surveyors remained a mystery but most of those involved were certain this was part of a significant fraud. One which was almost impossible to prove in Court.

However, Tony Lovelace was working on other interesting developments in the cases of the death of the boxing prodigy and of the body buried in the ghost pingo at Thompson Common.

Chapter 53

In the suburban beauty of rural Gloucestershire, early one Sunday morning, DI Tony Lovelace, accompanied by Sgt. Sally Parmenter knocked on the door of a large, detached house within a small estate of similar properties set in woodland surroundings.

They had driven from Norfolk the previous day and stayed, in separate rooms at a Premier Inn, and were sated by a full English breakfast, but were somehow thrilled by the job in hand.

The door was opened by a bleary eyed twenty year old woman with smudged mascara and wearing pink and light blue silk pyjamas.

"What? Ok God, what now?"

"Good morning, miss. We wish to speak with Mr.

Murray Flanagan, please."

"He's in bed."

"Good. Please ask him to come down and speak with us."

Gail's daughter turned and called up the stairs, "Murray. People to see you."

Tony and Sally stood at the doorstep for a further five minutes, their eyebrows moving in quizzical ways.

Eventually, wearing a pair of Gucci underpants under his thick red towelling dressing gown, Murray appeared at the door and merely said "Oh Christ, what now?"

"Mr. Flanagan, we are from the Norfolk Constabulary," said DI Lovelace, showing his identity card. "May we come in?"

"I'm not sure you can. What do you want?"

"OK, we can do this in public if you like, or in the privacy of your home."

"This doorstep is quite private thanks."

"Very well. Mr. Flanagan, we are looking into a series of incidents in Norfolk around eight to ten years ago, and in particular, a case where a young man attached to a boxing club in Norwich was unlawfully killed. We have evidence that suggests that you may know something about this."

Murray looked, blankly at the tall policeman, but felt his stomach churn.

"Also," continued Tony, "we wish to question you about a body that was found at Thompson Common. A black plastic bin bag has been retrieved from a location only a matter of yards from the site of the buried body, and we have some DNA evidence from the contents of that bag that we would like to share with you. You are not under arrest, but you will be if you don't cooperate with us."

Murray had been wrong.
This was not to be the end of his woes.
He was driven back to Norfolk to face the rest of them.

Chapter 54

And so, to autumn evenings, mists rising, the rustle of small mammals in the long grasses, the quiet passing of the barn owl hunting above those long grasses, the barking of foxes, harvest moon, shooting stars and murmurations of starlings. All great joys to Dave Wakefield.

He was enjoying his retirement and the way he was spending his time, but he still harked back to his working memories of clients and opponents he had faced.

But at least it was a time for contemplation.

It had been a warm afternoon and he had enjoyed a light lunch with Michelle with a few glasses of cool white wine. He felt mellow.

It was the contemplation of the good times, the great

achievements in his professional life, the disappointments at work by bad decisions made either by councillors, colleagues or even himself, and contemplation of the love of family and of close friends.

He was more content than ever, and the way he felt about his wife Michelle was maturing. "This is what real friendship is like," he thought and later that day whilst the mood was still with him, and after a comforting meal of corned beef hash with a glass of Merlot they sat together on the sofa watching a wildlife programme about the state of planet Earth and felt quaintly glad that they had lived in a time when life was good.

Not for everyone, but they felt they had been fortunate to live when they did.

As he mused about good times, he thought about the friends whose company he had enjoyed.

There was 'Chuck' Balls, Frank Park, 'Red' Herring, many other friends from his days in Round Table, those of his peers in his professional life, his kids who were more than friends, and, of course, Michelle.

His new friendships with the people at the Norfolk Wildlife Trust, and their astounding commitment to enhancing the quality of the landscape for the benefit of both all wildlife and for people to enjoy it. It wasn't just national treasures who could encourage a better understanding of the natural world and the dangers it faced.

He had felt the friendly companionship with Jane and with Sally Parmenter and had noticed the bond between 'Dolly' Parting and Darren Prescott.

Most of all, he really did hope that the friendship

between his old colleague Jane Seabrook and Jim Prentice would find its logical conclusion and was delighted to hear from her that Jim had indeed moved in, giving his children Philly and Zac the run of his home until such time as it proved sensible to sell it.

These were many of his friends.
Real friends.

Friends, as in those wonderful words of Henry Miller.

Not everyone can be your friend. It must be someone as close to you as your skin, someone who imparts colour, drama, meaning to your life.

Dave knew that his friends did just that.

A life without friends is no life, however snug and secure it may be.

The Thompson Body

Printed in Great Britain
by Amazon